DEAD BRANCHES

Benjamin Langley

READ UNTIL YOU BLEED!

DEAD BRANCHES

BENJAMIN LANGLEY

ACKNOWLEDGEMENTS

So many people have helped to make this book what it is. It's a product of many experiences over the years, since my youngest days. I'd like to thank my parents for making me believe that anything is possible, and for feeding my love of horror since the beginning. I mean, how old was I when I was terrified of 'Stop Boris', the game in which you had to shoot the giant spider with the laser gun? Was that an appropriate Christmas present? We loved it! Thanks for buying me 'Scream' comics, and of course, Horror Top Trumps.

I have fond memories of watching horror movies with my siblings and with my mum and my nan on Saturday nights throughout my childhood (starting with the Hammer House of Horror classics), and that spread to a love of reading horror. We should have known it would come to this!

I couldn't do this without the support of my wonderful wife, Lisa, and my two girls, Malibu and Georgia. We've had some great times together, and you always give me the time I need and the encouragement to develop my writing projects. Lisa, thanks for listening to my ideas, reading my drafts, and helping to make this dream a reality.

Huge thanks to my good friend Michelle Foster who gave me feedback on an earlier version of the novel. (Actually, she swore at me for what I did to one of the characters.) Our regular meetups keep me sane and being able to discuss and plot out ideas with you is so valuable.

Thank you, Pete Kahle, for believing in this novel. I'm thrilled to be published by Bloodshot Books. You're putting out some excellent work, and it blows my mind to think that I'm now part of that.

Don Noble, thanks for the awesome cover.

An early draft of this novel was part of my MA in Creative writing, so I'd like to that the staff at Anglia Ruskin University, particularly Colette Paul and Una McCormack. Thanks for the great advice, and all the recommended reading. I'll get through them all one day.

The first words of the novel (long since entirely replaced) were written on a delightful writing retreat at Le Verger in France. David and Michele Lambert are excellent hosts, and the opportunity to write in such a pleasant location really got the wheels turning on this one.

I'd also like to thank everyone that has supported me in my writing and given me encouragement in the writing groups and workshops I've attended over the years.

Finally, thanks to all the writers of stories out there that keep us filled with wonder, and all of the readers that are holding a copy of this book—hope you enjoyed it.

– *Benjamin Langley*

*For the friends we make
when we're young and innocent*

He's dying.
I read the words again to be sure.
The doctor says he's only got days left.

"What's wrong, Dad?" I look up, and see Charlie, already dressed in his school uniform. I hadn't heard him come downstairs.

"Hey, Charlie!" I pull him to me and into one of my inescapable bear-hugs. He's two months from turning ten, the age I was when I last saw my dad.

He squeezes free, proving my bear-hugs fallible, and looks at the letter in my hands. "Who's it from?" he says, his inquisitive face scrunched together as he looks up at me.

I won't say that he takes after me. I was naïve; he's a smart lad. But it's a common misconception that children don't know what's going on. Some people forget how curious they were when they were young. They don't remember that answers like, "It's nothing," or, "Don't worry about it," only encourage a curious child to seek their own conclusions. Sometimes the best answers are the ones that you find yourself.

"It's from my mother. Your grandmother." I don't remember the last time I let her see Charlie. It was never her fault, and it's not fair for me to keep him from her, but she's linked to too many bad memories.

"Your granddad's dying."

Charlie nods. He doesn't know what to do with the information. I'd not told Charlie much about my dad. Had I told him that he was a bad man? I'm not one for stories. Not anymore. Now he's older. I have to tell him. If I don't, then I'm as bad as my parents were. Mum said that they were only trying to protect us, but what harm would the truth have done? Not telling us was the easy option. And look at the damage it did.

It's a long time since I thought of that summer. It's a long time since I thought of Little Mosswick and its network of drove-ways and ditches that were our secret trails around the village. Don't believe the myth that Fenland folk are somehow special, that they have an affinity with the soil and share some kind of secret knowledge.

2 DEAD BRANCHES

Don't believe that there's an inherent goodness in that place. I made the mistake of believing their tales and trusting that they'd keep us safe. But the biggest reason why I'd find it so hard to go back is that, despite years of running it through my head before I locked it away for my own sanity, I'm still not sure of how much of it was even real. And now I have to wonder, can a creature like that even die?

PART ONE

Tuesday, 12th June 1990

Normally, you could hear the chickens clucking from a mile off. I don't remember if that struck me as odd right away, but then I saw the flurry of feathers, small, soft, white under-feathers, stained red, and sitting in the mud and I knew that something was wrong. Chicken wire jutted out of the coop at an ugly angle, twisted and torn away from the wood and there was a strong pissy smell like a well-soiled cat litter tray left to fester in the sun.

Reaching to open the door, I was most disturbed to find it cold. Heat used to radiate from the coop, but now it felt lifeless. I didn't have to open the door far before what was left of one of the chickens fell onto my foot. It was mostly still intact: head, wings, legs, but its side was a bloody chasm. I could see bits of bone inside and pinky-purplish flesh, still wet, glistening in the early morning sun.

Inside, the wooden panels were streaked with blood, and the straw was almost entirely lost beneath a layer of feathers. It wasn't until I saw a broken shell and hardening yolk smeared on a nest box that I started to panic. What if I went back without an egg? I could see Dad's face, puffy and red, and I could already hear the words "Useless boy", and then he'd pull on his boots and go stamping off, swearing about me under his breath. I had to find an egg. I pushed aside some of the straw, looking in the corner where they normally laid. The straw was sticky, and shards of eggshell clung to it, glued with half-set egg. In the other corner was another dead chicken, this one with a wing torn off, but behind that I was sure there was something egg shaped. I pulled a mangled chicken aside by a cold, hard leg and in the corner, there was a speckled egg. Proudly I gathered it and hurried back to the house where the smell of melting lard made my stomach turn over.

"You got some?" asked Mum.

"Something's happened," I said.

Dad was already glaring at me. "One egg? What good is one fucking egg?" He sneered, and then he looked me up and down, no doubt looking for something else to criticise, and as always, he found something. "What's that slarred all up the side of your top?"

I looked at one arm, saw nothing, and then at the other and saw the streaks of red on my white, school shirt.

"You've ruined your shirt. You must think I farm money. You must think I can just pull it out of the earth."

"Something's happened," I said again, but it was as if I had no voice.

Mum dipped a tea towel in the sink and came over to me. She started to scrub at the blood, but only succeeded in smudging it, spreading it further along the sleeve. "Whatever is it?" she asked.

"They're dead," I said, shaking my arm away from Mum. As I did so the egg shot out of my hand and smashed onto the floor.

"What the hell are you playing at, boy?" Dad said. He was rising out of his chair.

"They're all dead!" I said again, and this time he seemed to hear me.

"Who are?" he said, his brow furrowing, his eyebrows forming into one long hairy caterpillar.

"The chickens! Something's been in there. They're all dead."

As expected, Dad went over to the door and pulled his boots on. "Why didn't you say so in the first place?"

"Go up and get a fresh shirt," Mum said. "I'll clean this mess up."

We both looked down at the egg. The sight of the orange yolk, broken and diluting with the transparent white made me think of the stiff egg yolk in the hen hut and the gored bodies of the hens, so I dashed through the door.

My older brother Will was standing on the stairs. "What have you done now?" he asked, knowing it would wind me up.

I rushed past him, jutting my elbow out, trying to catch him in the guts on the way by, but I missed. I was in no mood for his games.

The chickens had been on my mind all day at school. I couldn't concentrate and thinking about them had made me short tempered. After school, my concentration wasn't much better. I'd just started my go on Super Mario Bros. when a knock on the door distracted me. I mistimed my jump and Mario landed in the open mouth of a piranha plant. Will laughed as Mario's death tune played and he reached for the joypad but then seven rapid bangs on the door drew us out of our bedroom. As we were halfway down the stairs, Mum called my name.

The door at the bottom of the stairs opened into the kitchen. Dad was sitting at the table chasing gravy around his plate with a piece of Yorkshire pudding. As usual, he had a smear of mud on his left cheek. Mum stood by the door, and outside was my friend John's mum. She always insisted that I call her Barbara, rather than Mrs Glover, but it felt weird calling adults by their first names. Mum urged her in. She looked out of place in our kitchen in her red and white supermarket uniform.

She came over to me. "Tom," she said, and put her hand on my shoulder. The knuckles were red. "Have you seen John?" A string of saliva hung between her lips.

"Not since school."

"Did he have any plans?" said Barbara.

I shrugged. Had John said anything? With the mood I'd been in all day, I couldn't remember. I'd gone home with my cousin, Liam, who had practically dragged me out of the classroom at the end of the day and was impatiently hopping around outside his brother Andy's classroom. We had a gang, the Crusaders. It was me, Will, Liam and Andy. We were originally called The Muskehounds, but we argued over who was Dogtanian, so we changed it. John had been hanging around with us so much that we'd had a secret meeting about whether he should be allowed to be a full-time part of the gang. We'd decided that he could, but we hadn't told him yet.

"Did he leave on his own?" said Barbara. The saliva string broke.

"I don't know. Sometimes he walks with Chris Jackson."

"I've been there," said Barbara. She took a huge gasp of air, as if she'd forgotten to breathe.

"Did he get home and go out again?" asked Dad, looking up from his dinner plate. Before waiting for a response, he picked up a knife and cut himself a slab of bread.

Barbara looked down at the tiles. She was never home when John got in. She worked in the new supermarket in Ely and John had the house to himself for a couple of hours. That was why he was always asking one of us over to play, so that he wouldn't be on his own.

"I'm sure he'll turn up," Mum said. She placed a hand on Barbara's shoulder. "You know what boys are like."

I couldn't pinpoint the exact moment that Mum was thinking about because there had been so many evenings when we'd been out all day, reinforcing one of our hideouts or trying to get a raft to float on the river, and then wandered home when it was already dark, but we'd never dare do it on a school night.

Mum was looking at Barbara with a sad look on her face, her hand still resting on her shoulder. I could never imagine the two of them as friends. Everything about them was different. Mum looked like a proper mum should, but John's mum looked more like one of those TV mums, with red lipstick and hair that didn't move, and they lived in one of Little Mosswick's new housing estates that Dad had sworn so much about when they were built.

"I should go," said Barbara. She stepped out of the door then turned to look back at me.

"Does he have any other friends I could check with?"

John didn't have many friends. The trouble was that he was smart, and he knew it, and people didn't like that. I shook my head and she turned away, her shoulders slung low. As

Mum put her hand on the door, I said, "Wait," and Barbara turned around. "Maybe Daniel Richardson? They hang out together sometimes."

Daniel and John *were* friends, but they'd fallen out when John had lent his imported Nintendo Gameboy to me and not him. But perhaps they'd made up. Perhaps John was over at Daniel's house trading Panini World Cup stickers. Maybe John was swapping his sticker of the World Cup trophy with Daniel, the sticker that I needed so badly to complete the first page. More than anything I wanted Daniel to have that shiny world cup sticker, even if it meant that I never completed my collection.

"Want us to have a bit of a look around? See if he turns up?" Dad said without looking up from his plate.

"No, I couldn't possibly ask you to…"

"It's no trouble. We'll send him straight home if we find him." Dad was already halfway out of his seat. He wiped his hands on his jumper and I wondered how he could even be wearing one in that heat.

"If you don't mind… Thank you." She looked at me, "And this other boy, Daniel?"

I told Barbara where Daniel lived, and she smiled before she hurried out of the door, catching her heel on the ridge, but not letting it slow her down on her way to her car.

"It's not right leaving kids that age home on their own," Dad said, after pushing another piece of bread into his mouth which distorted his voice. "Mothers should be home with their children."

He swallowed noisily then reached for his boots and sunk back into the seat to pull them on. "Couldn't very well leave her in that state though. Had to do something."

He stood up and called out, "Will!"

Will thudded down the stairs and peered around the door-frame.

"Come take a walk with me up along the drove, and down to the riverbank."

"Okay," Will said and went to fetch his shoes.

"You, boy," he said, glaring at me. "Take a wander around the back field. Take Chappie with you. He could do with the exercise."

We named our dog after the brand of food we fed him. We thought we were being original by not calling him Spot or Patch or Rover or Shep. He was a border collie, black with a ring of white around his neck and over his shoulders, and a patch of white around his left eye. We got him from the animal shelter. He'd been abandoned, so we had no idea of how old he was, but in the last year he'd slowed down. He didn't show any excitement when I fetched the lead, and he struggled to get to his feet.

"Come on, Chappie," I said, trying to muster some enthusiasm from him.

He shook after he stood, then looked at me with watery eyes, and put up no fight as I put him on the lead.

Our house was a couple of hundred metres from the main road which ran through Little Mosswick and was connected to the various fields that made up our farm by a series of droves. It had been so dry that the stiff grey mud had cracked and looked like the skin of an ancient dinosaur. Granddad Norman knew all of the names of the droves, but I only knew them by where they led to, or the streets in the village they crossed. I looked up along the drove that led up to the river, the one that Dad and Will were on, but I could see no sign of them. They'd already disappeared behind the row of elderberry bushes.

I gave Chappie's lead a tug. "It's me and you again."

He stopped to sniff the gatepost.

"How come it's always Dad and Will, hey Chappie?" I was almost dragging him along as I gazed down into the ditches on either side of the drove that separated the field of oilseed rape, which was alive with yellow flowers swaying in the breeze, from the potato field. "I'd rather be with you anyway."

I didn't know what I was looking into the ditches for. There wouldn't be anything down there. Those on the left were all bone-dry and had a bit of brown grass and a few bulrushes withering away in them. The other side was thick with nettles, with a few dock leaves sprouting at the very edges. At least if anyone fell in, they'd be able to ease the sting right away. I heard a rustling and pictured the horrible toad-like creature from the cover of the *Deathtrap Dungeon* Fighting Fantasy book that I'd been playing through. If anything was going to strike, it would have been when I was on my own. But John was strong, and he was smart; he wouldn't have been taken by a beast like that.

I wasn't scared, but I didn't want to walk along the ditches anymore, so a little way down the track, when we reached the entrance to the potato field, I decided to cut across it.

Chappie was immediately lost under the large green leaves, and I could only tell where he was by seeing where his lead disappeared, and from the odd quivering of the plants. I headed towards the back section of the field which was never planted up. It was home to a rusting Ford tractor that hadn't moved as long as I was alive. John was into old machinery, and liked to tinker with things, so I thought it was worth a look in case he'd wandered over there.

I kept my eyes on the tractor to avoid looking at the twisted old oak tree in the back corner. It was dead, and at some point, it had been struck by lightning, perhaps more than once, which had almost split the tree in two. There was also a scorch mark on its trunk like a gaping mouth, and the wild branches above were like the hair of some ancient creature, or the snakes of Medusa, and where some low branches had been cut short years ago it looked like it had stumpy limbs. In recent years ivy had started to grow around its base, giving the impression that it had returned to life like some kind of foul, brain-thirsty zombie.

I'd been scared of the tree ever since Granddad Norman put one of his glass eyes into a knot on the tree's trunk the day after he told us the story of how he lost his eye. It was not long after they bought the land, which hadn't been farmed since the Miller boys (whoever they were) had all been killed during the First World War, when Granddad Norman was still only a boy. My great-granddad wanted that land in use, so he gave Granddad Norman, and his older brother, Arthur, one day to clear it.

Once, there were sheds there, but they'd long since collapsed and the beams were half-buried in the ground. The best method Arthur and Granddad Norman could think of was to drag them out using chains attached to the tractor. They were all set to have the entire field clear, but then they set their sights on the old oak tree, and even though it was before the lightning strike, it already looked dead. They thought that it would come out of the ground as easily as those beams that had only been sunk a year or two. They didn't reckon on the ancient evil that was holding the cursed oak in place. They tied their chain around the tree, and Arthur started in the tractor. The engine roared and the chain dug into the trunk, and Granddad swears it was on the lean and it looked like it was about to go when he heard something ping. The last thing he saw with his left eye was the broken chain flying towards him.

It was all for the best, claimed Granddad, because if the tree hadn't taken his eye, then he would have had to fight in the war and, like Arthur, he might never have come home.

Putting his glass eye in the tree, the day after he told us that story, was his worst prank yet. He was spying on us from behind the old Ford tractor and he slapped the side of his legs and made a "Hoo-hoo," sound, as Andy ran off across the field screaming, and he kept laughing until he had to dab at his good eye with a handkerchief.

I couldn't look at the tree in case it was looking back and who knows what would have happened if I got caught in its evil glare, so I looked over to the new bypass. John wouldn't have been playing there. Not while they were working on it. We used to, when it was a huge pile of sand and rubble and it would be left unattended for days at a time, but he was more sensible than to play in the path of a steamroller.

Chappie sniffed at the tractor wheels and cocked his leg up at it and whined. There was a thin film of dust and dirt on the seat, and it was clear no one had been on it for a while. I lifted a sheet of corrugated iron, and flipped it over, watching the worms wriggle underneath. There was a strong earthy smell, but that was nothing out of the ordinary. We walked close enough to the oak tree to see that there were no footprints in the soft earth around it, but I wasn't getting any closer than that. We walked to the other side of the field and then I jumped the ditch while Chappie ran down and scrambled back up the other side. We had one of our old dens just off the path that led back to the farmhouse. This one we'd called Narnia, because, when we built it, I was obsessed with the TV series of *The Lion the Witch and the Wardrobe* which had been on TV a few months earlier. It was watching that which made me want to read all of the books. Our current base was across the other side of the oil seed rape field, and we called that one Moon Base One (Liam named it) and we had a smaller one, up by the school, which was The Broom Cupboard. Narnia was built where the dyke came to an end a couple of elderberry bushes met and formed a natural shelter. We used to climb down the dyke and hide under the bushes. All that was left in there was some sticks Will had sharpened with his penknife back in the days when we were still Muskehounds. When it rained hard the dyke would get wet at the bottom and Mum told us off for getting our school trousers muddy, so we gave it up. John didn't even know about this base though, and there was no sign of anyone having been there, so we wandered back home, passing the chicken coop on the way. Something bad had happened there. I saw those mutilated chickens in my head again, and then John's face. What if the same thing that had gotten the chickens had gotten John too?

Dad's boots were by the door. I walked in and he was sitting at the table. His face was red, and his hair was standing up, as if he'd been running his hands through it. He broke off his conversation with Mum when he saw me and stared until I looked away.

"He'll be all right," Mum said. She patted me on the back, and I slipped off my shoes.

"Can I give his house a call? To see if he's home?"

Mum turned away and picked up a tea-towel to wipe a cup which was already dry. "Better leave them alone," she said, looking down at the cup. "I'm sure he'll be at home, but his Mum and Dad will be having words with him."

Having words. That was adult speak for telling him off.

With that I filled a beaker with orange squash, ran in some water, and took it up to my room. It was the room at the top of the stairs, with the spare room on the left (piled high with boxes) and the bathroom on the right. Mum and Dad's room was on the other side of that, but we weren't allowed in there.

In our room, my bed was nearest the door and Will's was on the other side of the room which meant that he had to cross into my side to get to his, so he claimed that he had the better side of the room as it had more privacy. As the older brother, he deserved that.

On top of our shared set of drawers (top two for Will, bottom two for me) was our TV. We shared that too. It was a 21-inch Philips colour TV with Teletext and a remote control. Attached to that was our Nintendo Entertainment System, a joint Christmas present six months earlier. Will had already started playing again.

I walked over to the window and looked out. I was glad our bedroom didn't look out to the rest of the village; I didn't want to see the school and the estate John lived on. But looking out over the field brought me no comfort either as my eyes always came to rest on the oak tree. I pulled the curtains closed.

John and I had played football together at lunch time. Some of the boys pretended they were playing for Cameroon. Before Friday night the only thing we knew about them was a few names from the Panini stickers that we had and what was on the Top Trump card – they'd played at one previous world cup, and had drawn all three games, but after they'd beaten Argentina in the opening game of the World Cup their Panini stickers became the hottest property on the playground. A few of us stuck to being England players despite their draw with Ireland. We had a mini-Peter Shilton in goal, a little Gary Lineker up front and John was Paul Gascoigne.

By afternoon break it was too hot to play so we sat under the shade of the conker tree at the bottom of the school playing field. We argued. John was always bragging about having a

Nintendo Entertainment System which was imported from America. He could play all of the latest games, while we didn't get them for yonks. What's more, Dad didn't like the idea of games consoles so any new games for me and Will were limited to Christmas and birthday presents. John had finished Super Mario Bros. 3, while I was still playing the original. I'd been going over to John's house to play on his game, but that day I couldn't take any more of his showing off. But if I'd have gone, he'd be at home and everything would have been okay. Instead I'd have to go over to Liam's because he was so excited about his new set of Top Trumps which we didn't even get around to playing.

Will switched off the Nintendo, plugged the aerial back in, and picked up the remote. He opened Ceefax and called out, 'Belgium two, South Korea nil.' The South Korean team had two players on each sticker because no one knew who any of them were. Will turned off Ceefax and switched the TV over for the Netherlands vs Egypt match and beckoned me over to his bed which had a better angle for viewing the TV. I'd been looking forward to seeing Ruud Gullit, Frank Rijkaard and Marco Van Basten play for Holland. I'd never seen them play before, but I'd heard that they were like magicians. I'd seen clips of this wonder goal that Van Basten had scored in the European Championships two years ago. He volleyed it in from an impossible angle. There was no way that a normal human being could do that. These guys were more than that. They were super-human.

Halfway through the first half I found my attention wandering from the screen. I kept looking at the Gameboy – John's Gameboy – and decided I wanted one last go on that. I picked it up and realised that I'd placed it on top of *Deathtrap Dungeon*. I stared at the hideous toad creature, with its drool-covered fangs, and its multitude of eyes and quickly flipped the book over. I put the Tetris cartridge in the Gameboy and started a game. I cleared line after line and got my highest score ever, and then I turned it off and slipped it into my school bag, determined to return it to John in the morning.

Wednesday, 13th June 1990

I woke early. The machines were already at work on the bypass, but it wasn't the low growl of their machines that woke me. I re-checked my bag, making sure that John's Gameboy was still there, carefully wrapped in the school sweater that the bright light pouring through the crack in the curtains suggested I wouldn't need.

I opened the curtains to let more of the morning sunshine in, ignoring Will's groans as he turned away from the light and pulled his duvet, which he must have kicked off during the night, back over himself. It was a hazy morning; I couldn't see the old pumping station where the Little Ouse met the Great Ouse, which you could normally see on a clear day. I looked at the yellow machines, diggers, steamrollers and tipper trucks, and thought about how much closer they could have been.

A man from the Highways Agency had come to discuss buying some of Dad's land in order to keep the bypass as straight as possible. It would have taken a small chunk of the back field – the bit where nothing was planted, and that horrible tree stood. Dad could have put up a reasonable argument. He could have said that he wasn't selling because the further away the noise of the bypass was the better it was for him. He could have argued that he was planning to clear up that bit of land and plant it up, and it would cost him his livelihood to sell it, but reasonable argument wasn't something that Dad did.

Dad held a grudge against the parish council and as a result every type of council or Government official. First of all, there had been a land dispute with Peter Dalby (which meant I wasn't supposed to speak to Ian Dalby at school anymore) where they'd sided with the Dalby family. Then there was the planning application for a new shed for Dad to store crops in, which was turned down and he was still fighting. Dad's view was not so much you scratch my back I'll scratch yours, but if I can't have it, you can't have it either. So instead of turning them down he had them out to survey, waiting for them to make an offer, sat on it for weeks, and then turned them away.

Dad wasn't in a good mood. I'd gone downstairs to get myself breakfast, and he was already sitting at the table. He'd not shaved, so his face looked grey, and his eyes were puffy.

"Up early, boy," he said. "Shit the bed?"

He'd say this from time to time, usually when he was in a better mood, but his voice was low and flat, like when he was reading a letter out loud that had annoyed him.

"You want some breakfast, Tom?" Mum said, getting up from the table and taking Dad's plate with her.

"I was going to have cereal," I said, and went over to the cupboard and took out the box of Rice Krispies.

"Don't speak to your dad then," Dad muttered. He got up and went out of the back door. "Ignorant little shit," he said.

I looked up at Mum, and she looked at me and smiled. "Any plans for after school today?"

"Probably hang out with Liam and Andy," I said as I turned away from her, not wanting her to see how Dad had made me feel.

I didn't wait for Will because he liked to walk slowly and chat to people, sometimes older kids from the college, walking in the opposite direction towards the bus stop, as if he had set himself a challenge to arrive as close to the bell as possible, and I wanted to catch John on the playground as he arrived to say that I was sorry for not going over to play.

When the bell rang, I was still waiting. I told myself that he might be late. But John was never late. As the last few pupils deserted the playground and went into the school, including Will who punched me playfully on the shoulder as he passed, I looked out at the concrete and followed a crisp packet that scuttled along on the gentle breeze and a hard lump, like an undigested piece of meat, seemed to solidify in my stomach.

I was last into our classroom. I looked straight at John's seat, and when I saw it was empty, confirming that he hadn't used some kind of ninja-like skills to sneak past me, that lump in my gut seem to get bigger.

"Sit down, Thomas," said Mrs Palmer. She'd been our teacher since the September. She had dark brown hair with a ruler-straight fringe, wonky teeth, and always wore mustard-coloured cardigans. People said she smelled of cucumber, but I'd never noticed. She wasn't strict and, on some days, she would let us out to break early. Also, she'd taken me off the reading scheme and made me a free-reader, so I could read any book in the library, and it was her that said I was ready to read *The Chronicles of Narnia*.

That morning, she read out the register and when she got to the Gs and called out John's name (they were in surname order) we all turned to look at his seat. It was odd for him not to be there. It was odd for anyone to be absent and it usually led to stories spreading about the missing person having the squits, the squirts, or the runs, but it seemed different this time and no one said a word.

I felt sick. The lump in my stomach was breaking down and trying to make its way back up my throat. A couple of times I had to swallow hard to keep from vomiting, and I couldn't get the bitter taste out of my mouth.

"Can I go to the toilet, Mrs Palmer?" I asked.

She came over to look at my book.

"Thomas, you've not done a single one of these sums," she said, poking at my exercise book with her finger.

I hadn't even realised we were doing maths. "I'm desperate," I said, swallowing hard again.

"Okay, off you go. But I expect much more effort when you get back, or you'll be staying in at break."

To get to the toilets I had to go past the headmaster's office. Mr Inglehart was sitting at his desk, and I was sure that I could see a policeman sitting opposite him. I couldn't loiter outside there to listen in for two reasons: one, I was still about ninety per cent sure that I was going to throw up, and two, because Mr Jenkins, the school caretaker, was leaning on his mop at the end of the corridor. He was a whistler, but no one ever recognised any of the songs he whistled. His beard was so big and bushy that the end of the mop handle had become lost in it. He had a habit of marching children who were found hanging around the corridors to Mr Inglehart's office, and while that would have given me a better idea of what was going on in there, I didn't much want to chuck my guts up in front of my headmaster and a policeman.

In the toilets, I splashed some water on my face and took some long, deep breaths. I started to feel better. I went into one of the cubicles and locked the door. After a few seconds I remembered that this was the toilet that John had dropped the red food colouring into, making the water go a deep, dark red. Then I'd waited in the cubicle next door, and John in the one on the other side. We waited for someone to come in to see how they reacted. We could barely contain out laughter every time the toilet door opened. Unfortunately, the first couple of visitors were only using the urinals, and we needed someone to come into the cubicle to do a turd.

"The ideal scenario," John had said while plotting this prank, "would be for someone to come in, and not look before they do a dump. When they look round, they'll think they've shit blood!" He'd laughed so hard that he couldn't breathe until I slapped his back.

Unfortunately, that wasn't quite how it worked out, but the results were still hilarious. We heard the door creak open, and then, a few seconds later, there was a high-pitched girly scream, and heavy footsteps as someone fled from the toilets.

John and I dashed out of the toilets howling with laughter, and quickly made our way into the corridor to catch a glimpse of the girly screamer. It was a year-three boy in Andy's class called Jimmy Wilson.

It wasn't until the next week that we got wind of a significant number of year three kids pretending to be Ghostbusters. We found Andy on the playground and he filled in the gaps.

"Jimmy saw a ghost in the toilets," he said, his eyes wide.

It turned out that Jimmy's older brother, Gavin, who was at college, had been telling Jimmy for years that the toilets at the school were haunted, and this was the proof that Jimmy needed.

"So, what did Jimmy do?" John asked, winking at me and thinking about that girly scream.

"He says he yelled at it, and it dissolved into goo in the toilet."

"Right," said John, slowly and sarcastically. Then he looked around at Jimmy. "Hey Jimmy, can we play?"

Jimmy shrugged. "I guess you can be ghosts."

"No, I want to be a Ghostbuster. You be a ghost."

"But it's my game."

"I only want to play for a minute."

Jimmy sighed. He knew the rules. If a bigger kid wanted to join your game, then it was by their rules. "Okay, I'm a ghost." He raised his hands, wiggled his fingers, and gave off a ghostly moan.

John threw his hands up in fake-terror, and then started the longest highest-pitched scream I've ever heard and ran off into the distance.

At first Jimmy looked at him with a puzzled expression on his face, then the memory of his own reaction must have hit him, and he looked down at the ground sheepishly.

I looked across the field and spotted John. He'd finally stopped screaming and had collapsed on the field.

Before I even got close to him, I knew he'd be in another one of his giggling fits. I lay on the grass next to him, and his infectious laughter spread to me.

At some point Liam came trudging over and sat down beside us. "What's so funny?" he asked.

"Stupid kids in year three," said John between bursts of giggles. "Playing Ghostbusters."

A wrinkle formed on Liam's brow, his cheeks puffed out, and he pouted. "What's wrong with Ghostbusters?" he asked without making eye-contact, instead choosing to pick a daisy and toss it at his feet.

"Nothing, but these kids think ghosts are real!" John burst out into laughter again.

"Don't you?" asked Liam, throwing another daisy at John.

John shook his head. "I don't believe anything I can't see with my own two eyes."

"What about you, Tom?" asked Liam.

I kept my mouth shut.

I guess I'd been out of the classroom a little too long as Mrs Palmer was peering out of the classroom door when I wandered back along the corridor.

"Are you okay, Thomas?" she asked.

I wanted to say that I was worried about John, but I was afraid that if I did, I might start to cry, and I couldn't let that happen in front of the class, so I nodded my head, and figured that I better get stuck into the maths if I was going to have a break at all.

I dashed through the maths questions to make sure I was let out for break, but it felt even stranger then when we went to play football. Because John was one of the best players, he was usually a captain, and even though I was a bit crap he'd always pick me (not first, he had to get some of the good players in, but I'd never be left until the end). Without John to pick me, I was left until the end, when it was down to me and Stu who always toe-punted the ball and tripped over his feet. I got picked before Stu, but only because Will was insisting that Chris (one of the team captains) should pick me.

Chris was assigning roles on the team. He told me that I had got to be Richard Witchge, the Dutch player who'd come on as a sub in the game last night. "I'm going to be Gazza," he said.

"No," I said, without thinking.

"What do you mean?" he said. "It's my team. I can be who I like."

"John would normally be Paul Gascoigne," I said.

"Well John's not here, is he?"

"But you can't just take his player. Be someone else."

"Right, I'm swapping you out for Stu," he said, so I had to go onto the other team.

Everyone played as if everything was normal until Stu toe punted the ball into a group of girls (including Laura Matthews) who were making daisy-chains and they ran off with the ball and went and told Mr Inglehart, who liked to patrol the field to make sure no one was having too much fun, and partly to keep an eye on how his favourite pupils who played for the school football team were getting on. Surely, he was concerned about John? But he seemed to be acting normally. Maybe there was nothing to worry about. Maybe John was already back at home and he'd be back in school in a day or two, but something didn't feel right, and I didn't like it.

At the end of the school day I waited with Liam for Will and Andy. Liam and I were in the same class at school, and even though I was six months older than him, he was bigger than me in every way: He had bigger feet, he had a bigger belly, he was taller, and he had a much bigger head. The only thing I secretly suspected was smaller was his brain.

"Shall we walk round by John's to see if there's anything going on?" I said.

"Might as well. We'll have to walk past Shaky Jake's though." Liam did his awful Shaky Jake impression, for which he clenched his fists tightly and tensed up all of his muscles so his whole body shook until his face went red.

"Think he'll shout at us again?"

Liam sniggered. "Maybe if you walk into his yard."

"No way." I shook my head.

"Dare you." Liam shoved my shoulder with the palm of his hand and as I was about to grab him into an inescapable headlock, Will came wandering out of his classroom.

"Guess what?" Liam said to Will.

"What?"

"Tom's gonna do a knock-door-bunk on Shaky Jake." Liam was hopping from one foot to another and grinning from ear-to-ear.

"Watch he doesn't touch you with those stuttery old hands and turn you into a freak." Will then did his (better) Shaky Jake impression, which involved only shaking one hand, but holding it up towards my face.

"I'm not," I said, batting Will's hand away. "I was only saying we should walk round the long way to see if John's home."

Liam started clucking at me and flapping his arms, and then Andy jumped between the two of us and shouted, "Cowabunga."

Andy was only in class three, so still an infant, and he acted like to too, though I was always glad to have Andy around, as it meant that I wasn't the shortest.

With our rucksacks on our backs, together we walked down Main Street. We had to cross the road before we reached the Post Office if we were to go by Shaky Jake's house on the corner of Downham Close and Main Street. Waiting for a gap in the traffic, we were almost knocked onto our arses by the gust from a couple of heavy lorries that went flying down the road. Mum and Aunt Anne would have been angry with us for not crossing outside the school with Mrs Barnes, the lollipop lady, but that was for the little kids (Andy had us to look after him) and Mrs Barnes had crazy hair and worse so much perfume that it made you retch.

Shaky Jake had the relatively normal looking bungalow on the corner with the front fence which was rotten and bent away from the posts. Often, standing nearby was enough to rile him and he'd come running out of the house, sometimes holding a saucepan or a wooden spoon and he'd stand there on the spot and start shaking and then try to yell at us but he could never get the words out and spittle would go everywhere while the strands of his greasy fringe would flap around. One time some of the spit flew out and hit John on the hand and he tried to wipe it on us to give us the lurgy.

"Come on, let's go to John's," I said.

"You're not getting out of it so easily," Liam said. "Knock-door-bunk." He started to chant, and Andy joined in.

We saw the kitchen curtains twitch and thought he was about to come out, but then Will called out, "Look."

We turned around to see a police car drive past us and turn down Downham Close. We broke into a half-run and then stopped at the end of the road to see the car pull up outside John's house. Maybe they'd found him and were bringing him home. But only two policemen got out of the car. They went and knocked on John's door. We couldn't see who opened it, but a couple of seconds later they were inside.

Will started walking into Downham Close.

"What are you doing?" I said.

"Investigating."

We followed. We slowed to crawling pace as we got closer to the police car. I'd never been so close to one before. Will was first to peer in.

"Is he in there?" asked Liam.

Of course, he wasn't going to be in there. If they'd found him, they would have taken him in.

"No," Will said.

"What is in there?"

"Nothing."

"What's in there?" Liam said again, his voice high.

"I told you: nothing."

Liam, Andy and I all peered in at the same time. Will was right, there was nothing interesting in there at all.

"I guess they haven't found him," I said.

"So, what should we do?" Liam said.

"Why don't we go back to Moon Base One?" Will said.

"All right," Liam said. "We'll drop our bags home and then see you in twenty minutes."

Moon Base One was guarded by a dyke in a little spinney out by the field furthest from our farmhouse. A couple of hundred metres up from here the drove crossed the bypass but would lead on to Wissey Hill if followed far enough.

We'd used rocks to build a path across the dyke and hidden the entrance using some elderberry bushes. The advantage of the elderberry was that we always had plenty of the tiny berries at our disposal if we ever came under attack. We'd dug holes inside Moon Base One and cleverly disguised them with interwoven branches, so we could store provisions in there without fear of it ever being found. Will and I had been in there about five minutes when Liam pushed in through the branches.

"Look what I've got," he said, and held out a stack of cards.

"Horror Top Trumps? You've had them for ages," Will said.

"No, look," he said and as he went to show us the cards, he dropped them onto the ground. An evil face stared out at me from one of the cards with sickly yellow flesh. It had a beard and hair. Both with horrible curls (I always knew curly hair was a bad sign, and a good reason not to eat crusts), with two horns sticking out of his head. He had sharp fangs and was surrounded by fire. It was called 'Fire Demon'. I'd never seen this card before.

"Liam, what are these?" I said as I glanced at the other cards.

"Series Two. Thirty-two new cards. Check this one out." Liam picked a card from the floor and held it up to us.

"Horror rating one-hundred?" Will said.

It was called Death and had hideous long teeth and a finger pointing out of the card.

"No way," I said. "Only Dracula has a horror rating of one-hundred."

"Not anymore," Liam said. "And check this one out." He held up a card called 'Alien Creature'. "Who does that look like?"

It was a light-brown-coloured creature with dark hair in a bowl-cut and with ugly twisted teeth.

Will laughed. "Bloody hell. It's Mrs Palmer!"

I couldn't see it myself. The Alien Creature was much uglier than Mrs Palmer, and it had only two fingers on each hand, though its fur was the same colour as her cardigans. "It doesn't look anything like her," I said.

"You would say that, wouldn't you?" Will said.

"What d'you mean?" Liam said.

"Didn't you know? Tom always gets crushes on his teachers."

Liam and Will rolled around with laughter. It wasn't true. I didn't *always* get crushes on my teachers. There was one time, with Miss Wishaw, who had lovely long red hair, but that was it.

"Ooh! Mrs Palmer," Liam said. He pulled the card towards his face and puckered his lips. "I'm Tom, and I love you."

I let them laugh for a minute. "Where did you get them from?"

"Mum bought them for us. She saw them in the toy shop in Downham Market."

"Cool. We should have a game. Where's Andy?"

As soon as I said it, he jumped into the base. "Surprise attack," he shouted as he clung on to my back and squeezed as hard as he could.

"Get off," I yelled. He'd shocked me. For a second, I thought I really was under attack, but it's not like I was close to turning my pants into a lemonade factory. I guess with the Top Trumps in front of me with those horrible pictures and all of the possibilities running through my head, I was on edge. "Come on," Will said, collecting up the rest of the cards. "Let's play."

We played a couple of rounds and I got to see a few new cards. Some of these monsters I'd never heard of, like The Living Skull and Dr. Syn, and others were gory like The Fiend and Venusian Death Cell.

"What we should do," Liam said as he handed his last card over to Will, "is combine the two sets and play an epic game with all sixty-two cards."

"Sixty-four," I said.

Liam looked at me with a squint, his lip curled in confusion.

"Two sets of thirty-two would be sixty-four."

"You're such a bighead."

Liam took back the cards and started to clumsily shuffle them.

"Deal them already, will you?" Will said, tossing a berry at Liam.

"Let me shuffle them first."

"So, what do you think's going on with John?" I said.

Liam started dishing out the cards. "Well the police are involved. We know that."

"Maybe Shredder got him!" Andy said, his eyes wide.

"He could have run away from home," Will said. "He hated his dad."

"I don't know," I said. "I don't think he hated him." John and I had spoken about our dads a few times, and his didn't seem anywhere near as bad as mine.

"What do you think happened to him then, Tom?" Liam said.

I picked up my cards. The top one was The Sorcerer. Maybe something magical had happened to him. Maybe a great wizard had enlisted him to go on an amazing adventure where HE was the hero, like in one of my Fighting Fantasy books. Or maybe he'd uncovered a monster's lair, and it had captured him and taken him away. "I don't know," I said.

After a couple more games Liam checked his watch and said it was time to go home if they were to be back in time for dinner, and possibly catch the end of the Uruguay versus Spain match. Will said that he was going to walk back with them, and I said I'd walk round the long way across to the back field, just in case. They knew what I meant.

When I got near the end of the field, where it met the bypass, I heard a rustling in the dyke. It was overgrown with stinging nettles. I could see them moving. Over the sound of the heavy vehicles which were levelling the verges at the side of the bypass I thought I could hear something else, perhaps a groan. Maybe John had come for a walk all around here if he had no one to play with at home. I edged towards the dyke and the nettles quivered again. There was a slight breeze, but it didn't seem strong enough to swirl the nettles that way. I peered in but could see nothing through the thickness of the nettles. The grass was not trampled and none of the nettles were squished or broken as they would have been if something had fallen in. The machinery stopped and I could hear slow breathing. "John?" I said, and the breathing sound changed into a low growl. I thought back to our game of Top Trumps. The card that stuck in my mind was The Fiend with its sharp talons slicing through its victim's neck.

The machines coughed back to life, disguising a louder growl. The nettles seemed to part as if the thing was coming towards me and I ran down into field of oilseed rape. I could hear my feet, heavy against the ground and over the snarl of the machines I was sure there was another sound pounding the ground behind me. It was chasing me, and it was going to tear my head off. It had probably done exactly the same to John. I ran faster than ever. I could barely breathe, and my face felt like it was burning. I made it across the field, jumped the ditch and clambered up the other side onto the narrow drove which led straight towards home. I daren't look over my shoulder because I didn't know its powers. If it captured me in its gaze, I might have been under its spell and be forced to halt and I'd be powerless to stop it removing my head and feasting on my tender neck-flesh. As much as I didn't want to turn my head, a squeal, like the excited laughter of a toddler, made me look round before I could stop myself. I caught sight of that damned old oak tree, my toes hit something, and I crashed to the ground. I tried to listen for the approaching beast but all I could hear was my pulse, the blood racing thickly through my veins. I managed to glance over my right shoulder and could see the tree. Its crooked grin was wider than ever and the way its branches were shaking made it look as though it was laughing at me. I felt the breeze ruffle my clothes and cool my back, wet with sweat. Every second that passed I was sure would be my last, but the end never came.

Eventually I rolled onto my back, certain that the creature would be there waiting for me, mocking me, wanting to look into my eyes before he stole my life (and possibly my ever-living soul too – as I said, I was not sure of The Fiend's powers). At first, I was blinded, but when I shielded my eyes from the sun, I saw there was nothing there. I traced my path along the drove to where I'd fallen and stared at the tree root in the ground, I'd caught my foot on. It was almost black and covered in wet soil. It wasn't dull and grey and hard like the rest of the earth on the drove. The nearest tree was a good twenty metres away. The oak was even further away, but when I looked at its warped face, I was sure that was where the root had come from. It had tripped me, deliberately, and wanted to see me get eaten by The Fiend. Or maybe it controlled The Fiend and would have had me taken to it and it would have plucked out my eye. But what had stopped it? Did I have magical protection over me? Was I the chosen one, and destined to be a hero?

"Oi!"

I turned to see that it was Dad marching down the drove towards me.

"What d'you think you're playing at lying in the middle of the drove like you're dead?"

Why did he always have to appear at the worst time?

"There's a young lad missing, could be dead for all you know, and you make out you're a dead body. What are you, simple or something?"

"I tripped," I said as I got up.

"And look at the state of your bloody trousers."

I looked down and saw my dusty kneecap through the tear in the material.

"You think we're made of money, and can replace your trousers and shirts every time you act like a daft bugger?"

My face was hot, and I couldn't talk. I swallowed heavily and concentrated on breathing normally as I marched past him.

"What are you doing playing out in your school clothes anyway?"

It was an on-going battle to keep the tears at bay when it came to Dad and me. If he saw them, he could call me a sissy, or a baby, and that meant he definitely won. If I could make it to the house without crying it still meant that he won, but the defeat wasn't quite as humiliating. When protected from The Fiend by some kind of magical force I thought it might be because I was destined to be the hero, but what kind of hero has to struggle so hard not to be a cry baby? Younger brothers are never the heroes anyway. Look at *The Lion, The Witch and The Wardrobe*. Peter was no cry baby. I was more like Edmund, likely to betray my family and screw everything up for everyone.

After dinner, during which Dad kept going on about me ruining my school trousers, Will and I went to our room to watch Argentina play the Soviet Union. We'd all laughed at school when Argentina were beaten by Cameroon, because they were the world champions, and they were supposed to be amazing. They had one player, called Maradona who even thought he was God.

Because Argentina had beaten England in the last World Cup (which I was too young to remember) people didn't really like them, but they were playing the Soviet Union who were even worse. They were always the baddies in films, like Rocky IV, which we'd watched at John's before it was even released here, so I was cheering for Argentina. Then, with about ten minutes gone in the game, the USSR had an attack and the Argentina goalkeeper, Pumpido, ran out to get the ball and crashed into this Soviet Union player who was built like Ivan Drago, and then he just lay on the floor waving when all of the rest of the players kept playing.

"What's wrong?" I said.

"Dunno. Must be injured."

They stopped play for a long time and on the replay, I could see that his leg was curved like a banana when he tried to stand up. Watching it made my dinner come back in my mouth and all I could taste was a mix of bile and gravy for a long time. This wasn't right. Stuff like this wasn't supposed to happen at the World Cup. Goalie's legs weren't supposed to snap. Beasts weren't supposed to chase kids across fields either.

Best friends weren't supposed to disappear.

NOW

Of course it's raining. We don't have those long hot summers like we used to. It's another one of those factors which makes the childhoods of my summer, and particularly what I consider to be the last childhood of my summer, seem so unreal. I remember summers so hot that there was a constant haze, but now it's all broken promises of barbeque summers and regional flooding. I look down at my reflection in a puddle. Charlie's boot catches the edge of it, and it sends a ripple, distorting the image, and I have to wonder if my own memories of what happened back then are also distorted in some way.

It all still feels so real. Despite gaining a great deal knowledge over all the years since, I can't understand the logic of it all. I know that it felt as if I was being chased along the drove. To me, the sound of footsteps behind me was real, and the feel of a presence behind me was real, but it could have been the product of a vivid imagination spurred by the fiction I was feeding on and fuelled by a lack of facts from our parents. I can still see the pictures on those cards. Give me a name of any of those beasts from either series one or two, and I could draw it for you. I could probably make a pretty good guess at its stats too.

That's why Charlie isn't exposed to anything like that.

I leave Charlie at the school gate. He doesn't mind that he's one of only a handful of pupils in year five that are dropped off at school by a parent, and the reason for that is simple. I've told him of the dangers that await those that walk home alone, and he doesn't want to be the sexual plaything of a paedophile. Of course, I've explained how small that risk is as I don't want him cowering in fear every time that he leaves the house, but I'd be a terrible parent if I didn't make him aware of the genuine risks.

On the way back home, I drop my reply to Mum's letter in the mail, letter her know that we'll be there at the weekend.

These days, I communicate with Mum solely by letter. I'd email, but, unbelievably, they don't have a computer. For her communications with me, I have three very strict rules:

1.   Don't talk about Dad.
2.   Don't talk about the past.
3.   Don't tell me anything about Little Mosswick.

Mum sticks to these, so her letters can be rather short. They consist mostly of questions about how we are, and comments in response to the pictures I send her of Charlie.

When we meet, which I allow once a year near Christmas, and nowhere near my house, which she will never visit, I go over the rules again so that she is certain not to cross the line. When we speak, it is embedded firmly in the present. Victoria's death made this somewhat easier, as she can ask me how I'm coping, and tell me what a wonderful job I'm doing with Charlie. Am I? I know that she's only saying that to keep me on-side, still unaware that all I ever desired from her, back then and every moment since, was a little bit of honesty.

Could I have used her support when a reckless driver made me a widower and a single father before I was 40? Definitely. Did I take it? Not a chance. Showing emotional weakness may have opened a window to let him back in, and I wasn't going to allow that for all of the world.

Of course, when I go back there, I cannot expect her to live by those rules. There will be others too, people from that time who know what happened.

When I go back there, it means that it's time to deal with the baggage I left behind. But if he's really dying, then I guess it must be safe.

Now that he's dying, I can go back.

Thursday 14th June 1990

I made it to school early and I was hoping that the last couple of days would prove to be a waste of time when John turned up. He wasn't in the first wave of pupils that I expected to find him in, so I decided to slip into the school.

John's PE bag was still on his peg. I crept up to it, looking both ways to check that the corridor was clear. I didn't know what to expect to find in there but was hoping for a hint that he was in some way unhappy, or something that would tell me that he had a reason to run away. I lifted out his boot-bag and peered in at the football boots which still had clumps of mud and bits of grass on from last week's game. His World Cup Football Top Trumps were in there, with the case already scuffed up despite him only having had them for a week. There was nothing else in there, no note, no ancient artefacts, no clues, not even his P.E. shorts or top.

"That's not your bag, Master Tillbrook."

I looked up and saw Mr Jenkins coming towards me, holding a spray bottle.

"No, it's John's," I said.

"I know it's John's, and that's why you shouldn't be snooping in it."

"I'm sorry; I was looking for clues."

"Ah!" said Mr Jenkins. He stopped moving and gave me a smile. "Friends of yours, is he?"

I nodded.

"You know you shouldn't be in here before the first bell."

"I know."

"And if the wrong person caught you doing what I did, they might think you were thieving."

"I wasn't!"

"I know that, but not everybody is such a good judge of character as me. So why don't you go back out onto the playground and we'll pretend none of this happened, hey?"

Mr Jenkins followed me out, and then sprayed the window beside the door. He took a rag from his pocket and started to wipe. From the way his cheeks puffed out I could tell he was whistling. I was so focussed on Mr Jenkins' wiping action that I didn't notice Liam sneaking up on me, and he had his wet finger in my earhole before I had a chance to stop him.

I was still trying to wipe dry my ear when the bell went. Mrs Palmer stood by her classroom door and said hello to me as I entered. She greeted us all rather than shuffling papers at her desk or writing stuff on the blackboard as she usually did.

Liam jabbed me in the ribs as I stopped by my desk and whispered, "Alien creature." I didn't think it was funny, even though she was wearing one of those mustard-coloured cardigans again, but I smiled anyway and made a sort of fake-laugh noise which I think Liam thought was real.

Mrs Palmer didn't read out the register either, almost as if saying John's name would draw attention to the fact that he wasn't there again. Normally, a two-day absence would escalate the rumours from the previous day, leading to a diagnosis of the hyper-squirts, or in severe cases, the dynamite-shits. I turned to look at Liam, who always sat behind me. He was looking down at his hands. I made eye-contact with Daniel; he turned his head towards John's seat then shrugged his shoulders.

There was a knock, and Mrs Palmer went to the door.

"Pssst."

I turned around.

"What does transition mean?" Liam said in a loud whisper.

I looked down at the worksheet that Mrs Palmer had left on our desks, which was odd, because we normally started with PE on a Thursday, but couldn't see the word Liam had mentioned. Mrs Palmer was now standing at the door, talking to someone who was standing in the corridor - probably Mr Inglehart.

"What does what mean?" I said.

Mrs Palmer turned and glared, before turning back to her conversation.

"Transition."

"Don't know. Why?"

"Something I heard the teachers talking about. Might be a clue."

Mrs Palmer closed the door and turned her attention to us, meaning it was time to be quiet if we wanted to avoid sharpening pencils during break-time.

"Today," said Mrs Palmer, "we have a visitor. P.C. Wade will be coming in after break to speak to you."

From behind me, I could tell that Liam had put up his hand. He always made an "ooh" noise as he raised it, as if a question or answer had hit him with force. Without waiting for an invitation Liam said, "Is it about John, Miss?"

Mrs Palmer put a hand to her temple. "Liam, please don't speak until asked to do so."

I turned to see Liam shrink in his chair.

"But yes," continued Mrs Palmer, "some of you may already know, but John has not been seen since school on Tuesday. P.C. Wade would like to speak to each of you about John."

We all knew P.C. Wade. He was a regular visitor to the school. It was only a fortnight since his last visit in which he spoke to us about road safety. With the new bypass about to open the traffic flow through the village was likely to be reduced, but he assured us that our lollipop lady, Mrs Barnes, would still be there at the start and end of the school day to help us cross the road. Before that he'd spoken in an assembly about the danger of construction sites. I remember sharing sheepish looks with Will and my cousins, as well as John who'd come with us a time or two to mess about on the huge piles of sand and stone that were to be used for the bypass. We'd wander around the machinery while it was left unoccupied for the night, sit in the bucket of a JCB or try to throw stones over the top of the sand heap. One weekend we found a load of empty beer-cans pushed into the mound of sand, so we hadn't gone back. We didn't want to get caught messing around at the older kids' hangout.

We worked through the sheet until break. There was a pretty dull story to read, with questions to answer, and then you had to write the next chapter yourself. Normally I liked creative writing, but I could get into it at all.

When the bell went, Liam was quickly out of his chair, and he stood in front of my desk. "Let's ask if we can borrow the dictionary," he said.

It was always down to me to ask. If Liam asked it would probably be a no, but she seemed to like me. "Miss," I called out as I stood up.

"Yes Thomas?"

"Can I have a look in the dictionary?"

"Okay, but I have to go to a meeting in the staff room. I want you out of here before I get back."

I picked the big dictionary from the shelf by her desk and turned to the 'T' section. "Transition" I muttered as I flicked through the pages.

"Ooh!" Liam said and smudged his finger onto the word.

"Transition. The process or a period of changing from one state or condition to another."

"Oh," Liam said, and scratched his head. "What's that got to do with anything?" he asked.

"I don't know," I said, and looked at the mustard cardigan hanging on the back of Mrs Palmer's chair.

When we got in from break, Mrs Palmer didn't want us talking either before or after our interview, so we had to sit quietly and read. I know I stared at the same page for the whole morning, the words not sinking in, and from the lack of the sound of pages turning I guessed everyone else was doing the same. Every time the door opened, we'd all look up and try to read something on the face of whoever came back in. Whispers were hushed by Mrs Palmer's glare. We were going in by surname order. Liam went in before me because his surname is Carter. When he came back in his face was red. He embarrassed easily and didn't like to be questioned because he had this habit of always looking guilty, whether he'd done anything or not.

I had to wait until near the end. When Daniel Richardson went in, I knew I'd be next. John's mum would have spoken to Daniel on Tuesday night, and I guess he hadn't seen John either. A few minutes later Daniel returned. He walked back to his seat, sat down and sniffed loudly.

"Thomas Tilbrook," called P.C. Wade.

Liam's cheeks were still pink when he arrived at Moon Base One. Once embarrassed, he stayed that way until the next morning. He plonked himself down on the log we used as a bench. Will nodded at him.

"What did Wade ask you?" Liam said, looking first at Will, then at me.

Will shrugged and continued to scrape the bark from a stick with his penknife.

"When was the last time I saw him. If we were friends. Stuff like that," I said.

"What did you say?"

"I said that we were best friends, and I told them he didn't like being left home alone after school."

"Yeah, I said that too."

"I told them we'd had an argument that day."

"Tom!" Liam's cheeks reddened further than I thought possible.

"What?"

"They'll think you're a suspect."

"No, they won't."

"They will. Haven't you seen *The Bill*?"

"Shut up, Liam." I hadn't seen *The Bill*. Dad would never let us watch that, and I don't reckon Liam had seen it either, but I knew what he was talking about.

"They'll say you've got a motive."

"Liam," Will said, pointing with the tip of his penknife. "Leave it. Did they ask either of you if you'd seen any weirdos hanging about the village?"

"Yeah," I said. "Something like that. Asked if I'd seen anyone strange in the village."

"Me too," Liam said.

"What did you say?"

"No." Liam and I said it at the exact same moment, so I quickly blurted out, "Jinx," stopping Liam from speaking until released from the curse.

As Liam waved around his arms, hoping that Will or I would say his full name, Andy jumped into the hideout. As usual he was in his Teenage Mutant Ninja Turtle gear. He had a dustbin lid strapped to his back as a shell, and a bit of orange fabric with eyeholes cut out of it tied around his head.

"Hey, I got nun-chucks," Andy said. He pulled out his weapon. It was a couple of cardboard kitchen-roll tubes tied together with a bit of blue string. He held one tube in each hand and left them far enough apart for the string to be slack, and grimaced.

"Radical" Will said, rolling his eyes before going back to sharpening his stick.

Liam was peering out of one of Moon Base One's viewing windows by pulling the branches of the elderberry bush back. "Shush!" he said, ducking down lower.

Will punched him on the arm for breaking the conditions of the jinx.

"Stop," he said, with panic in his eyes as he pushed Will away.

"What's up?" asked Will.

"Someone's coming."

"Who?"

"Shaky Jake."

We were silent. Cautiously we crept into the corners of the base where we could peer out secretly.

Jake was striding along the drove, quickly moving from one side to the other and peering down into the ditches. I could see his mouth moving, and I could tell that he was saying something, but I couldn't make it out. It sounded like a bunch of nonsense noises, over and over, like some kind of chant. Maybe it was a spell of some kind, or a curse.

We watched him pass and walk off into the distance, and it wasn't until we couldn't hear him anymore that anyone dared to move or speak.

Eventually, I broke the silence. "Did the policeman come into your class, Andy?" I asked.

"Yeah." He tucked his nun-chucks into the side of his shorts. "He said if we had any information about John, we should tell a grown up."

"No one said anything?" I said.

Andy shook his head.

"What are we going to do?" Liam said.

"We're the turtles!" Andy said, "We'll find him then go for pizza."

Will closed his penknife. "We're not turtles. We're the Crusaders".

Andy looked at the ground. "But if we were the Turtles, we could be heroes and save the day."

"We can still save the day," Will said. He picked up the sticks he'd prepared and handed us one each. "Come on," he said. "We know this village better than anyone. We'll find him."

"How?" I said. I could feel the excitement building in us all. This was our moment. We were going to be heroes.

"We're going to take a walk back down to the school and follow the road along, take a look to see if maybe he fell into a ditch or something."

He was the one cut out to be the hero. For all my good intentions when it came to the crunch I'd probably hide away in terror and, if I was very lucky, I might be able to avoid turning into a cry-baby. I was like The Incredible Hulk in reverse, shrinking to the size of an infant when wound up. I suppose there's a chance I could drown my enemy in tears? I looked at Liam. He bent his stick with both hands then it slipped out of one and thwacked him in the side of the face. He was good to have around and would never let you down, but he wasn't the hero. Andy was laughing and swinging his nun-chucks. He was the comedy sidekick.

"Don't you think the adults would already have checked the ditches?" I said, and instantly regretting it, as I was proving myself to be a wet blanket again.

"They don't know them like we do," Will said, like any good hero should.

I took a stick and followed Will out of Moon Base One. Liam and Will grabbed the branches and pushed them back in place to hide the entrance. We'd flattened the tall grass around the outside and then collected rocks and branches to make an enclosure. Liam, Will, and I stepped over the thick mud at the bottom of the ditch which never seemed to dry out no matter how many days without rain we went. We clambered up the other side and waited for Andy who was checking that his nun-chucks were secure. He took a step backwards then ran towards the ditch. He took off and shouted "Cowabunga" in mid-air. Together, Will and I caught him to stop his momentum from carrying him over into the ditch on the other side. Then we started our walk back to towards the school, prodding our sticks into the ditch and random bushes as we walked.

"So, what do you think happened to him?" Liam said as we reached the school.

"He might have been hit by a car and fell into a ditch," Will said.

"But wouldn't the driver stop and do something about it?" asked Liam.

"Didn't when it happened to me," I said. I reminded them of what had happened the previous summer. I'd been cycling from Granddad Norman's cottage back towards the farmhouse when a lorry sped past. It didn't hit me or anything, but the gush of air caused me to lose my balance and fall into the ditch. I pulled the bike out, but the front wheel was buckled. I was only a couple of doors down from Granddad's and I was going to push it back there, but the this old woman, Mrs Johnstone, who used to work as a dinner lady at the school before she had her accident, saw me heaving the bike out and rushed over to me. She made me go with her into kitchen and put TCP on my knees and elbows even though they were barely grazed and before I had a chance to say no, she called home to say what had happened. When Dad turned up, he said, "Come on," to me and dragged me off the stool. The only good thing about being dragged away so quickly is that I only had to eat one of her soft old-people biscuits. Dad nodded at Mrs Johnstone and picked up my bike and tossed it in the back of his Land Rover.

"Poor boy never would have been hurt if you hadn't messed the council about with your land for the bypass," said Mrs Johnstone.

Dad didn't say a word to me all the way home. I never got my bike back. When I asked Dad what had happened to it he said it was too badly damaged, though I'm sure the wheel could have been replaced.

"Speaking of Mrs Johnstone..." Liam said. He shuffled through the Top Trump cards he'd just pulled from his back pocket. "Zetan Priest."

We all laughed. The character of the card had a mess of white hair, and a white face, just like hers. But the thing that most resembled her was the pink coat it was wearing. It was one of the least scary cards in the pack, but with a Horror Rating of 95, Killing Power of 91 and Physical Strength of 94 it was a powerful card to have. It goes to show that you can't really judge what someone is like by looking at them. I didn't know what a Zetan Priest was but figured it must be some kind of witch.

We continued poking our way along the side of the road until we reached Downham Close. We hadn't found a thing. I felt like Mario when he gets through the castle only to be told, "Thank you, but our princess is in another castle." John would like that joke, apart from him being the princess. I was about to share it with the others, but by the looks on their faces none of them would have laughed.

"What now?" asked Liam.

"Let's leave it there for today," Will said.

"We can't leave it," I said.

"I had a thought," Liam said.

"What?" I asked.

"You know I heard them teachers talking about that transition thing?"

I nodded.

"And you know when we looked it up, it meant changing from one thing to another?"

I nodded again.

"And you know Mrs Palmer is an alien creature?"

"What are you going on about?" Will said, and gripped Liam's arm, threatening a Chinese-burn.

"Don't," Liam said, wildly shaking his head.

"Get on with it, "Will said, "and stop saying 'you know' all of the time."

"Okay," Liam said. "What if this transition is a plan to turn all of us into aliens, just like her?"

But Mrs Palmer just *looked* like an alien, right?

"Think about it," Liam said, which sounded strange coming from him because he was often the last one to think about anything. "No one saw John leave school. He could still be there, locked away somewhere."

"Should we go back to check it out?" I asked.

"Be realistic. It'll all be locked up by now, anyway," Will said. "Plus Cameroon are playing Romania. We've already missed half of it."

I suppose a hero knows when to call time on a search.

We got home and Will and I played rock-scissors-paper to decide who was making everyone drinks. I went with paper, because Will is usually rock, but he'd changed to paper. I changed to rock, thinking he'd go for scissors, but he went for paper again. He never usually played the same way twice. He took Andy and Liam upstairs to watch the match and left me at the sink. I poured cordial in the bottom of each glass, and just after I topped up the third one with water, I heard a shout from upstairs, "Quick, Tom!" I filled the last glass, put them all on a tray and hurried up the stairs. One of the glasses tipped over, but most of the liquid remained on the tray, with only a trickle of blackcurrant juice landing on the carpet. As I got into the bedroom they were crowded around the TV.

"You missed it," Liam said. "Cameroon scored and he did a dance at the corner flag."

"Who did?"

"The Cameroon player."

"What's the score?"

"One – nil."

Cameroon were coming forward again and looked like they were going to score. I had to sort out the spilled juice. I kept imagining the sound of the front door going and Dad coming in and seeing the juice. Even though we'd seen him on his tractor when we came in, and he was miles away, it was as if he could travel great distances in an instant to catch me out.

I was about to go to the bathroom to get some toilet paper to mop up my spill when Cameroon raced forward again, and Roger Milla scored. This time I got to see his little dance in the corner flag.

I was smiling the whole time I scrubbed at the stairs carpet. Luckily, I'd made the juice weak and with a bit of soap scrubbed in there it couldn't be seen at all. There were a few bits of torn tissue stuck to it, but they were the same colour, at least. A purple stain would have been much more noticeable. It didn't take long either and I was back in the bedroom when there were only two minutes left and Romania scored to make it 2-1 to Cameroon. Suddenly, we were interested, cheering on Cameroon, hoping they could stop Romania from scoring another goal to equalise the game. As soon as it was over, I got out my sticker album. We looked at the Cameroon page. They were another one of those teams that had two players per sticker, as if no one expected them to be of any interest. I had all of the players and was only missing the shiny Cameroon badge sticker and the team sticker. But Roger Milla wasn't in there, and we figured that made him in some way special, because the Panini didn't even know who he was, but he'd scored two goals at the World Cup finals, and if that didn't prove that magical things could happen, then nothing would.

"Boy!" Dad shouted from downstairs.

Will was already down there. He'd gone to fetch drinks, and I had been wondering why he hadn't returned.

I started down the stairs, each step making me wonder what it was I'd done. Maybe Will had dobbed me in for something, but nothing came to mind. I looked at the spot where I'd spilt the juice, but there was no sign of anything. He couldn't know.

"Come on, boy!" he called again. "Your Uncle Rodney's here."

I stuttered down the stairs. Each footstep felt heavy. I could already feel my nostrils being invaded by his alcohol stink.

I pushed open the door to see him leaning forward on his chair, his backside barely touching it. His fingers were spread out and his whole hands jerked up and down as he finished telling his story, "So there I was, trousers around my ankles, and he says to me, 'No! I said show me you're willing!' Of course, I got out of there as soon as I could."

Dad was laughing like I'd never seen him, his cheeks looking like they were going to burst, and a huge smile spread all across his face.

I looked at Will, and he appeared as confused as I was.

Uncle Rodney turned to look at me. His top lip had a scattering of grey whiskers and his eyes were half closed.

"Thomas, my dear boy!" he said, and opened his arms to welcome me.

I looked over to Dad, to see if he was watching me. He wasn't, but if I hesitated too long, he'd soon notice. I walked over to Uncle Rodney.

Dad then looked at us and said, "You're Uncle Rodney knows someone that's giving away some chickens, so we'll have the coop back up and running in no time."

I thought back to the disgusting scene of the morning. I couldn't imagine ever opening the coop again without seeing the dismembered corpses. I was so caught up in that grim vision that I didn't notice Uncle Rodney move to slap me on the back in what he probably thought was a friendly way, but for me it was like being swatted by a mighty ogre; Rodney had enormous hands that looked comical at the end of his long, thin arms. I couldn't help but jerk forward, my hip crashing into the table. Teacups rippled before sloshing over the side and onto the tablecloth.

"You daft boy," Dad said. "Look what you've done."

"You always were a little unstable of foot," laughed Rodney as I went to grab a tea towel to mop up the spillages.

I was a little unstable of foot? He was one the one who fell of the stage every single year at the Mosswick Amateur Dramatic Society's summer performance. I never did find out what became of Macbeth as he crashed headfirst off the stage and had to be rushed to hospital for stitches. If he wasn't the originator and chairman of the MADS society no one would ever have cast him. I'm sure people only turned up to his shows because they were sure that he was going to make a fool of himself.

Will was narrowing his eyes at me from the table, where he sat next to Uncle Rodney. He was slurping a can of Coke through a straw. It had weird letters on it, like an O with a cross through it. Where'd he get that from?

"Would you like a drink, my boy?" said Rodney.

I looked down at the blue and white striped carrier bag by his feet and tried to glance inside. It bulged with colour. Uncle Rodney reached his hand inside and plucked out a can of Coke. It has the same strange lettering. He pulled the ring-pull off for me, and then handed me the can. As I was about to raise it to by lips, he put a finger on them to stop me. His finger tasted fusty. With his other hand he reached into his coat pocket and grabbed a straw from who knows where. He was a bit like a clown, or a magician pulling a string of hankies from his pocket, only these hankies would be a little bit dirty and tainted. The straw was a discoloured red. He dropped it into the can and it nearly bobbed back out again until I pushed it down with my fingers.

"Sit down, my boy," said Rodney.

I looked across the table to the seat by Dad, but as I was about to move over there, I felt hands on my hips. Rodney picked me up, as if I weighed nothing at all, and plonked me down onto him right leg.

Rodney's strength was always a surprise to everybody, because he wasn't big, as such. Yes, he was the tallest man I'd ever seen, but he was thin with it, and his hair, a dyed-brown-with-a-hint-of-red tangle of wiry curls, only helped further the clown look.

"No need to go all the way round there when there's a perfectly good seat here!" he said, and then he continued his conversation with Dad about people I'd never heard of.

Uncle Rodney spoke in a strange posh voice. It was nothing like the way that Dad or Granddad spoke, He liked to tell stories, so he was quite like Granddad in that way, but Rodney's stories were totally different; they were about the theatre and people with strange nicknames, like Bobbo, Wiggy, and Archer, that said strange things in the pub, The Merry Maidens, which was in the next village over, Great Mosswick (which was actually smaller than Little Mosswick).

Dad sat there taking it all in, nodding occasionally. He seemed to be totally fascinated by Uncle Rodney's nonsense.

I couldn't help but look at the way he moved his mouth when he talked, pushing out each vowel sound with his cheeks. There were some small scabs on his left cheek which caught the light every time he tipped his head back to drink his tea. He caught me looking at him and brushed at the side of his face. "Bit of a scrape with a razor blade," he said. "Hey, why don't you pick up the bag and see what's inside?"

Uncle Rodney always had the oddest chocolate bars. I picked out an orange packet with a brown bear on the front. The lettering said 'Bamse Mums'. I passed one to Will who tore off the corner with his teeth and bit straight into it.

I was more careful. I unwrapped it slowly and let the scent of the chocolate waft into my nostrils. It was shaped like a bear, and it looked a little soft, with melted chocolate clinging to the packet. Of course, it had started to melt in the kitchen. I took a bite to discover marshmallow inside. Flakes of chocolate fell from the bear, and onto Rodney's right trouser leg.

He looked down, and brushed the flakes away, but only succeeded in smearing the melted chocolate into his trousers, and then he let his hand come to a rest on my leg and gave it a squeeze.

I looked over at Will again. Now he was carefully stripping the chocolate away from the marshmallow at the foot of the bear. I did the same, carefully to as to ensure that no more fell onto Uncle Rodney.

"Time for your bath, boys."

I hadn't noticed Mum standing in the door to the kitchen. She often found herself something else to do when Rodney was around.

Will had a look of disappointment on his face, and noisily slurped what was left of his Coke, but I was happy to get away.

How could one member of the family be so different I thought? But then I looked across at Will, and Dad and saw how similar they were becoming. I looked at Rodney, who was blinking rapidly, as if he'd lost control of his eyelids, and I wondered if that was how I was destined to turn out.

Friday 15th June 1990

iam brought the Top Trumps to school. He was obviously thinking along the same lines as I was. He looked through the pack, put a card on the top of the pile and said, "Follow me."

It was break time. We weren't supposed to go into school at break unless we were going into the library, going to the toilet, or if we had a detention.

"Where are we going?" I said.

"You'll see."

We walked past the entrance to the library. Liam peered into the classrooms on the way. We walked past the first set of toilets. As we went by Mr Jenkins office (the one with the CARETAKER sign on the door) Liam peered in. He was in there gazing into a box and whistling something unrecognisable.

"Look at this card," Liam said in a whisper.

It was Ape Man.

"Hello Mr Jenkins," Liam said, causing the caretaker to turn around.

"You boys shouldn't be in here at break," he said then turned back to whatever he was doing.

It was lucky that he did turn because I could barely contain my laughter. They were practically the same person. Same big beard. Same eyebrows. Admittedly Mr Jenkins didn't have a massive club, or wear fur, but maybe his caretaker outfit was a disguise. He was certainly strong; we'd seen him carrying all sorts of things around the playground. And maybe that was why we didn't recognise any of the songs he whistled, because they were all so old, they came from the Stone Age.

We hurried back outside, lucky to avoid any teachers who would have told us off for being in at break.

"So, what do you think?" Liam said.

"He looks just like him," I said. "Mr Jenkins is the Ape Man!"

"But what do you think of him... as a suspect!" Liam's eyes were huge.

Could the Ape Man have taken John? "We better tell Will," I said.

Will was playing football. It looked like everyone wanted to be Cameroon again. We didn't have to wait long to see a goal, followed by a Roger Milla impression. When the bell went, we waited for Will to leave the pitch.

Liam held out the Ape Man card. "Who does that look like?"

Will shrugged.

"Mr Jenkins the caretaker," Liam said, nodding his head.

Will laughed and grabbed the card.

"Oi, Chris." He showed him the card. "Mr Jenkins."

Chris laughed and called over some other boys and shared the joke. One boy started making monkey noises.

Liam grabbed Will's arm and pulled him closer to whisper to him. Liam was rubbish at whispering. He was too loud, and he always breathed heavily into your ear, and his breath always felt hot and made your face clammy.

"What if Mr Jenkins has John?"

"Because he looks like the Ape Man you think he might be involved?"

"He's a suspect, right?"

"Give me the cards." Will held out his hand.

Liam sighed and gave Will the cards.

Will flicked through them then pulled out Fu Manchu. "Look at this one's moustache. He looks just like that bloke that works in the petrol station. Maybe he's got John locked up in the back of one of the cars!" Will dramatically held his hands up by the side of his face, and let his mouth hang open.

Liam took a sharp intake of breath and Will dumped the cards back in his hands and walked off.

"Do you think he could be?"

"Nah," I said, then had another look at the card. "But it's a pretty good match." And we sniggered all the way back to the classroom.

Mrs Palmer wasn't in there yet, and we were the first back. On her desk was a set of exercise books. I dashed in, swiped a couple, gave one to Liam, and hid the other in my PE bag.

"What did you do that for?" asked Liam.

"We can start recording all of our ideas in there," I said. "To help us find John."

At lunchtime we went through the cards looking for other matches. We wondered if we could find anyone for Mr Inglehart. When he first came to the school three years ago people said he was like *The Demon Headmaster*. The book used to be in the school library, but then it disappeared. At first we all thought that he'd had it removed to stop the rumours, but it turned out that he wasn't particularly strict, he never told anyone off for no reason, and he was good at training the football team, so the rumours stopped and everyone ended up thinking he was okay for a headmaster. The only card he looked a little bit like was Dracula, and as he was outside walking around the playground most lunchtimes, we figured he couldn't be a vampire.

Liam started chuckling as he was flicking through the cards. He covered his mouth with his hand.

"What?" I said.

"Nothing."

"No, what is it?"

"Well, you see this one?" He held out The Mad Axeman. It had a green face, and white hair. He had only one eye open. "Shaky Jake."

I nodded and started flicking through the rest of the cards when Laura walked by with Becky. Laura had her hair in pigtails, and she was always smiling. Becky had a fringe that came down to the top of her glasses and was always moody.

"Hey Laura," I said, and she came over. I could tell that Becky was trying to stop her, and in the end, she followed her over.

"Which of these three cards looks more like Shaky Jake?" I held out The Mad Axeman, Madman (yellow, lumpy face, brown hair, badly receding) and The Mad Magician (Long white hair, top hat, dark, creepy eyes and a weird smile).

"He hasn't got white hair, but his face is a bit like the magician's. His hair is more like the madman's."

"So, a cross between The Mad Magician and Madman then?"

"I suppose so," said Laura, and she started to walk away.

"Have you ever seen him do any magic?"

"No."

"Tell her about Mr Jenkins," Liam said.

I shuffled through the cards until I found Ape Man. "We reckon Mr Jenkins could be the Ape Man."

"That's mean," said Becky. "Mr Jenkins is a nice man."

Becky walked off and Laura followed her.

I stared at Liam, and he shrugged.

"What?" he said.

"What did you have to go and tell her about that for?"

"It's funny."

"But you made her go away."

"So?" I could almost hear Liam's brain ticking. "You fancy her, don't you?"

"No!" I said. I did though.

"Yes, you do!"

"Shhhh!" I said.

"Well I suppose it's a step up from Mrs Palmer. We couldn't have you hooking up with an Alien Creature."

"I never fancied Mrs Palmer."

"I'm not surprised. She's an alien."

"Let's get back to work," I said and flicked through the cards again. "How about this one: The Gorgon is Mrs Barnes."

Liam nodded. "Yeah she has hair like that. It could definitely be her."

"Okay, that's good." I picked up the next card.   "What about The Freak?"

"You're The Freak."

"No, you're The Freak".

"Freak."

"I know you are, but what am I?"

We didn't get much further.

At afternoon break Liam and I sat under the shade of a tree. Liam started pulling and then splitting blades of grass. Eventually he stopped and looked at me. "Do you remember when we were round at John's and he put that tape on of that TV show he'd recorded off Sky?"

John had satellite TV. He got to watch all of these cool American TV shows, like *COPS* and *WWF Superstars*. Sometimes he'd tape them and let us watch them, so we'd know who he was talking about when he went on about Hulk Hogan or the Ultimate Warrior or Rowdy Roddy Piper or Hacksaw Jim Duggan.

"Which one?" I said to Liam, because there were a lot of times, he'd taped shows for us.

"*Unsolved Mysteries* do you remember it?"

I thought for a second, and then it came back to me, "Yeah," I said.

"Do you reckon we could get in touch with them and they'd help us investigate?"

"Hey Liam," someone shouted.

We looked up, and the ball was trickling towards us.

Will was trotting over to collect it, so Liam got up and passed him the ball.

"What are you talking about?" asked Will.

"*Unsolved Mysteries*." I said.

Will picked up the ball, drop-kicked it back onto the pitch, and then sat down with us.

"That was the show with the crop circles at the start, right?" Will said.

"There hasn't been anything like that round here, has there?" I said.

"Worth keeping an eye out for," Will said. "Don't you remember – there was that bit about that lady who just caught fire on the show?"

"Spontaneous human combustion?" I said.

"Yeah, that's it!" Will said.

"What about it?"

"Wait," Liam said. "How about if that happened to John? He got really hot while we were watching that, and, remember, he was the only one of us who had a shell suit."

"So?"

"Tom! You're not thinking! Don't you remember anything? Like when Wade came into the school with the fireman and they did that demonstration of how easily shell suits could catch on fire? And that's why they were banned from school?"

"Liam, calm down," Will said, and he stood up and heading back towards the game.

"You're still not getting it!" Liam was starting to go a red. "What if he was wearing his shell suit – got really hot and then spontaneously combusted!" Liam stood up too.

"Where are you going?" I said.

"To tell Mr Inglehart, so he can pass it on to the police."

"No, Liam, I don't think that happened."

"But surely they have to investigate the possibility?"

"There would be some kind of evidence though, right? Scorch marks on the ground or something."

"Good plan. After school we can search for burn marks and crop circles."

I nodded my head. "Ace."

Liam sat back down.

"You don't think he's really gone forever, though, do you?" I said.

"I don't know, Tom."

"It's so weird. Nothing like this has ever happened before."

"How about when your dog went missing? That came back, didn't it?" Liam said.

"Chappie always used to wander off and come back," I said. But he'd not done it recently. He'd not done much at all recently.

"Yeah, but dogs are smart."

"John's smart too, Liam. He'll be okay."

After school we talked over our plan for the afternoon. "We could follow the drove round the back of the school. He might have gone off that way," I said. As you pass behind the school you can see into the staff room. We liked to mimic the teachers, make up pretend conversations they might have had about us.

We each picked up long sticks as we started our walk, except for Andy who plucked his nun-chucks from his rucksack. Liam thrust his stick into some elderberry bushes. There was a rustling and some birds flew out.

"What if John is out here?" Liam said.

"If we find him? Good." Will said.

"But what if I poke him in the eye, or something?"

"Didn't do Granddad Norman any harm."

"Seriously though," I said, "what if we do find him and he's *not* okay?"

"What do you mean?" Andy said.

"Nothing," Will said.

Andy looked sadly at the ground. He poked at a branch with his foot.

"He didn't mean anything," Will said, and put a hand on Andy's shoulder. "Those are some cool nun-chucks."

Andy smiled, and gripped the handles tightly.

"Let's keep going," said Will.

Around the corner were a group of older boys, Jimmy Wilson's older brother, Gavin, among them.

"Watchya Bill," Gavin said.

One of the other boys was smoking.

Will nodded towards them.

"What are you doing around here?" Gavin said.

"Hanging out," said Will.

"With a bunch of little kids?"

"My brother and my cousins."

"Wanna ditch them and come with us? Drew's pinched some fags from his dad."

"Better not," said Will. "I've got to look after this lot."

The boys walked on past us. Was that really the only reason that Will hung out with us after school? I suppose he was one of the cool kids, and sometimes I felt pretty far from it. I tried to forget it and looked through the gaps in the hedges towards the school, trying to look into each room to see if anything peculiar was going on, or if anyone unusual came in or out of the school. It wasn't until we got around to the back of the school playing field that we found anything interesting, just past the Broom Cupboard – our small storage area where we kept a few sharpened sticks and a couple of bow and arrows.

"Hey, what's this?" Andy said as he pushed aside some leaves. There were a couple of empty packets of Fishermen's Friend – sweets so gross that no child I know would ever eat them - and, partly covered by loose dirt and wedged under a protruding root, a magazine. On the cover was a woman in her bra and knickers. It was called Fiesta. We decided to take it with us as evidence.

We heard a twig snap and looked up. Coming from the opposite direction was Shaky Jake. He looked at us and then quickly turned around and hurried back the way he'd come, back towards his house.

From a distance, we followed him. The drove curved back round onto Main Street, a couple of hundred metres past the school, and opposite Downham Close. Shaky Jake had already gone into his house, and we could see his curtain twitching.

"Do you think we should report him?" I said.

"What for?" Will said.

"That's twice we've seen him snooping around. Perhaps he knows something."

"We can't report him for that though."

"Wade asked if we'd seen any weirdos hanging around. He's a weirdo," Liam said.

"Maybe he's worth keeping an eye on," Will said, and then he looked over Liam's shoulder. "Is that Dad's Land Rover?"

Dad sped towards us and broke sharply. He wound down the window. "Where the bloody hell have you lot been? Your mothers have been worried sick."

"Hi Uncle Trevor," Andy said.

"Get in, the bloody lot of you."

We all looked down at the magazine, which had somehow ended up in my hands.

"What you got there, boy?"

"Nothing." I moved it to behind my back.

Dad threw the door open, climbed out and spun me round. He took the magazine from me and looked at it.

"Bloody filth." He tossed it into the front of the Land Rover. "Get in. Now."

We all climbed into the Land Rover. The smell of smoke was thick, and it was hard not to cough. I'd never seen Dad smoke, though there were often packets of tobacco around the house.

Dad reversed into the drove and turned the Land Rover around. He dropped Andy and Liam off first.

Aunt Anne was standing by the door, she put up her hand, but neither Will nor I dared move to wave back.

"Thanks Uncle Trevor," Andy said, completely unaware of the extent of his anger.

As he sped towards home, he turned to look at me.

"We'll have to have a talk about your little magazine later."

Mum came out of the house to meet us. She must have heard Dad pull up. I saw him roll up the magazine and put it in the glovebox, and I caught a glimpse of what I thought was a bag of Fisherman's Friends. Mum hugged me first and then pulled Will in too.

"Go in and wash your hands ready for dinner," she said as she let us go. As we went through the kitchen, we saw that Granddad Norman was sitting at the dinner table holding a mug of tea. He was wearing his patch, so probably hadn't put a glass eye in.

"What have you lads been up to then?" he asked, and leaned towards us, using his walking cane for balance.

"We were out with Liam and Andy," Will said as he went over to the sink and turned the tap on.

"Your poor mum has been going out of her head," Granddad said.

Will had turned the tap up too high and water hit a spoon in the bottom of the sink and sploshed all over his top.

"We were looking for John," I said.

"That missing boy? He'll turn up."

I looked back towards the door, wondering why Mum and Dad hadn't come in yet. Maybe he was telling her about the magazine. I wish we'd had a proper look at it when we had the chance. I know Daniel's seen one before, because he kept going on about it like he was some kind of expert.

"What do you think's happened to him?"

Granddad tilted his head to one side. I looked up into the same corner to see what he was staring at, but it didn't look like there was anything there.

"Probably ran away from home to teach his parents a lesson."

Will was wiping himself down with a tea towel.

"Your dad ran away from home once, you know. With your uncle Rodney."

Will turned towards us, "Really?"

"You know your uncle Rodney's always putting on plays with his drama group?"

"The MAD Society?" I said, chuckling to myself.

"Well he's always been into that stuff; God only knows how as we never took him to see a show in his life. But when he was seventeen, he came out of his room with a suitcase and told us he was joining a traveling theatre. He never did want to work on the farm, no matter how much I was always encouraging him to help out. Your dad was completely the opposite. As soon as he could walk, he wanted to be out there. He'd ride with me on the tractor, and he could lift a bale of hay up over his head when he were six year old, so the last think I expected, was for him to follow Rodney out of the door."

Mum and Dad walked in. Granddad pointed. "And just like that, a couple of hours later he walked back in. He was pale white, like all the blood had run from his face. Reckoned he'd seen a shug monkey and had done a runner. Later on, he said he'd only come home because he was hungry, and Rodney had made no plans for dinner. It was a couple of years before we saw Rodney again."

Dad wiped his hands. "That story's a load of nonsense."

"You didn't hear it, you were outside."

"Yes, but I know how you tell it. I never ran away, and I never saw a shug monkey either. I walked with Rodney to the bus stop, and then walked home again when he got on the bus."

"Then why were you carrying your rucksack?" Granddad looked at me and winked.

"Are you heading home for your dinner?" Dad said.

"Why? Don't you have enough for me here?"

"Of course we do," Mum said.

"Well that's one of the reasons I came over. The other was to see if you boys fancied fishing on Sunday."

Will eagerly said, "Yes," and I was happy to have an excuse to be out of the house too.

Later, after we'd eaten and Dad had gone back outside murmuring "No rest for the wicked," as he headed out, I was able to ask Granddad what a shug monkey was.

"You've never heard of one?" he said, leaning back in surprise. "It's much like the black shuck in many ways." He must have seen the puzzlement on my face. "Don't tell me you've not heard of that either?"

I shook my head.

"You've heard of people seeing giant black dogs which suddenly disappear though, right?"

There had been something about it on an episode of *Unsolved Mysteries* that I'd watched with John once.

"It's much like one of those, only crossed with a monkey too."

"Have you ever seen one?" I asked.

Granddad leaned back and took a deep breath, as if he was about to launch into one of his epic stories. "No," he said.

"Do you know anyone that has?"

"Only that your Dad reckoned he'd seen one that time."

"Do you believe in them?"

"I believe what I've seen with my own eye first of all, but that don't mean that things I've not seen can't be true. I know there's a lot more out there than we can always make sense of, but what's to say that the shug monkey, the black shuck and the Fen tiger aren't all the same type of thing?"

I thought back to what had chased me the other day. Could that have been one of these things? Maybe the makers of the cards had collected all of these types of beasts together under the name 'fiend' because there were so many different names for them, and if there were so many different accounts, there had to be some truth in it, didn't there?

Back in my room I took out the exercise book I'd stolen and started to write down everything that I could think of, from Mr Jenkins, the Ape-Man, to spontaneous human combustion, confident that we'd be able to solve the mystery and get John back.

NOW

How easy I thought it would all be. Write everything down and it will all make sense. A quarter of a century later, it still doesn't make much sense. As a child, I believed that, as I grew up, the gap between what I knew and what I thought I knew would shrink. It didn't. Returning to Little Mosswick gives me a chance to move some of what I believed to be true into the confirmed column of my mind.

It was easy to make the decision to go back, but as I got close, I realised that I wasn't ready, so I pulled over in a layby on the A10 somewhere near Ely and looked out across the fields.

Charlie stopped fiddling around inside his mouth for long enough to ask, "What have we stopped for?"

"I'm not ready to go back yet," I said, and switched off the engine.

"You can see for miles!" said Charlie, craning his neck to get a better view.

I gaze across the checkerboard of fields. It's all so open, that it looks as there's nowhere to hide. It looks as though you couldn't possibly have any secrets in a place like this. I know better, and as I scan the land, I spot a corn silo, deep ditches that would allow you to cross this landscape unseen, and half a dozen dilapidated barns, the corrugated iron roofs curling away from rotting wooden beams. I know that not far from here is the river where there are more places to hide or to be hidden: under bridges, in drainage pipes, and at abandoned water works.

"Was it like this where you lived?" Asks Charlie.

"Worse." I say, not turning to face him, still looking across the fields.

The car rocks. I turn to see a police car speeding away, blue lights flashing, drawing my attention back to the road. It's time to go.

Saturday 16th June 1990

Will was still asleep when I woke up, so I left him there and went downstairs. Mum was alone in the kitchen drinking a cup of tea.

"Where's Dad?"

"He's bringing in the first potato crop."

"Did he go out last night?" I asked.

"No, why?"

"Nothing, I just thought I heard the door open." I'd been waking during the night a lot. Any sound such as the rattle of the window in the frame or a door closing lifted me out of my dreams, which, last night, had mostly been about monkey-faced dog creatures chasing me down the droves.

"Why don't you go up and wake your brother? Can't have him sleeping the day away."

"Can we go out to play?"

"Go wake your brother and I'll think about it."

Will was still asleep. His mouth was wide open. I was tempted in to drop in a Mojo from the last of my stack of penny sweets, but he snorted just after I unwrapped it, so I ate it myself instead.

"Mum says you've got to get up," I said as I shook him by the shoulder.

He opened his eyes and gave me a grumpy look. "What time is it?"

"Half past eight."

He looked at me even grumpier. "It's Saturday."

"Mum says we can go out to play."

Will shuffled up the bed into an almost sitting position, "Really?"

"She said she'll think about it."

Will threw himself back down. "Don't you know that 'I'll think about it' is adult speak for 'no'?"

"But we can ask, we might be able to do something."

"If we're not allowed out, I bagsy first go on Mario."

"But it's not fair," Will said. He tossed his crust onto his plate.

"How about I make us a picnic and we can go to the park," Mum said.

"We'll look like little kids." Will folded his arms. He had a smear of Aunt Anne's blackberry jam on his cheek.

Mum reached across and wiped off the jam with a licked thumb. "Don't be daft. I'm not going to hold your hand and push you on the swings and treat you like a baby."

Will rubbed his cheek dry with the palm of his hand.

"Can we take the football?" I said.

"Yes, you can play what you like."

"I don't see why we can't just go off and do what we like," said Will, his sulky face now supported in the palm of his hand.

"Because I want to know where you are."

"You never used to care. We used to be able to go where we liked."

Mum threw down the tea towel that she'd been holding. "That's not true William Tillbrook. I do care and I've always cared."

"So how come only now we're not allowed out."

"Because I never thought you'd be in any danger before."

I looked at Will and he looked back at me.

"If you want to sit around here all day and sulk that's fine by me," Mum said, "but I'm offering you the chance to get out for a bit, now what do you say?"

Will and I passed the ball to each other as we made our way along Main Street. As we approached Shaky Jake's house he passed it in front of him for me to run on to, and I passed it back again, but Will, and I swear he did this on purpose, lifted his foot so that it ran on to Shaky Jake's garden and came to a stop in one of his flowerbeds.

"Who kicked that onto that poor man's lawn?" asked Mum.

"It was Tom!" Will said.

"You let it go onto his garden on purpose!"

"Tom, go and get it. If Jacob sees you, I expect you to apologise."

If Shaky Jake sees me, I thought, I'm going to run.

With each step onto his grass I expected him to fly out of the house, no doubt wielding a knife or other deadly kitchen implement to murder me with, but I reached the flowerbed safely. I plucked the ball from within the flowers and was about to run from the garden.

Shaky Jake must have been out, I figured. Probably wandering the droves again for whatever reason he had. Maybe looking for other boys to kidnap.

"Will," I called, and drop-kicked the ball out of the garden.

He trapped the ball under his foot, and then beckoned me out of the garden.

I had other ideas though.

I crept towards Jake's window. The curtains were drawn, but there was a crack between them. To shield the reflection of the light I cupped my hands onto the window and peered in.

"Come away from there," yelled Mum.

I ignored her and looked into what was an old-fashioned living room. Inside there was a large dark-wood cabinet, recently polished to a shine. On it were dozens of framed photographs of people, but they were too far away for me to make out who they were. The only other thing in there was a sofa which still had a plastic wrapping over it, and it looked as though it had never been sat upon, and a coffee table covered in magazines.

"Tom, I swear, if you don't come off that poor man's lawn this instant, you'll have your father to answer to when you get home," called Mum.

I started to pull myself away from the window when I heard something from inside. It wasn't a cry, just a noise. A gurgle of some sort followed by a low grumble.

"Tom," called Mum.

"Quick," Will shouted. "Shaky Jake's coming."

I turned and moved to run, but my feet slipped out from under me and I fell face first into the grass. I scrambled up and managed to keep my balance as I hurtled from his lawn and looked with panic down the road.

Will was bent over double laughing. He managed to point at me but was unable to speak over the fits of laughter he was suffering with.

A quick lance down the road both ways told me that Shaky Jake was nowhere in sight, but when I caught sight of Mum's face, I could tell that she was furious, and that it was time to move on.

It was quite a way to the other end of the village, up by the social club where there was the big playing field. The best thing about it was that it had two sizes of goals, big ones and little ones, and we could move the little ones closer or further apart depending on how many of us there were playing a game. We usually used the little goals and the bigger kids and adults played on the full-sized pitch. The only time we'd play in the full size one was if there was no one else around and we were playing headers and volleys or Wembley.

Today there was an adult game on, where they had proper kits and a referee. The little goals were being used by some kids from our school that we knew, so we decided to join in with them. It was odd for a Saturday, because even though there were some of the dads in the football team a lot of people's mums were there too. Mum went over and sat next to Steven Farley's mum. He was in my class and we got on okay, but we weren't really friends outside of school.

There were about ten of them already playing.

"Can we play?" shouted Will.

Daniel Richardson, who was in goal, said, "It's Chris' ball, you'll have to ask him."

Chris was in Will's class. He was at the other end of the pitch, and we watched him score a goal. As they were making their way back for another kick-off Will went over to him.

"I'm on Chris' team. We're England. You're Holland."

I'd forgotten that England were playing again tonight, and against Holland, one of the best sides in the world. I was sure that it was going to be amazing.

"What's the score?" I said to Daniel.

"It's 4-3. We're losing."

After the game I was really looking forward to the real thing. I was expecting a close game, and goals too, but maybe not so many as in our game, which ended at 7-5 to England when Chris had to go home because his mum had to go to Downham Market to do some shopping. We did offer to sub in our ball to keep the game going but other people had to drift off with their parents too. As there weren't enough of us left for a proper game, we played Wembley for a bit. In the first game I went out in the second round and in the second I got knocked out in the first, so I went to sit with mum and have a sandwich and a pork pie and some crisps.

"Why are there so many adults out today?"

"What do you mean?"

"Normally it's only kids playing football or people watching the game."

"Aren't we allowed out to watch our children play?"

"You can but... it's not normal."

"People are worried, that's all."

"Because of John?"

Mum mopped at her forehead with a napkin. "It's hot today. I hope your dad took plenty to drink with him." She opened the flask and poured some orange squash into one of our little plastic camping cups. "You have a drink. Don't want you getting dehydrated after running around for so long."

"Where is he, Mum?"

"That's up to the police to find out. Don't worry."

"But he's my friend."

Mum ruffled my hair. "Why don't you go see if Will wants a drink?"

But Will was busy trying to get the ball past Daniel, so I left them to it.

After Will had finished winning his third straight Wembley competition and we'd finished the food we started to make our way back. I offered to carry the picnic basket and Will had the football.

"Can we walk back the long way?" I asked.

"Which way?"

"Up the drove at the end of Hereward Close."

"I don't see why not. Is that okay with you, Will?"

"S'pose".

Hereward Close was another one of those newer housing estates in the village. It came off Main Street then curled around to the left, but you could join the old drove and keep going straight for a while, then later join up with another drove (which might have been called Long Drove, but I can never remember which is which, like Granddad can).

A little way along the drove, in a field overgrown with wildflowers, there was an old military pillbox.

"Can I go inside?"

Mum shrugged then held out her hand to take the picnic basket.

"Are you coming, Will?"

Will shook his head and then bounced the ball into the ground.

The pillbox was at the edge of a field full of oil seed rape which was tickling all the way up my legs as I made my way through it. It was dark in the pillbox. I called out, but only my voice echoed back. I ducked my head inside and waited for my eyes to adjust. It smelt damp inside. Water must have come in when it rained and eventually it evaporates, but not before it starts to stink. I could just about make out the corners and the line of sludge along the bottom, so there was nothing much in there. I could see a sweet wrapper in the corner. I crouched down and reached out to grab it. It had a thin layer of slime covering it, and it had discoloured. It was a Stratos bar wrapper —another one of those chocolate bars that I only ever saw when Uncle Rodney came over. Maybe it was one I'd eaten myself, and it had blown away and drifted all the way here, or maybe Uncle Rodney had eaten it as he was wandering the droves. Either way, it wasn't much of a find.

I felt all itchy when I came out, and for the rest of the way home I couldn't stop rubbing my eyes. They were so bad I didn't notice Will throw the ball towards me and it thunked off the side of my head and into the ditch.

"Will, what did you do that for?" Mum said.

"I said 'catch'!" Will said, barely able to hold back from laughing.

"No, you didn't," I said and rubbed the side of my head.

"I did. You weren't listening. You didn't catch it, so you have to get it."

I looked down into the ditch and at the high stinging nettles that rose up out of it.

"You threw it, you have to get it," I said.

Mum sighed. "I don't care who gets it, just hurry up and let's get home."

"I'm not going down there," Will said, "I didn't head it into the ditch."

"Well, I'm not."

"Leave it then, for all I care," Mum said and started to walk away.

Will and I approached the ditch together. We could see where the ball had forced the nettles to part.

"Get a stick and we can drag it along," Will said.

I looked around for one, but my eyes had started to water really badly, and I could barely see. My nose had started to run too, and the snot coming out was so thin it was almost like water.

Will found a stick himself and used it to thrash at the stinking nettles. Their tops flew off and made it much easier to get over the ditch and have a proper look down. Will dragged it across the bottom, and the ball edged out from the nettles.

"Go get it then," Will said.

"You get it."

"I'm holding the nettles."

So, I went down into the ditch and dragged the football back with my foot, then threw it out of the ditch. Will moved the stick and the nettles pinged towards me, but luckily stopped before they touched my skin, but while they were moving, I could see something else among them.

"Give me the stick," I said.

"No," Will said.

"Come on!"

"Why?"

"I can see something."

"What?"

"I don't know. Clothes?"

"Will you boys stop messing about," Mum said. "You've got the ball; let's go."

"There's something else."

"Give him the stick so we can home," Mum said.

Will passed the stick down to me and I reached into the nettles. I dragged it closer and I could see that it was something purple. I took a step backwards and managed to get the stick all the way under it and drag it out. It was a bit of material, perhaps part of a t-shirt of something with a few holes in it and thick black grease marks.

"It's just a dirty old rag," Mum said. "Leave it alone."

I lifted it out of the ditch with the stick, and then climbed back out myself.

"How do you think it got there?"

"I would imagine it was just some rag used on a tractor and it blew off one day."

Will chuckled.

"What's wrong with you?" asked Mum.

"You said, 'blew off'," Will said, his hands crossed over his belly as he tried to stop himself from laughing.

Mum rolled her eyes and kept walking.

"So, you don't think it's important?" I said, with the rag hooked by the end of the stick.

"You still going on about that dirty old thing?"

"So, it couldn't be a clue about what happened to John?"

Mum opened her arms and urged me to come to her.

"I'm sorry, Tom," she said.

"He'll be okay?" I said and wiped at my eyes.

"I hope so," she said and then we made our way home and I didn't want to look into the ditches or check the fields anymore.

My eyes kept itching and my nose kept running all afternoon so that I was in no fit state to play Mario. I did try and got through the first world without so much as losing a life but then the sneezes started, and I ran into a Goomba because I couldn't see. Obviously Will thought this was hilarious and made out I was fake sneezing to hide how bad I was at the game. Mum had left us to play on our own most of the afternoon, and it wasn't until Dad came home that she called us down. She'd cooked a ham that we were going to have with some salad and potatoes.

"What's up, boy?" Dad said as I rubbed my eyes at the dinner table, "Have you been crying?"

"No," I said and looked at my plate.

"I think he might have hay fever," Mum said.

"Hay fever? You daft sod. You better get over that quick as I'll need you to stack the bales up in a few weeks."

I cut my ham and tried not to listen to him. The thought of it filled me with dread. Will would be raising the bales on to the top of the stack without a problem, while I'd struggle to get them higher than my waist.

"You hear me? What you should do is go out there and roll around in the fields,"

"Trevor," Mum said.

"Roll about in all the grass and the flowers; take in so much pollen and build up an immunity to it."

I had a mouthful of the ham. It was really juicy. I tried to focus on what it tasted like and its texture.

"Whoever heard of a farmer's son with hay fever. I bet you've been in your room all day playing on them silly games. That's why you get hay fever."

"We have been out today, haven't we Mum?" Will said.

Relieved, I relaxed in my chair a little.

"Yes, we had a picnic at the park, and then took a long walk back up the drove," Mum said.

"Alright for some! Long walks! Some of us have to work for a living."

"Shut up and eat your dinner," Mum said.

"Okay, okay, just teasing you. Miserable bloody lot you are."

Mum threw a tea towel at Dad and he let it rest on his face. He shovelled potato onto his fork and tried to put it into his mouth, pretending not to know the tea towel was there. I never knew what to expect from him, and didn't know if I preferred him when he was just in a grumpy mood or when he was trying to be funny, because when he was acting funny he could easily catch us off guard and suddenly turn the other way and me and Will could get into all sorts of trouble.

Dad seemed to be in a good mood, and it looked like it was going to stay that way. He even said that we'd be allowed to put the football on downstairs instead of sending us up to our room to watch it. "We had a job to do first," he said, and as if he was psychic, we heard a car horn beep from the yard outside.

"Come on, boys," Dad said, and went outside. Will followed quickly behind him, and I was a distant third.

Standing by his car was Uncle Rodney. He had one hand on his hip, and he was wearing a huge pair of gloves.

Dad peered into the back of the car. "Where are they then?"

"Ta-da!" said Uncle Rodney, and he opened the boot of the car, to the sound of clucking. A sea of brown feathers rippled inside, and then heads started to emerge, looking for the source of light. One seemed to rise above the rest, its wings sticking out and its feet looking for something to grab hold of. Quickly it was standing on top of another chicken, and then it jumped, landed in the dust, and started strutting towards me.

"Grab 'er," Dad said.

I waited until she was close and then pounced, but she darted out of reach. Meanwhile, Uncle Rodney was grabbing chickens by a leg, turning then upside down, and passing them to Will and Dad in groups of three in each hand.

After a couple of trips to the car they'd moved all of their chickens, and I'd managed to corner my one. I reached a hand towards her and she had nowhere to go. She moved low to the ground and I was able to reach out with both hands and grab her by the body. Proudly I held her out and walked towards the coop, but then she started to flap her wings and I had to hold her further away from me.

"That's no way to hold a bird," Dad said, and I could feel her squirming away from me.

Uncle Rodney was beside me in an instant and it seemed to calm her down. He took her from me and tucked her under his arm. He placed her into the coop. "And that makes thirteen," he said as he closed the door.

"Can we go and watch the football now?" asked Will.

"You can," Dad said. "As Tom was slacking off while we were doing all of the work, I think he should help your uncle tidy out the back of his car.

We all looked that way. Inside were so many feathers, and it looked like a fair bit of chicken poop too.

I trudged towards it. The blue rope in the back was peppered with downy feathers. For some reason there were also a couple of loose Panini World Cup football stickers, one of them was the shiny world cup trophy sticker.

"Let the boy watch his football," said Uncle Rodney, and he pushed the boot down with one of his massive hands. "I need to give the car a good clean out anyway."

I wanted to ask for the sticker, but Dad said, "Goo on then boy," and I hurried inside.

I was worried that England was going to get thumped because Holland were the European Champions, and last time they played Holland, they lost 3-1 and Van Basten got a hat-trick. The commentators were saying that England were using a 'sweeper system' which is something they use in other countries like Italy and Germany rather than England so I thought it might not work and Holland would end up winning, but England played some really good football. It was quite an even first half though and Holland didn't have too many chances to score so I was surprised because people were always saying how good an attacking team there were.

England got even better in the second half and they even scored two goals, but both of the goals were ruled out. First Gary Lineker scored, but it didn't count because the ball had bounced up to hit his hand before he kicked it into the net. Then, right at the last minute, England got a free kick and Stuart Pearce scored directly from the free kick, but the referee said it didn't count either.

"Why doesn't it count?" I said.

"I don't bloody well know," Dad said.

"It was obstruction," Will said.

"What was obstruction?"

"The free kick. It was for obstruction, which means an indirect free kick."

"So?"

"So, if it's an indirect free kick you're now allowed to score from it. It has to touch another player first."

"Well that's not fair."

"It's time you two went to bed," Dad said, and that was another thing we didn't think was fair either.

NOW

The closer I get to Little Mosswick, the more familiar it seems until I know every bend and dip in the road. As I round the corner, I can make out some familiar farmhouses, though there are some new housing estates blocking the view across the whole village. I feel almost glad that I can no longer see all the way across the land to my old home.

As I take the slip road into Little Mosswick I see another police car. Or, who knows, it could even be the same one. A police officer stands in the road, urging me pull over. After I stop, I wind down the window, ready for his approach. He's older than me by at least twenty years, I'd guess based upon the plethora of grey hairs in his beard. I don't recognise him but wonder if he was around back in 1990. He crouches down to look into the car. "Good afternoon," he says. "What's your business in Little Mosswick?"

"Visiting family," I say, the word sticking in my throat.

The police officer pulls out a photograph and holds it up for me to look at. "Do you recognise the child?"

It's John. The dimple in the chin, those blue eyes, the cluster of three moles on the left cheek.

"Sir?" Says the police officer. "Do you recognise this girl?"

I look at the picture again. It's nothing like John. Yes, she has the chin dimple and the moles, but she also has pigtails.

"Would you mind stepping out of the car?" says the police officer. He steps back from the car and speaks into his walkie-talkie.

"Dad," says Charlie. "What's going on?"

I shrug. I glance at the police officer and quickly realise that I don't have time to waste. I climb out of the car.

"Would you mind opening your boot for me?"

I hurry around to the back of the car and open the boot revealing the two bags I'd packed for Charlie and me.

The police officer bends down to look. He lifts the bags, one at a time, and feels underneath them.

"Where were you this morning between nine and eleven?"

"Miles away. We left our home in Oxfordshire at around ten o' clock."

"Can I take your name?"

"Certainly. It's Thomas Tilbrook. What's all of this about?"

"We're looking for a young girl. The girl in the picture."

"Who is she?"

"Her name's Jessica. She's a resident of Little Mosswick. She was sent to the post office for some milk and hasn't been seen since."

"Have you spoken to my dad?" I say, almost screaming at the man. "Have you spoken to Trevor Tilbrook?"

Sunday 17th June

O ur fishing trip would be a good opportunity to check out some of the other paths out of the village. I wondered if John might have decided to go fishing as none of us were about. We'd been fishing together a couple of times. He had to borrow one Will's old rods first time, but then his parents bought him a new carbon fibre one. He didn't really like fishing that much – he was never fond of putting maggots on hooks, and this one time when he caught a ruffe he couldn't get the hook out of its mouth and pulled it a bit too hard and blood went everywhere. That was all he caught, but Will and I have both caught some big roach there. One Monday he came in and told us he'd gone down there with his dad and they'd caught a massive pike that he claimed was bigger than the one on the cover to the Angling Times that was in the post office that week, but he'd never told us about anything he'd done with his dad before, so it made my chin itch. But maybe he did go fishing on his own. Not only that, it would give us the chance to see if the police were still searching around that area.

Granddad came around at eight. It was way too early for a Sunday.

"Time for breakfast before you go, boys?" asked Mum.

"Only if you've got plenty for me too," Granddad said.

"More than enough."

Granddad hadn't combed his hair (or maybe he had, and it was deliberate) so his hair was wild, like a crazy white mane. When it was like that, he reminded me of Aslan. Granddad was wise and strong and full of wisdom. I sometimes wondered if he was magic.

After breakfast we set off to collect Liam and Andy. They were eating their breakfast, and Granddad tucked away another bacon sandwich. We stopped off back at Granddad's house to pick up the fishing rods from his garage which had this smell like sawdust and engine oil, and because the windows were covered in a thick, green, mossy film everything inside looked distorted and other-worldly. There was a new smell today, over-powering the smell of oil, an animal stink.

Will tugged on my sleeve and then pointed behind me.

I turned to see three dead pheasants not more than a metre from my head. They had hooks through their beaks and were hanging from them limply. Once I could see them the smell was worse than ever, and I couldn't help but put a hand to my mouth.

"Don't you worry none about my pheasants," Granddad said. "Leave them to hang for a couple of three or four days and they'll be right tasty." He wasn't looking as he picked his tackle box from a shelf, and a heavy chain snaked off behind it, clattered to the floor, and coiled there.

"I'll pick it up later," he muttered. Looking at all of the other debris on the floor 'later' was not going to be any time soon.

We were walking towards the end of the village which didn't seem to be the quickest way to the river. Liam had been tasked with carrying the rods, and even though they'd been taken apart, so they weren't that long he kept turning to look into the ditches and clobbering Andy in the side of the head.

"Tom should carry the rods," Andy said.

I was already struggling with Granddad's fold-up chair. "Why me?"

"Because they're like Donatello's staff, and he's Donatello."

"We're not the turtles, Andy," Will said. He was having no trouble at all carrying the tackle box.

"We are the turtles."

Granddad stopped and turned to look at us. "Turtles? Whatever in merry Hell are you blathering on about? Of course, you're not turtles."

"We're the Teenage Mutant Ninja Turtles."

"Well that makes a whole lot more sense," Granddad said, scratching his head. "Anyway, I know you're not a turtle." He said as he ruffled Andy's hair.

"How come?"

"Because you're a money box." Granddad pulled a twenty-pence coin from behind Andy's ear.

Liam gasped and it made me smile too.

Andy muttered, "I am a turtle," with his bottom lip jutting out.

"Well, I ain't never seen a turtle in the river, but there have been terrapins dragged out of it."

"Really?" I said. I could see Will was shaking his head.

"Oh yeah, dozens of them. You boys aren't old enough to remember it, but I took your dad and your mum there when they were little. You know that big old house as you go around the bend on the approach to Ely?"

We all nodded, apart from Will who decided to overtake us and walk a little further ahead.

"The family that used to own that house, many years ago, they had a menagerie. Used to be the Duke of somewhere or other, I forget, who had the house and before my time they had lions and tigers and ostriches there. When I went, they only had a few of the smaller cats left; pumas, lynxes, stuff like that. What they did still have though was a tank full of terrapins. Only when they found out that the Duke's great grandson or great, great grandson had been diddling his taxes for years and had blown all of the family money they were going to lock him up. With no one to look after the animal he let what was left of them go, and the terrapins bred in the waters."

"What about the cats?" asked Liam.

"That's a story for another day. We're here now."

We were standing outside the entrance to old Mr Barnham's farm. Will had marched on fifty metres or so down the road and Granddad had to summon him back.

"What're we going in there for?" asked Andy.

Andy hadn't been fishing with us before, so he didn't know that this was the best place to get bait in the village.

As we wandered in through the gates the door to the shed, which had recently been painted black, swung open.

"Aye up, Teddy," Granddad said.

"Norm. Taking your lads for a spot of fishin'?" said Teddy. He must have been quite tall if he stood up straight, as he was almost as tall as Granddad Norman with his back bent and buckled like it was. His nose was long and pointed and the skin saggy and loose on his face. He led us into the shed where there was a counter, an ancient till, and several empty tubs. The smell was revolting. It was a sweet sickliness and the dust seemed to cling to the inside of your nose.

"What's it to be then boys? Worms or maggots?"

Andy's mouth dropped open.

"Well it's this little fella's first time," Granddad ruffled Andy's hair, "so I think we ought to have a pot of each."

"Worms and maggots? What a treat," said Teddy. "I normally do this out back, but as it's your first time..." Teddy opened the door behind him and grabbed a larger plastic container. He took off the lid and the sickly smell engulfed the room. He tilted the tub towards Andy so he could see the hundreds, maybe thousands, of tiny yellow maggots writhing around in there.

"Gross!" Andy said.

"You won't catch fish without bait." Teddy said. He thrust his long fingers into the container and picked up a handful of the maggots. He dropped most into one of the smaller containers but left a couple to wriggle out around on his hand to show Andy who looked away. "How would you like to pick out the worms yourself, young man?" Teddy laughed with his mouth wide open, showing the enormous gaps between his teeth.

Andy shook his head. "Granddad," he said, "can I wait outside?"

We left Granddad in there with Teddy Barnham. Andy still had a sickened look on his face, but Liam was grinning. "Hold these," he said, and pushed the fishing rods against Andy. He reached into his back-pocket and pulled out his wad of Top Trumps cards, both sets collected together and bound with an elastic band. He flicked through them and picked out The Sorcerer, an old man with long, pointed fingers, a huge nose and a cavernous mouth, almost devoid of teeth.

We were still chuckling about it when Granddad came out. "What are you boys laughing at?"

"Nothing," we said together.

"Well come on then. These fish aren't gonna catch themselves, are they?"

"How big can maggots get, Granddad?" Liam said as he looked into the pot full of them.

"Not much longer than your thumbnail. They hatch out into flies, see."

Liam was clearly thinking about The Maggot card from his Top Trumps. With a Fear Factor of only 66 it wasn't among the most frightening cards in the pack. The picture made it look huge though. Its head was twice as big as the human head which it was scratching with claws. I peered into the pot and watched them writhing.

"They don't even have limbs, or faces, or anything," I said. The monster version probably wasn't a maggot at all. Maybe it looked like one in some other way, but also had mammal features.

"Did you know," Granddad said, before setting his rod down to take up a more comfortable position, "that they sometimes put maggots on wounds to help clean them up."

"Urgh," Liam said, and shivered.

Andy shrank into himself.

Will cast his line into the water.

"Why would they do that?" I asked (after overcoming a slight shudder).

"They eat the dead flesh, which helps the rest of the wound to heal up quicker."

"That's gross," Liam said. "I wouldn't let them do that to me."

"Not even if it was the only way of saving your life? You might get blood poisoning without it."

But what it the maggot burrowed in too deep and got into your brain? Then you might turn out like The Maggot. I don't know if I'd want to live as a monster.

We'd only caught one fish when we came to stop for lunch, and that was a small perch on Granddad's rod.

"After we've had a bite, how about we go up a little further? Might have a bit more luck there," Granddad said.

I looked at Liam and he nodded back at me. It would be a good opportunity to scope out a different area.

"I know what you boys are thinking," Granddad said.

"We ain't thinking nothing," Liam said and started to go slightly pink.

"Your friend that went missing or run away. He might have come this way?"

"There's no harm looking," I said.

Will tossed a rock into the water.

"Well no one saw him walking along the main road. If he did come this way, then no one much would have seen him down this drove. Old Teddy Barnham has his fields left fallow. His boy doesn't want to farm it."

"How do you know no one saw him on Main Street?" Will asked.

"Police came to my door and asked if I'd seen him. Showed me a picture."

"So how do you know one else hasn't seen him?"

"Do you think I don't talk to my neighbours? What do you think I do all day now your dad won't have me help him on the farm?"

Dad had always said that it was Granddad's choice to give up working, and he often complained about how hard it was on his own. What Granddad was saying didn't quite add up.

"Anyway, I'm not doing a thing more until I get some grub in me. I'm famished."

After eating the sandwiches that Aunt Anne had prepared for us, we set off along the bank of the river. Granddad was telling us the names of all the droves and where they (eventually) led to.

"Would it be possible to track someone along here?" asked Liam.

"If you had the skills," Granddad said.

"Don't you have the skills?"

"Well in the winter anyone can follow footprints in the mud. This time of the year it's dry and cracked. You might make something out in the dust, but chances are the wind would blow it away."

"I saw this programme where they could tell from the way the grass was broken or flat that animals had walked by."

"Well why don't you keep an eye on the grass then and tell me what you figure out."

And Liam did exactly that, staring intently at the ground until we arrived at a spot sheltered from the sun by a couple of weeping willows. It was there that Liam beckoned us over to the water's edge.

"What's this, Granddad?" He pointed at a spot on the edge of the bank were the grass was flat. All the way down to the water the grass the grass was parted as if something had gone in there or crawled out.

"Well I can't see any footprints, hoof-marks or anything of the like down there," Granddad said.

"What could have caused it then?"

"I dunno. Small animal going down for a drink? Maybe someone was here and rolled something down the bank?"

"Like what?" Will said.

"I'm not a psychic. How about we cast in here and have a ponder on it?"

We had much more luck with the fish there, and Andy even got the hang of putting maggots on the end of the hook – though the worms were still more liable to wriggle away.

Once we all had our lines in the water I looked over at Granddad. "Has anything like this ever happened before?"

"What, a handsome old fella fishing with his four grandsons? I should think so."

"No, I mean, like John. A kid going missing."

"You hear about it from time to time on the news."

"And what happens?"

"Well sometimes they turn up, and well, sometimes it's not so good news."

"But has it ever happened here?"

"What in Little Mosswick?"

"Yes."

"Lots have things have happened here."

"But to kids? How about when you were young?"

"Well I suppose there have been one or two accidents. My eye. Teddy Barnham's brother drowned in the old pit which has been filled in now, though he weren't exactly a kid at the time."

"But nothing like this?"

"Well I don't rightly remember. It's not my place to give you a history lesson, is it? Now keep an eye on your float or you might miss a bite."

After about an hour or two, with us all having caught a fish apart from a Granddad who kept missing his float go under, Granddad got up and peered into the water again at the point where something had been rolled in.

"Clamber down and have a look to see if anything has been dropped in there," he said.

"No way. I'll slip," Liam said.

"I'll do it!" Andy said, jumping up and dropping his rod to the floor.

"I think it needs to be one of the bigger boys," Granddad said. "Though you are awfully brave for volunteering."

"Let me," Will said.

"If we make a chain – Will at the front, then Liam then Tom then me then Andy we can keep a hold of Will and make sure he don't fall in. His Mum'll have my guts for garters if I bring him home soaked."

"Mum! What about Dad, what'll he say?" I said.

"He's not the one to be scared of; I can tell you that for nothing. He thinks he's the big man, but I remember when he was just a little boy."

"Did you take him fishing?" asked Andy.

"Yes, but he never had the patience for it. Always thought sitting around was a waste of time."

That sounded about right; he was always going on about how sinful time-wasting was.

We formed our chain and Will headed down the bankside. Liam had his fingers in Will's belt loops, and I had hold of the back of Liam's pockets. Granddad had a firm hold on me, and Andy was somewhere behind. Will kept edging forward until he was close to the edge.

"Anything?" called Granddad.

"I can't see. It's too dirty."

"Okay, let's back up."

We took a couple of steps backwards when Will shouted, "Stop."

"What is it?"

"I found something."

"What?" we all cried.

"Sweet wrapper."

"A sweet wrapper? That's not what we were looking for!" Granddad said. "Come on up." He continued to back up.

Will grabbed the wrapper and showed it to us when he got to the top. Fisherman's Friend.

"Bloody litter bugs," Granddad said.

I starred at Will, urging him to say something about the sweets we'd found before. I couldn't find a way to put it into words.

"Boys," Granddad said, "why don't you pack the rods away?"

"But it's still early!" Andy said.

"It's probably nothing, but the more I look at it the more it looks like something was dumped in there. It's probably a load of old rubbish, but I want to let someone know so they can check it out."

"I saw them by another bit of the river the other day," I said, remembering the police cars up on the bank.

"They've got divers and snorkels and all sorts of things, so if there's anything down there they'll find it."

"Is it John? Could someone have chucked him in the river?"

"No, nothing like that. He would have flattened the reeds. Probably just a fisherman getting rid of some broken tackle, but we have to keep our eyes open."

All the way home I was thinking about what might have happened. If John had gone that way what reason would he have to dump anything in the river? He wouldn't get rid of his clothes or any of his possessions, unless he'd done something bad and was trying to get rid of the evidence. And the sweet wrapper didn't add up there either. That certainly wouldn't have been John's. I remember we tried some once and they made us gag. I don't remember where he got them from, he always had loads of sweets given to him, so we were going to share them, but they were so disgusting it was like a pebble that dripped acid on your tongue. We both spat them out in the bushes then ran to his house and downed a pint of water. We figured that if they were the kind of sweets that adults bought it would explain why adults didn't eat as many sweets as kids.

I thought about what had been lurking in the ditch the other day and what had chased me. Could that have been some kind of amphibious creature that came and went into the water and that point, but could also survive in the dykes?

"Liam, can I have a look at your cards?"

He got them out of his pocket and handed them to me. I was sure there was nothing in the original set, but I didn't know the new ones well yet. There were a couple which caught my eye; Terror of the Deep with Killing Power of 72 and a three-pronged trident, Creature from the Black Lagoon with Killing Power of 73 and clawed fingers on webbed hands and The Slime Creature with Killing Power of 68 and a spear and some kind of weird trunk. None of them filled me with fear, in the way that The Fiend had.

Granddad hurriedly threw the fishing equipment in his garage and then said that we should be okay making our own way home from there. We stopped a little distance form Liam and Andy's house.

"What do you think it was then?" Liam said as I gave the cards back to him.

"There were some under-water ones, but I'm not sure."

"Add them into your book and we'll see what evidence comes up."

"There's no point thinking about monsters and stuff like that," Will said. "John probably just ran away. He might even have already come home."

"What about the sweet wrapper?" Liam said.

"It doesn't even mean it was the same person who ate it as the ones at the school."

"But not many people can like them. They're disgusting. It's got to be some kind of evidence."

"Evidence of what?"

"That someone was spying on the school, and kidnapped John," Liam said. His face changed after he said it, as if suddenly understanding the implications of what he was saying.

"That's why it's stupid talking about monsters. Monsters don't eat cough sweets, even really, really gross ones."

"But what about aliens?" said Liam.

"Where's your Granddad?" Dad said as he saw us walking down the drive.

"Home," Will said.

"What, he left you to walk back here all by yourself?"

"We've done it thousands of times Dad."

"You might have done in the past, but that was before."

"Before what?

"I'm going to have to have a word with that daft old sod," he pulled the keys to his Land Rover out of his pocket, got in and revved the engine hard. He barely gave us a chance to get out of the way before he flew past and off towards Granddad's.

All the noise brought Mum out. "You're back early boys," she said. "Where did your dad go in such a hurry?"

We told her what we'd seen and what Granddad was doing.

"Oh, I know what I was going to give to you!" Mum said and she urged us to follow her inside. From the cabinet under the sink she pulled out a Burrows Bookshop paper bag. She handed us a book each. As soon as I saw the familiar green spine of the Fighting Fantasy series I smiled. I'd played through all of the books I had so many times the pages were worn. Will took hold of *Battleblade Warrior*, which had some kind of lizard monster riding a pterodactyl, and Mum handed me *The Secret of the Scythe*. Will wasn't as keen on the books as I was and he cheated, skipping the fights and using bookmarks to alter his choices.

I dashed up to the bedroom and studied the book in more detail. The cover had a dark-hooded skeleton on the front with a huge scythe. It looked more like the Top Trumps Devil Priest rather than Death, but I knew it was supposed to be the Grim Reaper from reading the back cover:

Dare YOU travel to the other side?

Only the desperate would travel the perilous paths into the Underworld to confront the Grim Reaper. Yet it is there that you must go if you are to unlock the secrets of the scythe and bring back your master, the great wizard Hexor, from the brink of death.

Can you defeat the Grim Reaper and his dastardly puzzles, or will the dead-eyed wanderers of the Underworld devour your very soul?

Part story, part game, this is a book in which YOU become the hero! Two dice, a pencil and an eraser are all you need. YOU decide which routes to take, which dangers to risk and which foes to fight!

I looked at the cover again. The Reaper stood in a dark forest, where only the tree trunks were visible, each of which had a glaring pair of red eyes. Off to the left was an orange glow, a hint of fire.

I grabbed my pencil case and pulled out a pencil, and then had to search for a dice. As usual they turned up under my bed. That's what you get for playing Fighting Fantasy at night. I also found another set of Top Trumps down the side from the Super Top Trumps series. Tractors. I'd never played them.

I rolled the dice onto the book and scored terribly. You roll one dice for skill and one for luck and add 6 to each to give you a score out of twelve. I got nine skill, and eight luck. For stamina you roll two die and add the score to twelve. I only had one dice, so I rolled it twice, scoring six overall to make my stamina only eighteen.

I didn't get far into the book at all on my first play-through. I encountered a goblin after a poor luck roll meant he spotted me hiding in a bush. I beat him, though he did quite a bit damage to me and I was down to thirteen stamina. I came across a cottage on the road and decided to rest there to recover some of my strength after being invited in by what was described as a 'kindly old lady'. I should have paid more attention to the witch-hazel shrubs growing up beside her house; that was a huge hint that I shouldn't trust her. Anyway, she poisoned me, and I fell into a deep sleep where I was confronted by a nightmare demon which I nearly beat, but a run of bad dice rolls meant that I lost. I don't think I'd ever been beaten by a Fighting Fantasy book so early. At least this one would be a challenge.

Will had already lost interest in his (though I spotted several torn pieces of paper on his bed that he'd used for bookmarking) and had switched on the TV to watch the build-up to the Egypt versus the Republic of Ireland game, which was in England's group. Every match in the group so far had been a draw, so if either team won, they would be top of the table and probably go through to the next round. It wasn't a good game and before half-time I'd picked up *The Secret of the Scythe* again.

Will interrupted me at some point during the second half. "Granddad was acting weird today."

"How?"

"Normally when you ask him a question there's a crazy story to go with it."

"Granddad's stories aren't crazy."

"That's not what I meant. Over the top. Exaggerated."

"Like the story about the terrapins?"

"Exactly. There were probably one or two which were thrown into the water, but not '*hundreds*'."

"Don't you believe him?"

"It's not that. Sometimes he likes to make them more exciting."

"So?"

"Don't you think it was odd when you asked if any other kids had gone missing?"

"What about it?"

"There was no amazing story."

"Maybe there was nothing to tell?"

"Or they don't want us to know."

"They?"

"The adults. Can't you see they're not telling us what's going on?"

"With John?"

"With everything. They tell us it's wrong to lie, but they do it to us all of the time."

I could see that Will was really upset. Tears were welling up in his eyes and he kept rubbing his forehead as he was talking.

"Let's go downstairs and ask them if there's any news about John," he said, shuffling off the end of his bed. He waited by my bed for me to move, but I could imagine Dad getting angry if we asked questions.

"See?" Will said, as if reading my mind. "There's no point. They won't tell us anything. They'll change the subject."

"We should ask at school. See what our teachers say."

"They'll do exactly the same thing, I bet."

NOW

What was the point of those Fighting Fantasy novels? Until the summer of 1990, I couldn't get enough of them, and I would have told you that it was because it gave you choices and made you feel like you were in control of the story. Since there was only one good ending, you might have to play it through a dozen times or more before you got there, which I suppose made it a challenge, but learning the path through the book wouldn't be enough either, because you were forced to battle monsters by using dice rolls, so you could know exactly what you were supposed to do, and still fail. Much like life in many ways.

I drive slowly through the village. I pass the playing field where I spent so much time kicking around a football without ever developing any level of skill. There are so many new houses in this part of the village, that I can hardly recognise it. Row after row of identical houses. I've never been a fan of these kind of housing developments, and they seem utterly out of place here in Little Mosswick.

I pass a new building on my right and am surprised to see it labelled Little Mosswick Primary School. What happened to my old school? I'm surprised to find that I feel as if I have been slighted by this in some way.

As I approach the post office, I see another police car parked outside it. I also notice that it's grown an extension – a Chinese take-away that also sits askew to my memories of the village.

Continuing through the village, I notice change, with no further housing developments, leaving the Little Mosswick that I remember. It feels as though the old Little Mosswick has been left behind, as if they've tried to move the heart of the village to one end, but all they've done is turned Little Mosswick into a Frankenstein village, held together with the ugly stitches of new roads. Maybe the whole place should have been left to die. I'm glad I was taken away in 1990. I'm glad I didn't come back sooner. Maybe I've returned too soon?

If I had a die, I'd roll it and let that decide if I should stay or go.

Monday 18th June 1990

Will was right.

"The police are still investigating," Mrs Palmer said when Liam and I approached her when the rest of the class went out to break. "I'm sure they're doing all they can."

"Do you think he'll be okay?" Liam asked.

"You boys go and get some fresh air. When there's news to tell, you'll be among the first to know."

"Don't you want us to stay in and tidy your cupboard?" asked Liam, nodded towards the locked door.

A wrinkle appeared on Mrs Palmer's brow. "Why? Whatever would you want to spend your time doing that for?"

"To be helpful," I cut in, as Liam looked lost for words.

"That's very kind of you, but it's all perfectly square in there. Off you go."

"She's definitely hiding something," Liam said when we were out in the corridor.

I wasn't so sure. Mrs Palmer seemed way too nice to be an alien.

"She's definitely an alien," Liam said. "How do we even know she's not involved?"

We stopped off in the toilets, and on the way out of the school we had to pass Mr Inglehart's office. We could hear Mrs Palmer in there with him, along with a couple of other teachers.

"We have to prepare the pupils for transition," I heard someone say, and then it sounded like someone was moving towards the door, so we dashed outside.

"See" Liam said. "They're still moving ahead with their plans."

"What can we do about it?"

"We have to get into the staff room. They must keep something secret in there."

"Maybe it's not an alien invasion plan. Maybe it's something innocent," I said, thinking about how much Mrs Palmer had helped me.

"But it all makes sense. Remember last year when Ian Dalby had to have ages off, and they just told us he was sick? And since then he never plays, and he hardly talks to anyone? Maybe they turned him into an alien."

"What about John?"

"They've got him now. He's going through the... transition... and he'll come back, but he won't be the same."

"But what would be the point in turning kids into aliens?"

"We won't see it coming, Tom. When they launch the alien invasion it will be through us kids."

At lunch, Liam and I met up with Will to decide on our plan for our search after school. We decided to walk up to the River Wissey and follow the bank the other way from where we'd gone fishing along up past the new bypass. There's a good view of the cornfields from there, and while I didn't like Liam's alien idea, I didn't want to rule out anything.

As we were chatting Becky Reid barged into our circle. "Tom, I need to speak to you," she said. Ignoring her was not an option.

I followed her to the step by the infant entrance, where no one else was around. "Laura daren't ask you herself, so I'm doing it for her."

I felt panicky. Was Becky going to ask if I liked Laura? What would I say if she did? The only person I'd told that to was John. What if I said I did like her, and Becky said that she didn't like me back? But what if I lied and said that I didn't, and she did like me, and it would hurt her feelings?

"Laura wanted to know if you'd heard from John," Becky said.

"No," I said, and the panic disappeared, only to be replaced by disappointment. "No one knows where he is."

"Okay. That's all she wanted to know," Becky said before turning around and marching off.

"What was that all about?" asked Will when I returned to the group.

"Did she ask you out?" Liam said.

"Did she want to snog you?" said Andy, and he kissed the back of his hand sloppily.

"No. Yuck. Nothing like that. She asked about John."

"You two would make a good couple," Liam said. "You're both bigheads!"

At the end of the school day, Aunt Anne was waiting at the school gate.

"Have we got to go somewhere?" asked Liam. He ran his tongue across his teeth and looked as if he was pondering something.

"I'm taking you straight home. Tom, you too, I'm giving you a ride."

"But why, Mum?"

"Because I say so, that's why."

"But we have to continue our search for John," Liam said, he glared at me, wanting me to take over the argument.

"I don't need a lift, Auntie, I can walk it."

"Your dad asked me to make sure you went straight home, so as soon as Will and Andy are out that's what we're doing."

Andy's class were out next. Andy handed his mum a sealed envelope. She put it in her handbag to read later.

Will eventually trudged out the main doors with his hands in his pockets, chatting to some girl. When he looked up and saw us all waiting, he trotted quickly away from her.

"Who's your girlfriend?" Andy said and over-exaggerated a laugh.

"Leave him alone," said Aunt Anne, and beckoned us towards her car. It was unusual for anyone to come pick us up from school since we were in the infants, and even then, someone would only drive to pick us up if we had to go somewhere straight after school. It seemed strange to drive within the village but looking out of the car window there seemed to be so many fewer children walking home alone. Children pushed the cycles they normally rode on while walking beside their mums, or an adult would be with a cluster of children, urging them to stay close and take caution when crossing the road. Maybe the aliens had landed after all.

Aunt Anne said that Liam and Andy could stop over for a while to give her a chance to stop for a cup of tea with mum. They didn't speak to each other while we all made drinks of squash. As usual, Andy had turned the tap on too high and water fountained out of his cup and all over his feet. When he slowed it down to a trickle, he was left with a drink not nearly as bright an orange colour as ours. As soon as we left the kitchen one of them pushed the door closed behind us. I could hear chairs scraping across the tiles as they moved closer, probably to talk about us. We might have been in trouble for some reason. It's not like we don't often play out after school and go wandering where we want, so I don't know why they got so serious on Friday. When I asked Will about it, before we went to sleep, he said it was probably because they were worried about what happened to John, but it wasn't like we were planning on running away or anything.

We put the television on and checked BBC and ITV, but there was no football on. That wasn't right, there had been a four o'clock game every day since it all started.

Will knelt on his bed and checked the World Cup wall-chart. "No games until later. Argentina play Romania and Cameroon play the Soviet Union, but both are at eight." He switched the TV to back to BBC, where Andi Peters was deep in conversation with Edd the Duck about the spate of quack circles which had been appearing in the studio. Whatever was happening on screen wasn't sinking in. I blocked out Andi Peters singing the theme tunes and found my gaze drawn to the window. I looked out across the fields to where the old oak tree stood. Its branches seemed to be hanging lower, as if hiding something. I tried to look out further to the west, to see if I could see all the way to the riverbank, to where the police cars were parked previously.

Teenage Mutant Ninja Turtles finished. I hadn't even realised that it was that they'd been watching.

"Do you wanna play football?" Andy said. At least he'd been paying attention.

"Or we could say we're going to play, but then go off and explore," Liam said.

I nodded and Will headed for the door. We bundled down the stairs and into the kitchen. Mum and Aunt Anne gasped as we crashed through the door.

"Can we go play football?" Will said.

"Only out in the yard," Mum said.

"Can't we go down the rec?" Will said.

"No. You'll stay in the yard or not go out at all."

We went out. I dragged the football from under a hedge then we passed it to each other as we jogged towards the barn.

"Who's going in goal?" Liam said.

"Tom," Will said.

"Andy," I said, knowing I'd have a better chance of scoring against Andy as he was almost a foot shorter than the rest of us.

"No," Andy said, "That's not fair."

"Well why don't we dib for it?"

Will did the ip-dip-dog shit song, and it turned out Andy was going to start in goal anyway. He didn't mind, because the rhyme had chosen him completely fairly. So, he enthusiastically dived for the ball as first Will banged one into the corner of the goal we'd marked on the shed, and then Liam put one over his head. There was some debate over whether it might have hit the crossbar, but as it was hard to tell exactly where the crossbar would be. Then I had a shot and it sliced off my foot and off across the yard. I went after the ball. It had a black splodge on it. I traced the path of the ball back across the yard to where it had picked up its stain. There was a black patch on the ground. Was it a burn spot? The grass looked dead around it, and some of that was black too – but it didn't really look singed. I must have been staring a long time because Will had trotted over, followed by Liam, and then Andy. Liam looked at me and was clearly thinking about the burn spots we were supposed to be looking out for. What if John had exploded right there? But there were always some remains, like a stray limb or a shoe or something.

"Oil," Will said.

"It's burn, isn't it?" Liam said.

"Nah, definitely oil. Touch it."

Liam looked at me. I reached out towards it

"What the bloody hell are you lot doing?"   Dad was marching over to us. "Don't touch that it'll get all over your clothes."

"What is it, Uncle Trevor?" Andy said. He had to look up so high to look Dad in the face that he was squinting.

"Tractor's leaking oil. You should know better than that, Tom. Are you soft in the head or something?"

"We were only playing football," Will said.

"Playing football in a pool of oil. Daft bloody kids."

"No, by the barn."

"Well you'll have to stop now anyway; I've got to move the combine. Go on, get out of here."

I picked up the ball, forgetting about the oil on it until it was all over my hands.

We went back into the house, to find Mum and Aunt Anne drinking tea in silence. Will, Liam and Andy went back upstairs, and I went over to the sink to wash my hands, but I couldn't get all of the oil off. The soap didn't seem to touch it unless I really scratched at it, then Liam shouted, "Tom, quick!" I wiped my hands on a tea-towel, leaving a dirty black stain.

I ran up the stairs to see them gathered around watching Newsround. There was a story on about crop circles.

"There's been more of them!" Liam said, then, whispering to me, "The aliens are coming."

Mum served a beef stew with dumplings and mashed potatoes for dinner.

Dad rubbed his hands, said, "Lovely grub," like he always does, and picked up his knife and fork.

"So," Will said, holding his fork close to his mash, "how come we weren't allowed out after school today."

"Never mind that. Eat your dinner," Dad said, his words distorted as he kept a piece of beef in his mouth by wedging it between his tongue and his teeth.

"But it's not fair," Will said.

"I'll tell you what's not fair. That poor boy that's gone missing," Dad said.

"Trevor," Mum said, and Dad shovelled more food into his mouth.

"How about," Will said, ignoring Mum's glare, "if we went straight over to see Granddad tomorrow? Liam and Andy too? Well go straight there."

"I don't know," Mum said. "I'd prefer you to come straight home."

"Go straight there, and call home the second you arrive," Dad said. "And I'll pick you up from there at dinner time."

"Surely we can walk back from there. It's only five minutes."

"Leave it, otherwise you won't be allowed to go at all," Mum said.

"But..." Will said.

Dad jerked his arm out, pointing at Will with his knife. A bit of mashed potato flew from it and landed on my lip. I brought my hand up to wipe it away.

"What's that on your hand?"

I look down at the black smears of the oil I couldn't get off.

"I thought I told you not to play in that bloody oil."

"It got on the football." I said. "I didn't see it."

Dad wasn't listening. He was out of his chair. He leaned across the table and grabbed my hand and yanked me off my chair and around the table.

"You're bloody filthy." He shoved me towards the sink. "Your mum's cooked you a lovely meal and you come to the table in that state."

My lip started to quiver. I hate it when it does that. I didn't know what to do.

"Wash your hands."

I turned on the tap, grabbed the soap and rubbed it on my hands. It wasn't coming off. Then I sniffed and I heard his chair scraping.

"Wash your bloody hands, boy." He grabbed my hands and pulled them under the water.

"Sit down and eat your dinner," Mum said.

"Water's not even hot. Cold water won't clean it off." He turned the hot tap on further and turned off the cold. "Now wash then properly."

I put my hands back under the water for a second then picked up the soap again to lather up my hands. When I put my hands back under the water it was so hot, I pulled them back out again so fast I caught dad in the stomach with my elbow.

"Wash the fuckers," he said, and grabbed both wrists and forced my hands back under the water again.

"Will you two stop messing about and eat your dinner," Mum said.

The water was so hot I couldn't hold back any longer and I cried out. Dad let go of me. My hands throbbed. They were pink.

"Sit down," he said.

By the time I got around to the other side of the table he was already shovelling food back into his mouth. Will was looking down at his plate and eating slowly.

When I tried to bend my fingers to pick up my knife and fork, they hurt too much, and I had to put then down again. Dad stared at me, swallowed his mouthful of food, and said, "If you're not going to eat it, you can go to bed."

I got up. The chair scraped so loudly that I thought it was going to make my head explode. I didn't look back as I opened the door, my hands burning as I gripped the handle, and headed towards the stairs.

"Well, the boy's got no respect," I heard him say, "coming to the table like that. He must be simple or something."

When Will came up about an hour or so later, I was in bed. I'd wrapped my hands in a flannel I'd soaked in the upstairs bathroom to try to stop them feeling so hot and throbbing so much.

"Hey," he said, in a whisper, and perched on the end of my bed, "Wanna sit with me and watch the football?"

I shook my head. I didn't want him to see my hands.

"Do you mind if I put it on?"

"That's okay."

"I snuck you up this." From his pocket he pulled an Orange Club biscuit. "I thought you might be hungry."

"Thanks," I said, and he put it down on the set of drawers by my bed, put the TV on, and sat on his own bed.

"Still nil-nil."

Will sat and watched the rest of the match and I watched him as the sun went down and the room got darker, he started to glow green from the light of the television.

Even though I was only half paying attention to the football I realised that because it ended one all, both teams went through to the next round. No wonder people always said Argentina were cheaters, they probably arranged it beforehand. They had so many magical players, but they still decided to cheat. Perhaps that was the difference between good and evil, both could be magic, but evil could also be corrupted. After the game they showed the result from the other match. The Soviet Union had beaten Cameroon four-nil. What had happened to Roger Milla? Cameroon had been beaten by the biggest villains of all. How was that even possible? The table showed they still went into the next round though, so the magic was still alive, but with my hands throbbing it felt as though evil was winning.

Tuesday 19th June 1990

When I woke, I found my face cold when I'd slept on a wet patch from the flannel. One of my hands was still very pink and on the palm were a couple of small blisters. Every time I had to move my hand, I winced. There was no way I could get away with wearing gloves in June, so I spent most of the school day trying to hide my hands under the desk when in class, and in my pockets during break, and grimacing as I slid it hiding. No one really noticed them, which was good because I wouldn't have known what to say. I couldn't say it was Dad being horrible, because he only wanted me to wash my hands and probably didn't realise the water had gotten so hot.

At break I didn't want to play football when everyone else did because I couldn't run around with one hand in my pocket, so I said I didn't feel very well and watched from the side of the pitch. All of the goals were celebrated with a Roger Milla style dance and people were laughing and joking. It was like everyone had forgotten about John, and he was the one who started the Cameroon copying when he shouted, "Omam-Biyik" when he scored the first goal at break eight days ago. Then he turned to Brian Harper, who was in goal, and copied Barry Davies, the commentator and said, "It will go down as goalkeeper error."

I went back into the classroom. Mrs Palmer was setting up a Bunsen burner on her desk and had already got out some beakers.

"Hi Tom, the bell hasn't gone."

"Miss, how come no one talks about John?"

Mrs Palmer took a step towards me, "There's really not much to say."

"It's like everyone's forgotten about him."

"Mr Inglehart is in touch with the police every day, and as soon as there's some news they can share, all of the teachers will get together and decide how best to do that."

It was odd that she was willing to say more to me alone than she had to me and Liam. It was things like that that made me think Liam was wrong, and she wasn't an alien. "Normally when someone's off sick or on holiday you ask someone to make notes for them, but you haven't done that for John."

"You seem like the ideal person to do that job."

The bell went.

"Okay Mrs Palmer, I will."

"Tom, what's have you done to your hand?"

I put them behind my back. "It's a... heat rash. It's too hot."

"Let me see."

She bent down and took hold of my hand as Daniel Richardson walked in.

"Tom and Mrs Palmer sitting in a tree," he said, and stared at us.

"K-I-S-S-I-N-G," said Brian Harper, who was following behind him.

"Daniel, Brian, you've earned yourself a detention at afternoon break."

"Ah, but Miss..." said Daniel.

And Mrs Palmer urged us all to sit down as she was going to show us an experiment and she wanted us to write down all of the equipment used and then the method of how she did the experiment. She gave me an extra sheet of paper so I could make a second copy for John, and it felt like everything might be okay again.

"So why were you and Mrs Palmer holding hands at break?" Liam said at lunchtime.

"We weren't."

"You were. Daniel saw you. He told me."

"She was just looking at my hand."

"Why, what did you do to them?"

"I burnt it on a hot tap."

"That was stupid."

"Yeah," I said as I saw Andy come out.

He had a big smile on his face. He kept trying to say something, then breaking down with laughter. He took several slow, deep breaths then looked at me and said, "So, Tom, I hear you've got a new girlfriend." Then he was laughing so hard he was bent over double.

"What's all this?" Will said, who arrived as Andy was practically wetting himself.

"Nothing." I said.

"People saw Mrs Palmer and Tom holding hands," Liam said.

"Tom, that's gross," Will said.

"She was just looking at my hand."

"You told her what happened?"

"No! I told her it was a heat rash."

"Why lie?"

"You're a poet, and you didn't know it," added Liam.

Will give him a glare.

"I don't know; it was the first thing that came into my head," I said.

"You know what, Tom," Liam said, "You can be really weird sometimes." This set Andy off into another bout of laughter which kept going and going.

"What's wrong with him?" Laura Matthews appeared at the edge of our circle, with Becky Reid lingering behind her.

"Nothing!" I blurted out quickly. I didn't want her to hear about Mrs Palmer and me. Not that there was anything between Mrs Palmer and me, but I didn't want her hearing the stories.

She nuzzled her way into the circle, "What have you done to your hands?" she asked.

I couldn't say nothing again, I'd sound like an idiot, so I held it towards her.

She held the back of my hand and looked at it really closely. "That looks painful. Does it hurt?"

"A little," I said.

"How did you do it?"

"Burnt it."

"I hope they get better soon."

Liam then edged her out of the circle. "We were having a private conversation," he said, emphasising the word private.

Laura looked hurt. She turned around to chat to Becky.

"Liam, that was rude," I said.

"Just 'cos you fancy her," he said.

"I don't," I said, and instantly felt bad. Laura was still close. What if she'd heard?

"You do something stupid like burn your hand, and the prettiest girl in the class starts cooing over you," said Liam, going red.

"Maybe Tom's not the only one who fancies Laura," said Will. "Come on, let's go play some football.

We didn't have to cross any roads to get to Granddad's, that's why our parents let us go without being looked after.

"Thinking about going to Granddad's makes me wonder," Liam said, "What if John got one of those brain parasites, and it sent him crazy and he went running off into the wild?"

"It's possible," I said. We knew all about brain parasites from Granddad Norman because one time he had one. He said it was on his fortieth birthday. He was ploughing a field when he felt a bump. He thought perhaps a beam had snapped or a mouldboard had come off or got twisted, so he stopped the tractor and had a look. Sure enough, one of the mouldboards was bent right over.

He looked on the ground and there was a big bit of bog oak. He picked it up and carried over to the end of the field by that old oak tree, and when he threw it down, he felt something fly up and hit him right where his left eye used to be. Then he reckons he felt something squirming. He says it was like when you let a worm wriggle around on the palm of your hand, only inside his head. He couldn't stop scratching, so he ran all the way back to the farmhouse. This was when Granddad still lived there, and he tells us that if our Nanna was still alive, she would have confirmed it, but he was speaking fluent French. I don't know if Nanna could speak any French or not or what he was saying, but he says it's true. The only way he could get rid of it was to stick his head in water. Apparently, parasites don't like the cold. So, Nanna fetched his pipe so he could breathe then filled the sink with water. Granddad thrust his head into the water and held it there for well over an hour, until he could feel the parasite wiggling its way out of his ear. When he felt it slip out, he pulled his head out of the water. Trouble is he's had his head under the water for so long he'd washed all the colour out of his hair. From that day on it was completely white, despite Granddad never having had a grey hair in his life before that day. He showed us the parasite once. He kept it on a jar in his garage. It looked like a dried-out slug.

As we arrived at Granddad's house, we saw Uncle Rodney driving off. He gave us a wave with one of his ridiculously large hands. He'd done a good job cleaning his car, the red paint gleaming in the sun. We let ourselves in to Granddad's house and found him at the kitchen table staring at the newspaper. He'd got his glasses right on the tip of the nose. There's no glass in the right eye of the glasses. He reckons he doesn't need that as he's only got the one good eye. I couldn't see the point of taking the glass out, but he says one day he might find a use for it. I doubt he'd ever be able to find it again though as he probably only put it in one of these tin cans or boxes that are filling up his garage.

When he heard us, he looked up and said, "Yello, boys. Your Uncle Rodney's just dropped me in the paper," he said, holding it up to show us before quickly turning it over and putting it under a stack of mail.

Before he hid it, I caught a glimpse of some of the headline, seeing the words, 'CONCERN GROWS' and the outline of a picture which I pretty sure was John.

"No school today?" Granddad asked.

"We're finished. It's half three," Will said.

"Half three?" he said. "Finished school? In my day you'd stay at school until gone five then go home and do a full day's work in the fields. You boys have got it easy..."

We all joined it with the end of the sentence, "you don't even know you're born."

"You didn't really used to stay at school until five o'clock, did you Granddad?" asked Andy.

"Truth is I don't even remember. I know I went, but that's about it. Got a nasty bang on my head one time and can barely remember a thing from the first ten to fifteen years of my life."

"What happened?" Liam said.

"Well you can't see the scar, because it's under my hair, but you can still feel it."

We took turns. He guided our fingers through his thick white hair to feel the ridge on the top of his head.

"If my brain had been any smaller, chances are it would have fallen right out of the gap."

"But what happened?" Liam said.

"Patience, young man, I'm coming to that."

"Was it the tree?" I said.

"Was it heck! As if I'd give that old thing another chance to do me in. No, I was working on the combine harvester, you know, the red one, opening up one of the sides to clear out a blockage when the unloader swung down and cracked me on the head. Blood everywhere there was." Granddad paused and looked at us. "Not impressed?"

Liam said, "I thought it might have been and evil spirit, not a bit of combine."

"Who's to say it wasn't an evil spirit knocking down the unloader pipe, trying to bump your dear ol' granddad off, hey? Did you stop to think about that before you went and called my story boring?"

"We didn't say it was boring," Will said.

Andy had his hands on the table, his fingernails digging into the varnish. "Evil spirits can do that?" he said.

"I never said it was or it wasn't. I'll leave that up to you to decide. Anyway, you boys don't want to be cooped up in here with me all day. What are you up to?"

"What happened after you called the police?" Will said.

"I assume they investigated it. They don't give you feedback. But I did see them head back out that was with the sniffer dogs, and one of their Land Rovers followed them down there not long after that."

"No other news then?"

"They might have found something; they might not. I'm as in the dark as you are. So, is that why you came to see me today?"

"We wondered if you wanted to take a walk with us. Just up to the river and along the bank a little way," Will said.

"Ah, so that's it. Up to a little snooping."

"Oh, no, Granddad," I said, "We just thought it might be nice to get some fresh air, what with it being such a lovely day."

"Such a lovely day," mimicked Liam.

I ignored him.

"You think I was born yesterday? As it happens, I could do with getting on the move; my old bones get so stiff if I sit still for too long, and what harm did a little bit of snooping ever do anybody?"

We walked from Granddad's cottage along Main Street, past the village sign.

"So, if we head up Wissey Drove, then head back along Catchwater Drove that'll bring us to Long Drove and we can follow that back to the farmhouse," Granddad said. He knew all of the names of the droves, how long they were, where they went to and which was the quickest way to get from one place to another.

"How do you know all of this, Granddad?" I asked.

"When you've been about as long as me, not much passes you by. Besides we used to drive cattle down these droves, back when there was money in keeping cattle."

We turned down Wissey Drove. I'd felt irritated all day, but as soon as we headed down this path, I could really feel my eyes start to itch. I kept scraping my tongue with my teeth to stop it from itching.

"Whatever are you doing?" Granddad said.

Liam looked round and saw me pulling a face as I scratched my tongue, and he covered his mouth to hide a laugh.

"Itchy tongue," I said to Granddad.

"Well, you know what they say about getting an itchy tongue?"

"No?"

"Means they're about to find some luck."

My heart raced. Was today the day we were going to find John?

"Come 'ere," Granddad said.

I walked over to him, thinking that he was going to give us some great idea which was going to help us.

"You got something in your hair," he said, and reached towards me. He brushed the hair beside my head, then in the flat of his hand help out an old coin.

"Was that in your hair!" cried Andy.

No. It wasn't. Granddad's favourite trick normally made me laugh, but what that coin represented this time was a spark of hope fading away.

"Aren't you going to take it then?" Granddad said.

I forced a smile. "Thanks," I said. I popped it in my pocket, and then gave my eyes a rub.

The grass soon gave way to a grey mud path with two deep grooves running along it with tractor tyre marks in odd places where the ground was a little wet. Mostly it was all dry and cracked where we hadn't had any rain in so long. I looked down at the ground then at the wrinkles on Granddad's face. In Mr Johnstone's field we saw the back of the trailer which had the massive banner on it. It faced the village so people would see it on the way out. It was for Truckfest, which was over a month ago, but he hadn't bothered to take it down yet.

We reached the point at which the drove met the river. There was a wooden bridge across it. Andy ran up onto the bridge.

"We don't wanna go that way Andy," Granddad said, "You'll end up at Twelve Mile Bank and we'll have to trace our steps all the way back."

Andy jumped, listening to the sound of his feet as the hit the wood.

"See that building by the river down there," Granddad said, pointing to a mostly ruined brick building that spread, somehow, halfway over the river. "That's an old pumping station. I used to have a cousin who worked there and looked after the drain."

Andy wasn't listening. He went back to the drove and pulled up a handful of blades of grass from a clump. He dropped it off the bridge and watched it as it drifted slowly under. He turned to the other side of the bridge and waited.

"Why isn't it coming?"

"Probably sunk," Liam said.

"Or it got stuck," Will said.

Liam went towards the bridge too, but instead of crossing onto it went a little way down the bank to look under it.

"For Christ's sakes don't fall in, Liam. Your mother will string me up by my delicate bits if I bring you back soaked to the skin and covered in bog slime."

Liam bent down to peer under the bridge. Will and I went over to make sure he didn't fall. Will leant off the bridge and had hold of the back of Liam's school trousers, and I was holding on to Will to make sure that Liam didn't pull him in. This activity was beginning to become a bit of a habit.

"Well?" Will said.

"It's dark, but it looks like there's something in there," Liam said.

"What is it?"

"I don't know – have you got a stick?"

"Andy, go get a stick," Will said.

Andy went over to the trees on the other side of the bridge and looked around at the ground.

"There aren't any."

"Break one off."

Andy bent a low branch down. He jumped to put more of his weight on it, but it only bowed further without breaking.

"Can I borrow your knife, Will?"

"I can't get to it from here," Will said, "Can you get it out of my pocket, Tom?"

"Or you could use this one," Granddad said. He pulled the thickest Swiss Army Knife out of his pocket that must have had about a zillion different tools on it. He pulled one out. "Try the saw."

Andy took it. His eyes were wide, and he nearly tripped over my legs as he went back across the bridge. He pulled the branch down again and started sawing at it. It broke within a few seconds and the bit still attached to the tree bounced back up and thwacked him in the face. He didn't let it bother him though and grabbed the branch and dragged it along the bridge and held it out for Liam.

"Go back up onto the bridge and watch what comes out," Liam said. I could hear him grunting as he pushed the branch into the water. There was a slurping sound, like when you get a welly-boot stuck in mud. Will tensed up suddenly and I could see his arm go tight.

"What is it?" shouted Liam. Will relaxed and then let go as Liam made his way up the bank.

"Just a log," Andy said.

Will and Liam joined him on the bridge and watched it bob away down the river. I stood by the side pinching my nose, which had started to run badly, and I had no tissue left to mop it up.

"He could have fallen in though," Liam said.

I thought about the police car by the bank of the river earlier in the week.

"What do you think happened, Granddad?" asked Liam.

"I don't rightly know. Police are out there doing their best, and that's a good thing."

"But shouldn't they have some kind of clues by now?"

"Truth is they probably do, just not ready to release the information yet is all."

"Which way should we go?"

"Keep going up this drove, as I said before." Granddad rolled up the sleeves of his cardigan and we continued along the drove. Andy was walking up high on the riverbank, and Liam followed behind him, looking across into the fields in both directions. We reached the point at which the new bypass crossed the river.

"What used to run along there was called Dark Fen Drove," Granddad said, pointing along the path of the bypass. "See, these council folk they know the old roads had the best paths through the fen, that's why they followed it along this way. Of course, they did want to cut across our land to save a bob or two and keep it straight, like a Roman road, but the lay of the land don't always allow for that."

Granddad swatted a bug off his forearm, and a noticed a scar there I hadn't seen before.

"How'd you get that one then Granddad?" I asked.

"I've told you that one before, I'm sure I have."

We all shook our heads.

"What, I've never told you about the time I got mauled by a Fen Tiger?"

Andy gasped, and we all closed round Granddad.

"Maybe this'll make up for that boring old story I told you about cracking my head open." He leant forward on his stick, so his face was no more than a foot away from any of ours. "We'd had a few bad storms and a lot of trees had come down over the winter – it was the same winter that lightning struck that old oak tree – you know, the one that had my eye out – and with the east wind sweeping through all ferocious it blew most of the debris off the land and into the ditches. Well the second we got a bit of rain all the fields got waterlogged. The ditches up by Catchwater Drove were too full of junk to properly function so the water just came back up onto the land. Well we couldn't have that; they would have been unplantable for the season and what with us having two little ones and another on the way there was no way we would be able to make ends meet without being at full capacity. Only thing I could do was clear the ditches and make sure the water could run off. And that's what I was doing when it happened. I pulled out all of these branches – bigger than that one Andy had off that tree – but there was something else in the bottom. As I got closer, I could hear this kind of purring – but not like you'd hear from a cat, much deeper than that. Then it opened its eyes. There were shining out of the mud and I scrambled back, fell in a heap onto a bunch of the branches still down there. I tried to climb out, but my trousers were snagged on something, and this shape in the mud, it started to grow. The eyes got closer to me, and it sniffed me. Well I put up this arm to protect myself from it and it claws at me and tears that scar into my arm. I shouted out and tried to struggle away, but only succeeded in snapping some of the branches I was laying against. Don't ask me how but I kind of fell into them. They were all around me like a cage – but it was protecting me because the creature couldn't get through to me. I don't know how long I was in there but eventually something scared it off – a gun shot from a couple of fields over, probably Carter's farm – your great granddad on your dad's side," Granddad nodded towards Liam and Andy, "He was always out shooting. Liked to catch himself a pheasant. There was a time or two he'd bring one over to us and we'd have it off him in exchange for something. Anyway, the beast was scared, and it ran off. I saw it take off across the field, shaking off most of the mud as it went. Well I knew what it was because I'd heard stories about the Fen Tiger, but I didn't believe them until that day I was nearly eaten up by one of them."

Fen Tigers, black shucks and shug monkeys. Were they real? Where were they coming from? Where did they hide?

"So how did you get out of the cage?" asked Liam.

"Well, once that thing was gone, I was able to pick it apart, one branch at a time. Tore my trousers to shreds getting out of there though. When your grandmother saw me, she didn't know what to say. A right state I was. Of course, I had to go back to finish clearing out those ditches, but let's just say I didn't jump into another ditch without making sure there wasn't already something else down there waiting for me." Granddad smiled at us, then laughed as he stood back up straight again.

"You know you told us about the Duke and his little zoo," Andy said.

"Yes."

"It that where the Fen Tiger came from? One of the escaped pumas?"

"You know what, young man, I think you may well be right."

That didn't sound right to me. There was something much darker at work than that.

Granddad pointed with his stick, "We'd better get a move on or your mothers will carve me up for dinner, and this old flesh won't be good eating."

Granddad turned down what must have been Catchwater Drove with Andy following close behind him. Liam nodded at me.

"What?"

"Something else to add to the list."

"What list?"

"Tom! Don't you pay any attention? About what might have happened to John. Fen Tiger attack."

Liam trotted off to catch up with Andy.

"I've asked Granddad about that scar before," Will said.

"And?"

"He never said anything about a tiger. He said he couldn't remember."

"Well... maybe he remembered," I said.

"It's not the kind of thing you'd forget." And Will set off to catch up with the others.

We'd turned onto Long Drove and the farmhouse was in sight. I was trying to avoid looking at the oak tree, so was looking down into the ditches as we walked. The tree always made me feel weird when I was with Granddad because I couldn't stop myself from thinking about what it had done to him. I kept seeing his eye go flying out of his skull, and no matter how hard I tried not to think about it the eye always ends up going into the tree's mouth, and it chews it up and laughs. Of course, if it's right that it wasn't hit by lightning until after this point then it wouldn't even have had that scorch mark on it that looks like a mouth, but I can never think of sensible things right away and end up thinking of it in the worst way possible.

Because I was looking down, I didn't see who was walking towards us. Liam had to drop away from Granddad's side to poke me in the ribs.

"It's crazy old Shaky Jake, look!" he said, "Think if we go 'Boo' at the right time he'll fall into the ditch?"

Jake was paying about as little attention to us as I had been to him. He was looking down into the ditches on the other side and muttering.

"How do?" Granddad said as he got closer.

Jake looked up. He was blinking a lot, and he licked his lips a couple of times, as if he was trying to decide if he should say anything or not. In the end he decided not but nodded his head in a more deliberate way rather than one of his twitches.

"What did you speak to him for?" Liam said when we were a little way clear of Shaky Jake.

"Why shouldn't I say 'ello?" Granddad said.

"He's crazy. He comes out of his house and chases us down the road."

"And what do you do to make him chase you? I know how you boys go looking for sport."

"But this one time," Andy said, "He had this knife and it was all bloody and if he caught us, he might have stabbed us to death."

"Don't be daft."

"It's true," Liam said.

"Will? Were you there?"

"It's true. Sort of," Will said. "We were standing by his kitchen window, and I say he was cutting some meat."

"And why did he chase you?"

"Tom was pulling faces at him."

"You were too!" I said.

"Have you ever stopped to think that if you didn't go out of your way to wind him up, he wouldn't react the way he does, and then everyone wouldn't say he was crazy? If you left well enough alone, he'd keep himself to himself and no one would be any the wiser to whatever his problems are."

Granddad stopped walking and leant on his stick. "Now you boys run on back to the farmhouse, and I'll catch up with you in a minute or two."

And we left him there. We took a slight detour off the path to head to Moon Base One for a quick meeting.

"So, what have we got on John so far?" I asked.

"Nothing. We've got nothing," Will said.

"No. Not true," Liam said, "We've got loads of people from the Top Trumps, and we keep hearing the teachers talk about transition."

"Rubbish. We've seen no sign of him. The police are probably doing better than us, and this is *our* village."

"But what about some of the stuff Granddad was talking about today?"

"Like what?"

"Bog slime. What if something pulled him into the river? There are cards which show water monsters. What about evil spirits attacking him? What about the Fen Tiger?"

"You can waste your time on all that crap if you like," Will said, "But I'm going home before Granddad beats us back to the farmhouse, because then we'll be in real trouble."

Andy dashed to the base entrance and peered out, "God, I can't see him. What if he's already back?"

We jumped across the bank and ran down the drove and back alongside the field. We were sure Granddad had dashed for the farmhouse and dropped us in it until we looked back down the path and realised he hadn't moved at all since we left him. We went into the house. I could hear the television on in the living room, which was odd, because Mum never put the TV on during the day. I made some drinks of squash which we all downed straight away, so I made some more. Mum must have heard the tap running because I heard the TV switch off and then she came into the kitchen. She stuffed a tissue into her sleeve.

"What were you watching?" Will said.

"Anglia News."

"Why."

"Oh, no reason, someone I knew was going to be on there, that's all."

"Really, someone you know is going to be on TV? Who is it?"

"No one you know. Don't worry about that. Now do you boys want a drink?"

Surely, she could see the drinks in our hands?

"Whatever's wrong with your eyes?" she said, looking at me.

They felt like they were burning now. My tongue was also sore from where I'd scratched it so much, and even the inside of my ears tingled.

"They've been itchy all day."

"Hay fever," she said. "I must make you an appointment with the doctor, get you some medicine."

Dad had just wandered in, with Granddad just behind him. He must have heard her.

"He still whimpering on about having bloody hay-fever?"

"I wasn't," I muttered.

"Ain't no good living round here having hay-fever. You better shake that off quick-sharp."

There was nothing I could say. My eyes were welling up. It was the hay-fever. That's all.

"Liam, Andy – make sure you've got all of your stuff and I'll run you home."

I waited until they were gone until I snuck upstairs to the bathroom where I stared at myself in the mirror, leaning in close so that the only thing I could see were my eyes. My lower eyelids were puffy and bloated, and the whites of the eyes looked almost yellow, as if a thin layer of pollen had coated them. Thick red veins zig-zagged towards my iris. In the corner of my eye, the side by the nose, was a load of gunk. I dapped at it with the toilet tissue. This was the itchiest part. It was like a little red ball, and I thought, if only I could pluck that out, it might get rid of the itching. It might get rid of the hay-fever. It might stop me from being a stupid little cry baby. There was a pair of nail scissors on the windowsill. I could just stick it in there, and pop that bit of the eye out no problem. I picked up the scissors and slipped my thumb and finger through the holes. With the back of my other hand I wiped at my eyes again. I scrunched my knuckle into the left eye, and could feel it pulsing inside, trying to push back away, but I didn't care as it had stopped the itching. I was going to do it. Cut the bad part out and live a better life. I took by fist away from my hand, and everything through that eye seemed dull, and unreal. I moved the scissors towards the eye, but my vision hadn't cleared enough.

"Tom." There was a knock at the door. It was Will.

"What?" I said, annoyed.

"Come on. You've been in there ages. I need a piss, and the football's going to start in five minutes."

"Go downstairs," I called through the door. The scissors started to feel awkward in my hand, the finger holes too tight around my fingers.

"I can't."

"Why not?"

"It stinks. Dad must have been in there."

I laughed. There was no way he'd dare say that if Dad was home. I had to let him in after that. I put the scissors back on the windowsill and opened the door.

I added to the page on the Fen Tiger, which I'd put alongside the shug monkey and black shuck, to my evidence book. It was just an exercise book from the stash we'd nicked from Mrs Palmer's desk drawers one afternoon when she'd been called into a meeting and the substitute was late. I flicked back through and looked at some of the headings. RUN AWAY, HIT BY LORRY, ABDUCTED BY ALIENS IN SCHOOL, SPONTANEOUS HUMAN COMBUSTION. Underneath each I'd written EVIDENCE, but there was nothing but speculation under each. At the back of the book was a separate section to record evidence that we couldn't put against a possible cause. The only thing I'd noted on there was FIESTA and

FISHERMEN'S FRIEND, but they could have been there for ages so we couldn't definitely say they were connected.

I had West Germany versus the Colombia on in the background. It ended 1-1 to the Germans, but I didn't see any of the goals except for in the replays at the end of the match. I was too distracted by my book and trying to pull it all together to make some kind of sense. Each of the Top Trumps creatures we'd talked about had a page, and some were linked to people in the village.

"What do you think about John?" I said to Will after he turned off the TV.

"He probably ran away."

"But don't you think he would have said something to us before?"

"Do you tell your friends every time something bad happens at home?"

I looked down at my hand, which was almost back to its normal colour, but the skin was peeling off in some places around where the blisters had burst.

"Well what about some of these other ideas?"

"What? Aliens? Fen Tigers? It's all bullshit."

"Isn't."

"Yes, it is, Tom."

"But Granddad said..."

"Don't believe everything Granddad tells you."

"Why not?"

"I mean, do you really think that if he had a parasite in his brain it would turn his hair white?"

"So, what should we do then?"

"Keep a look out. Listen."

Then the door creaked open and we both stopped talking and it made me think of the way Aunt Anne and Mum stopped talking the other day when we kept going into the kitchen. Mum was standing at the door.

"Bedtime, boys," she said and stood looking at us for a minute. "And don't forget to brush your teeth."

She was talking to us like we were five and six again. I can't remember when she last reminded us to brush our teeth because she knows we always do it. But she even watched us do it too, and then even went as far as tucking us into bed.

A little while after she was gone, when I think Will had already fallen asleep, I heard the front door open. It was probably Dad going out to check something on the farm or maybe to let Chappie out for a wee.

Wednesday 20th June 1990

I woke early and took Chappie for a walk around the field. Mum insisted on keeping an eye on me and said I had to stay in view of the house at all times. It has rained overnight and as I walked slowly around the field with Chappie, we encountered several clusters of horrible brown slugs. They were that mustard colour which reminded me of Mrs Palmer's cardigans, and, since Liam was constantly going on about it, alien creatures too. These were odd slugs. Why weren't they black? Could it be that they were alien slugs? Chappie stopped to sniff at one of them, and, surprisingly for him, chose not to eat it. He'd eat anything, but maybe he drew the line at alien servants. The alien theory was beginning to sound like to most likely, given that nothing else we'd come up with made any real sense at all.

I took a shortcut across the field both to stay in Mum's view and to avoid going too close to the tree. I'd not forgotten how it laughed after it had tripped me up. I could see someone walking up along the back drove though. They must have come from up the end of Hereward Close. I squinted and looking at the way the man was fidgeting as he walked, I was sure it was Shaky Jake.

"What's he doing walking around there?" I said to Mum when I got back, pointing at the tiny figure almost out of view on the drove.

"Who dear?"

"Shaky Jake."

"Don't call him that, Thomas. It's not nice to call people names."

"But why's he walking around like that?"

"He can walk where he likes. The droves aren't private property. Hadn't you better be getting ready for school?"

At school we were spending the morning at the church to sing some hymns and learn a little about the history of the building, which meant that we'd have to spend the morning with the vicar, Reverend Lloyd Meath. He came into school from time to time and brought his guitar with him and told us stories about Jesus and sang hymns. He had a habit of closing his eyes for a really long time while talking, and his hand gestures were really over the top. We often saw him after school outside the vicarage where he spent a long time tending to his garden. We didn't like to get caught in conversation with him though because he was way too serious, so if we saw that he was out there we'd cross over the road to avoid him.

The whole class had to walk together to the church, with Mrs Palmer leading the way and Mr Inglehart following us. It seemed a bit over the top considering we didn't even have to cross any major roads.

Liam and I were towards the back. I told him about seeing Shaky Jake acting weird this morning, and he said that we should probably try to investigate him a bit more. I don't know how we were supposed to do that, but it seemed like a good idea. As we walked through the gates, I held back a little and looked at the dates on some of the gravestones.

"Look," I said to Liam. "There's a girl there that was only nine or ten when she died." I pointed to the gravestone and felt a hand on my shoulder. I looked round to see Mr Ingehart.

"Keep moving boys," he said, and urged us into the church.

Liam and I managed to get on pews towards the back for the hymn-singing part, so we were able to mouth the words and continue our conversation. "1952 – 1962 it said. Surely Granddad would have remembered that."

"What was the..." begun Liam.

Mrs Palmer was looking at us. A fraction of a second later we joined in with the hymn too until her attention was elsewhere.

"The name?" Liam said.

"Don't know. Ingehart stopped me reading the rest."

After listening to the vicar go on about caring for each other and the tale of the good Samaritan we did some rubbings on various bits of stone inside the building.

"Can we do a rubbing on the graves?" asked Liam.

Mrs. Palmer quickly moved him to one side, where Reverend Meath couldn't hear. "No, you can't do a rubbing on a grave! How is that showing respect to the dead?"

"Sorry," he murmured, with his cheeks reddening.

"Could we do some from outside the building though?" I asked.

"Well I don't see why that would be a problem. Do not step on any of the graves though!"

"Of course, she said yes to you. She loves you," said Liam, and stuck his tongue out.

We carefully made our way around the church yard, pretending to take rubbings at appropriate spots.

"Look," I called to Liam, "Ernest Barnham. Must be Teddy's brother that Granddad was talking about."

"How old was he?"

"Fifteen."

"I thought Granddad said he wasn't a child?"

"I guess Granddad was wrong."

We continued to work our way around the graves.

"There's Nanna's," I said. Then one a couple of spaces down caught my eye. "Liam," I said, "Who was Enid Tilbrook?"

He shrugged.

"June 1931 – May 1952. She would have been only twenty when she died."

"Was she Granddad's sister?"

After school it was Mum waiting by the gates. With so many parents there it was oddly quiet when we came out. I'd updated Will at lunch time when we were back at school, and he said there was no point asking Mum about it. I ignored him. "Mum. Who was Enid Tilbrook?"

"I don't know, dear. Why?"

"We saw a gravestone with her name on it."

"She's probably some distant relative."

"Can we go see Granddad?"

"You're not going to bombard him with questions?"

"No, it would be nice to see him, that's all."

"You saw him yesterday."

"And it would be good to see him again today."

"Well I suppose, but only for a few minutes. I've got to get dinner on."

But when we got to Granddad's house, he wasn't there.

"I suppose we ought to go home then," Mum said.

"He might have gone for a walk. Can we follow the path that goes around the back of his house and comes out the end of the village?"

Will gave me a puzzled look.

"Go on then," Mum said, and the five of us set off on a diversion. The path led us behind Teddy Barnham's house and farmyard. The shed where he bred maggots wasn't painted quite so well out the back. As we moved on a little further, we saw why. Teddy was halfway through painting the side and hadn't got to the back yet. He was standing on a small set of stepladders, with the tin of creosote in one arm and the brush in the other.

"Poor old chap. He doesn't have a single family member good enough to help him out and he has to struggle on all by himself," Mum said.

He didn't look like he was struggling though. He was standing straight up instead of bent and crooked like we'd seen him at the weekend and the job didn't seem to be bothering him at all.

"Hello Mr Barnham!" shouted Andy.

He looked round and gave us a wave. "Back for more maggots young fella?" he shouted.

"Not today," Andy said.

"Have you seen Granddad?" shouted Liam.

"I can't say that I have."

And with that we gave him a wave and continued our way, without coming across Granddad before we were back on Main Street.

At dinner, just after he'd finished and before he got down from the table Will said, "Tom saw something interesting at the church today, didn't you, Tom?"

"What's that?" Dad said.

I didn't want to ask him in case he turned funny, but now if I didn't it would be just as bad. "We were looking at the gravestones and we saw one for Enid Tilbrook. We wanted to ask Granddad who it was."

"I can tell you that," Dad said. "She was your granddad's cousin, or more specifically your great-granddad's brother's daughter."

"She was only twenty when she died," I said.

"Is that so?"

"Do you know what happened to her?"

"Can't say that I do. Are those plates gonna wash themselves?"

Will washed, and I dried. My hands were still really sensitive in water, so I was doing all I could to avoid that. After we'd finished washing up, I had another go at *The Secret of the Scythe*. My rolls for skill and luck were much better this time, but a couple of bad stamina rolls left me seriously weak. I stayed on the road and beat the goblin without hiding which meant I got the first hit in, and I didn't go into the witch's house at all. There was an option to snoop around, but I thought it was probably best avoided altogether. Just past the house was the entrance to the Underworld. You had to go in through the mouth of an enormous dead tree. As you approached, you were attacked by tree roots. I put the book down and stared out of the window at the tree in the field. Could it really be a gateway to Hell? And if it was the gateway to Hell, could something have emerged from there to take John?

NOW

Last year, Charlie had a piece of homework in which he had to produce a family tree. I was powerless to avoid thinking about my own family, and the names I'd have to put on there. As much as I wanted Charlie to do well, I simply couldn't do it.

For the first time since I asked for his daughter's hand in marriage, I gave Victoria's dad a call. They hadn't seen Charlie lately (entirely my fault – I didn't have anything against them, I'd just blocked them out of my mind), so they were more than happy to take him for the weekend and work with him on their part of the family tree.

When he came back home, Charlie was quiet. At first, I thought that he'd had a bad weekend, which made me think I should keep him from his mother's side of the family too, but eventually he showed me the piece of work he'd produced with his grandparents. It was fantastic. They'd taken Charlie back generations, and halfway across the world with their family tree, and what's more, they'd presented it beautifully. I hadn't been entirely honest about my reason for sending Charlie away to work on this project, and, thinking that they were being considerate, they'd left plenty of room on one side of the tree for Charlie to trace back his family on my side.

"Maybe I could just make it up?" Charlie said, staring at the blank side of the paper after listening to my outburst about my family.

"We don't make things up," I told him.

"What can we do about it then?"

I got out a pair of scissors, taking of the space where we could have put by side, and sent an email to his teacher, explaining that I didn't have anything to do with my family, and didn't want Charlie getting caught up with it. I thought that would make it okay. When Charlie got the homework back, the teaching had praised it highly. When Charlie brought it home, he put it in the bin.

Thursday 21st June 1990

It was the day of England versus Egypt. A win would put England through to the next round, and defeat would boot them out of the tournament. Wherever John was I knew he'd be excited for this one too. At break, it was all anyone could talk about (apart from some of the girls). Egypt had already drawn with the Netherlands and the Republic of Ireland, so they weren't going to be easy to beat. But through all the excitement I kept turning my mind to John.

Chris punted the ball towards the football pitch and said that he was going to be Gazza. There was no way he was good enough to be Gazza, and if John was here, he would have been him.

"I don't think you should be Gazza," I said.

"Doesn't matter what you think. You're playing for Egypt," he said. So, I decided I wasn't playing at all and walked off. Liam followed, which was good because he was on the England team and it would have left the teams still even.

"Do you think John will be allowed to watch the football, wherever he is?"

"John could convince them to let him," I said. I felt a tear trickle down my face. "He always was pretty persuasive."

"Do you remember that time he talked Mr Inglehart into letting the whole class come down to watch the match against Hilgay?"

"That was ace. We cheered every pass and every tackle!"

"Hilgay looked scared."

"No wonder he didn't let us do it for the next game."

"What's it going to be like next year?"

"What do you mean?"

"Will and his class will have all gone up to big school. We'll be in the top class."

"It'll be strange. I always imagined John would be with us. The three of us would be like the kings of the school." In truth, I'd imagined John and I as the kings of the school and hadn't thought about Liam in this little fantasy at all.

"John will come back. He's got to."

"Should we be doing more about it?"

"Like what?"

"Like have a good look in the staff room to see what the teachers are hiding."

"Now?"

"No, we'll do it at lunch time."

We sat and watched the others play for a while and when the ball came rolling our way after Chris had hit a shot a mile wide (he's no Gazza) we decided to re-join the game.

I couldn't focus through the science experiment that we were supposed to be doing. Mrs Palmer had had to go into her cupboard to get out some of the equipment, and Liam had quickly jumped up to help her get stuff out.

"Do sit down, Liam Carter," she said.

"Thought you could use a hand, Miss," said Liam, and held his arms out to take whatever she had to hand out.

"That's very kind of you." She sent him into the cupboard, and he came out carrying a stack of beakers shortly after.

After handing them out, Liam came over to me. "It's clear," he said.

Together, we worked on the experiment very badly. We measured out the wrong volumes, adding too little of the substance so that nothing happened. That was probably a better outcome than what happened to Daniel and Brain though, who managed to put too much in, and had their mixture bubble up and foam up over the top and onto their textbooks. While muddling through we formulated a plan, and when Mrs Palmer let us out for lunch instead of rushing for the canteen, we dashed around the back of the school.

Apart from kids heading towards the canteen, we encountered no one. We got all the way around the back of the school, so that we could see into the staffroom window. This allowed us to scope out where we needed to look if we were able to get in. There was a small area that we couldn't see which looked like a good starting point. Otherwise the staffroom full of nothing other than comfy chairs and bits of paper pinned to the wall.

"If the plan's on one of those," I said, "we'll never find it."

"But it's empty at the moment," Liam said. "If we don't go now, there might not be another chance."

We went into the school through the side door, so we were quite sure that no one had gone into the staff room as we made our way round. Carefully I turned the handle and was surprised to see it open. Before I stepped inside, I took one last glance at the sign on the front.

STAFF ROOM. NO ADMITTANCE TO PUPILS.

I gulped as I stepped inside, and Liam quickly followed. It smelled strongly of coffee, and there were newspapers strewn on the tables.

"I really want a go on one of those seats," said Liam.

"We don't have time to mess about."

"But they look so cosy."

I walked over to the corner we couldn't see through the window, the part which had been partitioned off. Behind it were a bunch of pigeonholes, half of which were crammed full of paper, and another door. "Where do you think that leads?" I asked. It couldn't go anywhere, surely. There wasn't room for much, as it was on the external wall, and it definitely didn't lead outside. Was this the portal to the alien base? I looked round, waiting for Liam's response, but saw that he was slumped in one of those chairs.

"Liam, this is important."

"So's this," said Liam.

I looked around expecting to see him pretending to be asleep. Instead he was holding a newspaper. "NO NEW LEADS IN MISSING BOY CASE".

"What's it say?"

"Not much more than in the headline. It's been eight days..."

I heard a laugh from outside. It sounded deep. Maybe Mr Inglehart.

"Quick," I said. "Hide." But there was only one place to go: Through the door. I waited until Liam was beside me, and then pulled it open, half expecting to see John in there attached to a bunch of machines and wires, or to see stars and planets, but instead it was stacked with exercise books and textbooks going back decades. We bundled in and pulled the door closed and were stuck with the smell of mouldy books for the rest of lunchtime.

Luckily, we could hear the conversations going on inside the staff room. They weren't very interesting, and Mrs Palmer only said nice things about our class, but they did give us an idea about when the room was clear, and we were free to make our way back to our classroom.

"Why don't you come over mine to watch the game?" said Liam. "Bring everything we've gathered so far, and we'll see what we've got. It might give us something to concentrate on."

"And hide that newspaper somewhere," I said.

Liam looked down. I think he'd forgotten that he was holding it as he'd had it so long. Quickly he stuffed it into his P.E. bag, and we went back to class.

Mum and Dad were more than happy for us to spend the evening at Aunt Anne and Uncle Alan's house. After dinner, which included ice cream topped with the magic chocolate sauce which instantly went hard so that you have to crack it with the side of your spoon, we went up to Liam's room. Will stayed downstairs with Andy. He said that he didn't feel like talking about it.

I got out my exercise book and started to flick through the pages. "We said that he might have run away. What evidence do we have for that?"

"Nothing," Liam said.

"Well, not nothing. We know he wasn't happy about being left at home on his own, but is that enough to make you run away?"

"No. I'd love it if Mum left me alone once in a while."

"But if it was every day?"

"True."

"What evidence have we got against him running away?"

"He never told us. I think he would have done."

"Also, if the police thought he'd run away I think they'd have questioned us a bit more."

"Okay, so he might have run away, but there's no evidence for that. What's next."

"Hit by a massive lorry. That's out. Surely if that was the case, they would have found him. We've walked all the way up and down the village and not seen a thing."

"What else?"

"Kidnapped."

"By aliens."

"Aliens is one of the possibilities for kidnappers. But a non-alien could have taken him."

"We have motives for aliens though. Remember, 'transition'."

"Plus, I saw a bunch of weird alien-looking slugs."

"But what else can we do? We've checked the staff room. Where else is there?"

"We have to keep our eyes open and listen for possibilities. What else have we got?"

Liam got out his Top trumps and spread them on the floor. He pulled out the Alien Creature and put it to one side. "Oh, and remember, Mrs Johnstone is the Zetan Priest."

"But we don't really have a motive for that."

"Do Zetan Priests need a motive?"

"You don't even know what a Zetan Priest is."

"So, neither do you."

"Well if we're going on look-alikes Teddy Barnham looked like The Sorcerer, and I swear he has to have some kind of powers to do that painting he was doing the other day, plus to put up with the smell of the maggots.

"That's another motive there. Granddad said maggots can feed on dead flesh."

"You don't think John's dead, do you?"

We were both quiet for a while. Liam was eyeballing the cards. "Hey," he said, pointing at The Hangman (Horror Rating 88), "he looks like your dad."

I grabbed the card and looked at it. "He doesn't look anything like that."

"He has the same hair."

Liam was right, he did have the same hair. I picked up The Cannibal (Physical Strength 93), who was completely bald. "Well if we're going on hair, this one looks like your dad."

We both laughed, then another card caught my eye. "This is odd," I said, pointing at the Beast card. For some reason the hairy, green creature was on a stage. "Reminds me of Uncle Rodney."

"Uncle Rodney's never on stage for very long though; he normally falls off!"

"You know who I've seen wandering about in the village more than usually lately?"

"Who?"

"Shaky Jake." I picked up The Madman card (Killing Power 69). His mouth was tight, and his eyes were closed, exactly how Shaky goes when he's wound up, and his hair was exactly the same too: brown, receding, and sticking up in random tufts.

"He might even be an alien too."

It would certainly have explained why he was so weird.

I don't even remember watching the first half of the football because I was still thinking about the cards. Liam had left them in his room when I wanted nothing more than to look through them all again. But, by the time the second half had started, and England had missed their first chance I was interested. Because only a win would mean they were through for sure we all got a bit worried every time they kept giving the ball back to Egypt. Luckily, we didn't have to wait until the last minute for a goal or anything as Mark Wright scored when there was still half an hour to go. We were cheering on England to score more goals, but they didn't, but we knew that would be good enough. At the end of the game the people in the studio showed us the table and said that because Ireland and Holland had ended 0-0 it meant that England finished top of the group. Because the games from group E were played earlier in the day, it meant we found out that England would be playing Belgium in the next round.

Mum came in not long after it had finished. "Are you boys ready to go home?"

"Where's Dad?" Will said.

"He's having a chat with your uncle. Come on, it's late and you've all got school in the morning."

We went outside. Uncle Alan was leaning in and talking to Dad through the Land Rover window.

"Well, thanks for the update," said Uncle Alan, "I'll catch you later." As we passed him on our way to the Land Rover he said, "See you later boys," and then started chanting, "Engerlund, Engerlund, Engerlund."

If England had gone out of the tournament, I don't think I could have taken it. The fact that they had got through, that they had survived the group stage made me think that John was probably still be okay too. All England had to do was win the tournament and everything would work out just fine.

NOW

Having watched England in a number of tournaments since, I've learned now to depend upon them too much.

Driving through the old part of Little Mosswick makes me see that this place is still as sick as ever. But if he's dying, if he's really dying, then maybe that's what the village needs to be healed. If I don't see him go, then I'll still think he's out there. Maybe I need to see him die too before I'm healed.

I continue to drive through, with the old parts of the village starting to show through more and move. I pass Downham Close and slow down as I pass the place where Shaky Jake lived. The whole house is gone now, the foundations grassed over into what should be a pleasant green, but there's no one enjoying it. Beyond it, on the road where John used to live, I can see a number of For Sale signs. People have given up on this area.

A little further down the road, I come to a stop outside the old school building. The gates are closed, long since chained together, but behind it the building is still standing.

"My old school," I say to Charlie, and nod towards it.

"What was it like?"

"Up until year five it was a fun place to be. I liked the teachers. I worked hard. I had good friends."

"Then what?"

"Everything changed. I didn't go back, but I guess that there were too many ghosts wandering the corridors."

Charlie leans closer to the window, staring at the school.

"Not real ghosts. You know I don't mean real ghosts, right?"

"Yes Dad," says Charlie with a sigh.

"What is it, Pal?"

"You always do that."

"What?"

"You'll talk about a ghost or a monster or a skeleton in the closet and then insist on explaining that it's not a real ghost, or monster, or skeleton."

"I don't want you getting mixed up, that's all."

"They do teach us about metaphors and similes at school, you know, Dad," says Charlie with a smile.

"They taught me too," I say. "Didn't stop me getting confused."

I pull away from the school, and less than a minute later I'm turning down the drove towards my old house. From the outside it hasn't changed at all. The house had stood for a couple of hundred years without change, so why would my twenty-year absence make any difference.

As I pulled up around the back of the house and looked into the field, I saw that there had been one enormous change. Our fields were covered in solar panels.

The old witch had been right.

Friday 22nd June 1990

I opened the kitchen door and Mum and Dad stopped talking. It was becoming a bad habit.

"What's up?" I said, and they looked at each other.

"You want some breakfast? I can do you some bacon," Mum said.

"No thanks. I'll have some cereal."

"Your dog's missing," Dad said, and Mum stared at him.

"What do you mean?"

"I let him out for a pee last night, after we got home, but he didn't come back in."

"Where did he go?"

"How the fuck should I know?" He rose up out of his char.

"Did you look for him?"

"I gave him a shout this morning."

I grabbed my trainers from by the back door and sat at a chair at the kitchen table and pulled them on.

"We'll take a look for him later," Dad said as he sat down again.

Mum was cutting bread for the bacon sandwich she was making Dad. "You've got school. Have some breakfast now and look for him later."

"No," I said and left them at the dinner table. How could they be so calm? Didn't they care about anything?

Even though it was early it was already warm, but it wasn't just the warmth I felt right away, as soon as I was in the open, I could feel my eyes start to itch and the back of my throat felt scratchy. Even the inside of my ears needed a good itch. I tried to get the itchiness out of my head by thinking of the places Chappie would normally lead me to when I took him for a walk. We had a couple of usual routes, but it had been a couple of years since he'd bounded off looking for an adventure or going to sniff at a hole in the ground. I walked out towards Main

Street as the worst thing I thought might have happened was that he's been hit by a car. There was a little bit of traffic going through the village, but it wasn't too heavy. I looked down the road both ways but couldn't see any new roadkill. The fox that had been hit a few weeks back was practically flat now, but that was down by the end of the village after the last of the houses where people start to speed up again.

I crossed over the road and looked down into the ditch. I seemed to be spending a lot of my time staring into ditches recently, even though they all pretty much looked the same, filling up with nettles and no clear sight of the bottom. But if anything had fallen down there, I would have seen it. We never came down onto Main Street on our walks though, so I figured he probably hadn't come out this way. I walked back past the house just as Dad was coming out.

"Any sign?" he said.

I shook my head, "Not yet."

"I'll check the sheds, you take a walk around the back fields, and don't leave my line of sight."

And I thought, what if the tree got him? I looked across to it. The branches were shaking even though there was next to no wind. I looked away quickly, but knew I had to take another look at it. I stared at the ground for a bit, counted to ten then looked up. There was definitely something at the base of the tree. I hurried up the drove, but before I got to the entrance to the field, I realised there was someone standing nearby.

"Hey, young man."

It was Mrs Johnstone. She was in her dressing gown.

"Hello," I said, confused by her presence. "What are you doing here?"

"One day, you'll be farmers of the sun," she said.

I saw someone running down the drove towards us.

"Have you seen my dog?" I asked.

"You'll find him dead," she said.

"Mum!" came a shout from the drove. The man running towards us must have been her son.

"Won't be the only one to die!" she said, leaning close to me.

The man arrived. Out of breath, he grabbed his mum's hand. "Come on, Mum. You're not supposed to wander off alone."

He started to lead her off, then turned back to mouth 'thank you' to me.

I didn't have time to worry about whether Chappie was dead, as I heard a whimper. I listened. It seemed to be coming from the ditch on the left, it sounded like the noises Chappie made when he was asleep, and I always figured he was probably having a dream or something. I looked down and could see him curled up at the bottom of the ditch with flattened nettles all around him.

"Chappie!" I called, and he looked up. He tried to struggle onto his feet, and after a few seconds he managed to get into a more upright position. I slid down into the ditch beside him, flattening more nettles so they didn't sneak up my trouser legs and cover me in stings. He was breathing heavily but seemed to be comforted when I stroked the top of his head. He licked at my wrist, and when he seemed more comfortable, I put my arms underneath him and lifted him up. He felt so light and it was easy to plonk him down just out of the ditch. I didn't even notice that my hands had been in stinging nettles until I glanced down and saw how blotchy they were.

Chappie was okay walking back to the house, even though he was slower than usual.

"Found him then?" Dad said from the shed. He had his overalls on and already started work on one of the farm vehicles. So much for helping me look for Chappie. I didn't expect him to, but he followed us back to the house.

"There he is!" Mum said as we walked it, and it annoyed me, as she acted if he'd wandered back himself and she was the first to notice. He went straight to his bed and curled up into a ball.

"Is he all right?" I said, looking at Mum, then Dad, not knowing if either would give me an answer.

"He's getting old, that's all," Dad said.

"Let him have a rest and we'll see how he is later," Mum said. Then she must have caught sight of my hands, "Oh look at you! You must have got stung. Let me put some lotion on it."

She got this slightly purplish bottle of liquid out of the pantry and a bag of cotton wool balls and insisted in covering my hands in the goop.

"Oh dear," she said, "it must be a bad sting. The skin's peeling."

Dad had already gone back out again by this point, but I didn't feel like telling her that the only reason the skin on my hand was peeling was because Dad had burnt them the other day as I got the feeling that she'd tell me not to be daft even though she was right there and saw him do it.

When I arrived at school Liam was excitedly hopping from foot to foot.

"What's up with you?" I said.

"You know you said we should keep our ears open?"

"Yes."

"Guess what I heard Mr Inglehart talking about in his office."

"What were you doing in his office?"

"Nothing, I was crouched down outside the window. Guess what I heard him talking about?"

"Who was he talking to?"

"I don't know. Now guess what I heard them talking about!"

"Why were you crouched under his window?"

"Tom! Guess!"

"I don't know. A school trip?"

"No."

"I give up."

"No, guess."

"Mrs Palmer's stick insects."

"Now you're being silly. Guess properly."

"I don't know, Liam. Tell me."

Liam stopped hopping from side to side, leaned in close, and whispered, "Transition."

Will, who had been listening patiently so far, rolled his eyes and walked away, calling, "See you losers later."

"I'm not a loser. You're a loser!" cried Liam, triumphantly, and then turned his attention back to me. "So, what are we going to do about it?"

"What exactly did you hear?"

"Well I don't remember what they said exactly."

"What did they say, roughly?"

"Something about having to move on with the next stage of transition before it was too late, and how they couldn't let the current situation stop them from moving forward with year six."

"Will's in year six."

"We've got to warn him."

"Why didn't you say something before he left?"

"He called me a loser! I got confused!"

"Come on; let's go."

Mr Inglehart appeared at the door and started calling pupils in for the start of the school day.

"What are we gonna do now?" asked Liam.

"If we run to his classroom, we might be able to get to him in time."

Liam sped off first, and I followed behind. Mr Inglehart was talking to a couple of girls in our class, so he didn't seem bothered by us going in in such a hurry. We were in the corridor and heading for Will's classroom when the door to the caretaker's cupboard swung open. Liam had to swerve out of the way, and his legs collided with mine. We both fell in a heap.

"That's why we tell you not to run in the corridors. We say it again, and again, but nobody listens until someone gets hurt."

I looked up to see Mr Jenkins standing over us, holding his mop as a Neanderthal might have held a spear. His eyebrows now seemed to meet in the middle, and his beard was thicker and more menacing.

I untangled my limbs from Liam's and scooted away from Mr Jenkins on my bottom.

"Go on," said Mr Jenkins. "Get up. Don't tell me you've broken something. That's the last thing we want to be dealing with right now."

Liam and I awkwardly stood and started to move away.

"Hold on just a minute. Someone needs to give you two a serious talking to. What if one of the infants had been in the corridor? You could have knocked them down, and they might have cracked their skull. We can't be having that, can we?"

"No, Mr Jenkins," Liam and I said in unison, and started to walk away.

Again, Mr Jenkins stopped us, lifting the mop slightly as a barrier. "What else?"

"Sorry, Mr Jenkins."

"That's better. Now off you go." He still held up the mop as a barrier. "And remember, your classroom's that way." He nodded with his head, pointing towards the corridor which led to Mrs Palmer's classroom.

We had no choice but to take that path.

Mrs Palmer urged us in from the doorway to her classroom and gave us a bit of a telling off for running late. She told us to sit down, and then she did the register, and told us to get our P.E. kits on.

"What are we gonna do?" asked Liam in one of his noisy whispers.

"Right," said Mrs Palmer. "Tom, you change in that corner." She pointed to the area by the sink, near to where the stick insects were kept. "And Liam, you go to that corner." She was pointing at the book corner where the comfy beanbags were.

The class changed in silent, and soon were we out on the field laying out cones to make lanes for a relay race. I had managed to sneak back over to Liam, and we were dropping cones out together when I looked up and saw Will, and the rest of his class, heading across the playground and towards the school gates.

"Look," I said to Liam, and nodded towards them, with one eye on Mrs Palmer.

Liam was less discreet. "Will!" he shouted.

"I've had enough of you two already today," cried Mrs Palmer. A vein was bulging in her neck. She never got angry. "You're going to sit out this activity, and you'll be spending break-time with me too." She split us again quickly, pointing to spots on either side of the field where we were to sit in silence, facing away from each other.

As I sat alone, looking at the horses in the neighbouring field I wondered why Mrs Palmer was so edgy today. Maybe she was nervous about whatever plan the school had for the year six class and Will. I tried not to think about what might be happening to them. Were they being beamed onto the spaceship, one at a time, ready to be strapped into the alien machines to have their brains wiped? Maybe Will would be too smart for them and would have fled before they were able to start the transition process. And if Will had escaped, maybe he would be able to sneak aboard the alien ship, and free the rest of the class. He could come face to face with the alien master and use his strength and wits to defeat him and save the entire planet. He had, after all, been sneaking his penknife to school since John went missing. I kept looking to the sky, waiting for the inevitable explosion, but perhaps defeating the aliens was taking rather a long time, as Mrs Palmer called us back in before there was any activity.

Until break time Mrs Palmer had us working on maths problems using long division. She had brought both Liam and me to the front, but on opposite ends of the row, so we couldn't talk to each other. While we were working silently, she kept looking at different documents on her desk, and she was scratching a spot over her right ear frequently.

Eventually break-time came, and Mrs Palmer released the rest of the class. Once their noise had disappeared from the corridor, she looked at each of us, and then sighed. "What has gotten into you boys today?"

Liam looked nervous. He was tugging at a bit of loose skin by one of his fingers. I could tell that he was desperate to put it into his mouth and tear it free.

"I'm sorry, Mrs Palmer," I said, looking down at the desk.

"Sorry only works if you mean it. You can't start chatting again mid-lesson just because it takes your fancy."

"We were worried about Will, Miss," Liam said.

I didn't want to have this conversation. I didn't want Liam to expose what we already knew, which would put ourselves at risk.

"Tom's brother?"

"Yes, Mrs Palmer," I said.

"What do you have to be worried about? Is he not well?"

I looked up. "We saw his class go off somewhere, that's all." I looked over at Liam, but he wasn't looking at me. He was staring intently at Mrs Palmer.

"Where are you taking them?" he said in a voice which I think was supposed to be menacing, but it made him sound dumb.

"They're at Methwold High School for an induction day. Didn't your brother tell you, Tom?"

"He must have forgot," I said.

"In a month's time he'll be finished here, and then in September he'll be at Methwold High School, and you two will be year sixes, where we don't expect any chatter whatsoever."

I had one more question to ask. If she was ever going to tear off her human flesh disguise and devour us both, this was the question that was going to prompt it. "What's transition?" I said and shuddered.

"Transition? As in transition from primary school to secondary? It's days like today when Will gets to have a look around the secondary school he's going to."

I nodded. I looked over at Liam whose face was screwed up and reddening.

"I'm not going to have you two sitting around when you're on detention," said Mrs Palmer as she stood up. "Go sharpen all of my pencils."

"How do we know she's telling the truth?" Liam said at lunch time while shoving the remainder of his sandwich into his mouth.

We were sitting under the shade of one of the trees on the edge of the field updating Andy on what had happened that morning. He'd been particularly worried because he hadn't seen us at break and thought we may have been eaten by a teacher. He even went as far as peering into the window of our classroom, risking a telling off from Mr Inglehart and being dubbed a 'Nosey-Parker', to find out where we were.

"I used my Turtle Power to stay hidden though," Andy said, with a smug grin. "So, do you think Mrs Palmer was telling the truth?"

"We'll know when Will comes back."

"If he comes back."

"Don't say that, Liam; he's coming back."

"What makes you so sure?" Liam stood up. "We've been talking about what happened to John, and before you all agreed that aliens might have taken them away, and we found all that proof of it, so why do you believe Mrs Palmer and not me?"

Andy stood up too and whispered in Liam's ear. He then broke down into a fit of giggles.

"Well they were holding hands," Liam said, laughing with Andy. "That's why you believe her, and not me. Just you wait till I'm right. When none of them year sixes come back maybe then you'll believe me."

Don't say that," I said. I could feel myself getting hot and angry. I tried to get up, but while I was pushing myself up from the ground Liam pushed me back down and walked away with Andy without looking back.

At least I wasn't going to get into trouble for talking to Liam after lunch, as I had no intention of talking to him whatsoever. For a second, I thought I might have to, as Mrs Palmer had us working in pairs on a junk-modelling project. Even worse, we were asked to make rocket-ships. Normally I'd work with Liam on those kind of things (our potato-printing artwork was awesome), but I couldn't think of anything worse than having to stare at his ugly, podgy face. Plus, with us working on rocket-ships he'd probably think they were for the alien fleet to attack with, or something stupid like that.

"Liam, Tom," said Mrs Palmer, and I feared that she'd throw us together, but maybe she saw the way my face screwed up and took pity on me as she said, "I'm keeping you apart after this morning's performance. Liam, you work with Brian, Tom, work with Daniel."

I'd barely spoken to anyone else since John went missing, so in some ways it was nice to talk to Daniel Richardson. We kept on the subject of our junk model pretty well, suggesting ideas to each other. It was nice to work on something together properly, as Liam would normally go blundering ahead. I looked round and laughed to myself when I saw that he'd managed to stick two of his fingers together with the glue.

Daniel had been casting glances at Mrs Palmer for a while, and when she was talking to some of the girls (yuck) at the other side of the room he said, "So have you heard anything about John?"

I shook my head.

"I heard someone say he might have been abducted."

Not aliens again. Liam was spreading rumours all around the school, it seemed, when it was supposed to be our own private investigation. "Did Liam tell you about his alien idea?" I asked.

"Aliens? No! Who made that up!" Daniel could barely stop himself from laughing, and his raised voice made Mrs Palmer look over, so we hurriedly started holding pieces of junk next to each other to make the main body of our rocket.

"So, you've not heard anything?" asked Daniel again.

I shrugged and tilted a fizzy pop bottle at an angle to see if we could use it in our model.

When we were let out for class at the end of the day Will was already waiting with Aunt Anne on the playground.

"See!" I said smugly to Liam.

"Don't be such a bighead. You think you're so cool, but do you know what? You're not." And with that, he swung his elbow down and caught me in the gut, knocking the wind out of me. He looked round and gave me a 'don't tell' look.

I couldn't if I'd have wanted to and took the lift home with Aunt Anne in silence.

"How come you never told me you were going up to big school today?" I said to Will as we walked in through the front door.

"Big school? Only babies call it that," laughed Will. "You're on drinks duty." He ran upstairs and left me to get us some squash. First of all, though, I went to see if Chappie was okay. He was asleep. His drink bowl was empty, so I tipped a glass full of water into it to top it up, then I made drinks for Will and me.

Carefully carrying the drinks upstairs, I thought about how angry Liam had been. Had I been unfair on him? I couldn't see how I had. His idea had been wrong, that's all. As I got into the bedroom, I saw that Will had already put the N.E.S. on to play Punch Out.

I glanced out of the window, feeling bad for hurting Liam's feeling, even though he'd been the one who elbowed me in the stomach. Maybe he felt as bad as I did. I looked all around outside until my eyes fell on the tree. I'd forgotten about it until I saw the oak tree's branches swaying, but there had definitely been something under the tree earlier, and if it wasn't Chappie, which I had originally thought, then what was it?

"Hey Will," I said.

He stared at the screen and dodged to the left as he pressed the buttons on the joypad.

"Will," I said.

"I'm busy."

"Come check something out with me."

"No." He leaned to the left then ducked, but his character, Little Mac, was getting a bit of a pounding on screen.

"Please," I said.

"Later," he said, and tapped furiously at the buttons as Little Mac got to his feet. I stood by the door and watched him win the fight, but then he started the next one without even turning to look at me, so I figured I was on my own.

"Where are you off to?" asked Mum as I was putting my shoes back on again.

"I left something outside when I found Chappie this morning." I lied.

"What did you leave out there?"

"My goalkeeper gloves." I have no idea why I said that, it was the first thing that came into my head. Maybe it was because the football was sitting by the doormat, so I was thinking of football, but couldn't say football, because it was right there, and, well, she could see it.

"If you had your gloves out there why ever did you take them off and get your hands all stung, you daft little monkey?"

"Um... Chappie doesn't like me stroking him with gloves on." This was true.

"Okay, well go fetch them and come straight back where I can keep an eye on you, and for Christ's sake don't go falling into the nettles. You're stung up badly enough already. I should probably put more lotion on your hands."

"Can it wait until I come back?" I asked.

Mum nodded, and I sprinted out of the house.

It was probably going to be a load of rubbish anyway, that's what I told myself as I entered the field. Maybe something the people working on the road had thrown over the dyke and it had come to a rest by the tree. Maybe a polythene bag had blown from the yard across the field and got stuck at the base of the tree, and it just looked bigger because it had all torn open. But the closer I got the more I started to dismiss all of the boring possibilities. There was definitely something that looked red, the same colour red as our school jumper.

It was torn in loads of places and there were patches of a much deeper red all over it, and mud smeared haphazardly on the front. I picked it up without ever thinking that I should leave it as some sort of evidence. I had to know if it was his. I looked into the neck as the label inside, and sure enough, sewn on with red cotton was a name tag that read 'John Glover'.

I looked down at the ground by the tree. There were footprints. I bent down to look closer, but only got a waft of that maggoty smell that always permeated from the ground around the tree. The footprints pointed towards the tractor. I followed them. The corrugated iron I'd lifted the other day had a footprint on it too, and beside it a large red circular stain, with a smaller partner beside it. John had been here, and he was hurt. I looked around the tractor, but there was no further sign of him, so I kept walking in a straight line from the tree. I tried to imagine where he'd come from, but I couldn't make any sense of any of my thoughts, but surely there was only one place he was heading: to the farmhouse. He'd escaped from whatever beast had held him, fled across the field, and was on the way to our house to call for help; that was the only possible answer.

But he'd not made it there.

Had the beast given chase and reclaimed him?

I followed the quickest path out of the field onto the track that led to the farmhouse. Surely that was where John would have gone.

Then I saw it. The gap in the tall nettles beside the ditch on the other side. He'd run, and he'd fallen in, and now he needed my help.

I dashed over as quickly as I could, his jumper still in my arms, and looked down.

It was him. John. Lying there, on his side his feet lost beneath a blanket of nettles. His face was down, but I knew that haircut. Mum wouldn't let me have mine shaved at the back like that.

"John," I said, in a whisper, like I was scared of waking him up. I got in closer and bent down and said "John," again but he still didn't react. It was too quiet. I couldn't hear any breathing. I couldn't hear the wind rushing through the grass anymore either. Everything was completely still. I swear I could hear my blood flowing into my heart, and it being pumped around my whole body. I edged into the ditch, closer to John, and put a hand on his shoulder.

"John," I said. He was cold. I shook him a little, in the same way I do Will when I'm sent to wake him, but there was no stirring. I pulled on his shoulder and his body fell onto its back. His mouth fell open and his skin was white apart from around the neck where it was all purple and blotchy, and there was a large wound on his forehead.

"John," I said. I tried again, only louder this time, and I kept saying it until I was almost shouting it, but he couldn't hear me, and he would never hear me no matter how loud I shouted it.

I don't know at what point I clambered out of the ditch and ran, but that's what I did, all the way home, still shouting out John's name, and then Dad was shaking me and all I managed to do was point to where I'd run from.

Later there were police but by then I was inside again, and Mum had put a blanket around me even though it was hot and I was drinking tea that I don't really like and it had about five sugars in it but I drank it anyway and then I wanted more and I wanted to go back outside to see what was going on but I couldn't even move or tell Will what happened when he came down; even though he was asking me questions, I didn't know how to work my mouth properly to answer any of them.

PART TWO

NOW

Charlie's used to death. He overcame the death of his mother with maturity. After the accident, when she was lying in the hospital bed, unresponsive, I never told him that everything would be all right.

I remember the horrified look of the nurse as I explained to Charlie, who was seven at the time, that his mum's brain was dead. That meant that she wouldn't be waking up again. We were going to turn off the machine, and he'd have to deal with that.

Together, we cried, but I never told him that it was all going to be okay. I was never going to give him false hope. Hope is a castle on the sand, and it's only a matter of time until the tide turns.

Ridiculously, I did hold out hope for a miracle. I clasped my hands together when they switched off the life support. So, when the heartrate monitor flatlined, when the castle collapsed, I broke all over again. That's what being brought up with lies will do to you.

And don't think I gave him any of that crap about going to a better place either. The only place other than here is worse, much, much worse.

Friday 22nd June 1990

don't know how I got into bed, but I knew it was much later because there was football on the telly. Will was sitting on the bed and as soon as he saw that I'd opened my eyes he shouted, "Mum," and she must have floated upstairs because I didn't hear her feet on the steps at all and there are three that are creaky.

She sat on the side of my bed and started stroking my hair. My forehead felt clammy and my hair felt all yucky with sweat, probably because I'd been under the duvet in the middle of a hot June day.

"Are you okay, Thomas?" she said, and I didn't know what to say.

"Do you want something to eat?"

I shook my head.

"You really should have something. How about a nice ham sandwich?"

I shook my head again.

"What about a big bowl of chicken soup?" And that sounded like the best idea in the whole world.

While I was sitting at the kitchen table, (and getting to the kitchen had felt like an incredible effort) slurping some soup from the spoon, Dad came in, and P.C. Wade was with him.

Dad put his hand on my shoulder, and I jumped a little. "P.C. Wade would like to ask you a few questions."

I nodded and pushed the soup bowl away from me. I'd eaten about three quarters of it without really tasting it.

"So, Thomas, you know me from school," said P.C. Wade.

I nodded again.

"I need to ask you a few questions about... what you saw this morning."

I said, "Yes," and he held his notepad and pen out ready, but he didn't write down anything after that question.

He asked me when I first saw the body and I told him about going out to look for Chappie, and then I suddenly remembered how poorly Chappie had been in the morning, so I got up and checked on him. He was drinking water from his bowl and he seemed to be alright, so I sat down again. P.C. Wade wanted to know if I'd moved the body at all, and I said that I had, because I thought I could wake him up and he shook his head and started to write.

"When you came in, your parents say that you were holding a jumper. Where did you find that?"

"It was by the tree."

"Did you know it was John's?"

"I looked at the label."

"How did you know where to look for the body?"

"I saw blood nearby, and I followed it in a straight line."

"Did you disturb anything else?"

I couldn't think. I wanted to retrace my steps. I was struggling to believe that any of this was real. "Can I go out and see him again?" I said.

"We've removed the body," said P.C. Wade.

"Oh," I said, and I got down from the chair again because I figured that there wouldn't be any more questions. P.C. Wade left a few minutes later after having one of those whispered conversations with Mum and Dad outside the front door.

"Whatever did you want to see the body again for?" Mum said when she came back in.

"Because I ran away and left him before," I said. "It felt wrong."

Upstairs, Will was sitting on his bed cheating at *Battleblade Warrior*.

"Good book?" I said.

"Not bad," he said and put it down.

"So, what happened today?" I said.

"I don't know. They told me to stay out of the way."

"Didn't you see anything?"

"I was watching out of the window, but I couldn't see anything."

"Did you see them take the body away?"

"No. Mum kept giving me jobs to distract me. There were loads of police down there. They had cars on the bypass and police Land Rovers on the drove and on the field."

"Did they say what happened?"

"No. He's dead, that's all I know."

"I never thought that would be it."

"Be what?"

"That he'd be dead. I always thought we'd find him, or he'd come home."

"Me too."

"Thomas," called Mum from downstairs.

I opened the door and called back.

"Your uncle Rodney's here. He wants to see that you're okay."

"Tell him I'm fine," I shouted back.

He came creeping up the stairs a second later. For a tall man he was incredibly light on his feet. It must have been all of the acting. "My dear boy," he said as he saw me. He kept moving closer, until he was looming over me. He bent down and wrapped his arms around me in an awkward hug. "What a terrible, terrible thing for one so delicate as you to experience." He let me go, and I edged back into the bedroom, where Will was looking up at us secretly over the top of his book.

"And the poor boy was dead when you found him?" asked Uncle Rodney.

I didn't want to talk to him about it. He didn't even know John. I nodded but said nothing.

"Such a tragedy. Life is a precious thing, and a young life all the more precious." He came forward to hug me again, and he held me for about half a minute without either of us saying a thing. When he let go, somehow, he had a chocolate bar in a blue wrapper in his hand. "For you," he said, and handed it to me. It was a 'Stratos' bar, and with that he went back downstairs.

"Do you want it?" I said to Will, who was still peering over the top of his book.

"You don't?" asked Will

I shook my head and held it out to him.

Will took the chocolate bar and tore the end of the wrapper off. He took a bit, and before he finished swallowing his mouthful he said, "What did he look like?"

I couldn't answer right away, and it wasn't until after he'd taken another mouthful and then gulped it down noisily that I answered, "Like John... only... different."

"Different how?" His voice sounded like his mouth was gloopy with chocolate.

"You know, like the wax works in Great Yarmouth, how they look like real people, but they're not?" We been on holiday there the previous summer. The beach was nice, and there were some good rides in Joyland, but the waxworks were creepy, and half of them were of people I'd never even heard of.

"Yeah."

"It was like that, only not. He looked a bit like a wax work, only he wasn't, he was real. It was like he wasn't actually there."

"I've never seen a dead body before," Will said.

He was the lucky one, I thought.

Saturday 23ʳᵈ June 1990

I was woken by the sound of someone shouting my name. I didn't recognise the voice. It wasn't Dad, or I would have been up straight away. It wasn't Mum's soft shout either. It was a sad, desperate shout, and it lured me out of my bed.

When I was on the stairs, I heard another shout, but this was definitely Mum's voice, "You stay up there, Tom."

As I stopped, not knowing what to do, I heard it again, "Tom".

I had to go see. I came to the kitchen door and went to push it, but someone was leaning up against the other side.

"I'm sorry for what happened," I heard Mum say, and her voice sounded close, the other side of the door, so I assumed it was her leaning against it, "But you have to go, now."

"Tom," said the voice again. It was a woman's voice, that's all I knew.

"Hello?" I said.

"Tom, it's me," said the voice. It didn't help.

"Mum, let me in," I said. "Who is it?"

"It's Barbara. Mrs Glover... John's mum."

I felt Mum's weight shift away from the door, so I opened it and went into the kitchen.

"I'm sorry," she said, looking at Mum then at me, "but I had to come."

She looked so different. She wasn't wearing any make-up and her hair was scruffy and limp. She was wearing an old t-shirt which was so long it almost came down to her knees and there were a few stains on it, like she'd spilt something and mopped most of it off.

"Can you show me where you found him?" she said.

Mum came between us. "You don't have to if you don't want to."

"It's okay," I said. I understood why John's mum would want to see where he was, and it felt right to take her back there.

"I didn't get to see him until he was at the mortuary. We had to identify the body, even though we all knew it would be him," said John's mum as we walked across the yard and up onto the drove.

Dad glared at us from the yard. I watched him march inside as we followed the track along the drove to the point in the ditch where I'd found John.

Mrs Glover had heels on, and she put her hand out for support as she struggled across the mud, so I helped guide her between the rows of potato plants.

As we got a close a gust of wind came from nowhere, and John's mum gasped.

I turned to face the wind and found myself glaring at the tree. I swear the shape of its mouth, the big scorch mark on it that looked like a mouth, had changed, like it had turned up at the corners into a laugh.

We couldn't get close, as the police had put tape all around the area, but we moved to the edge of it. "He was there," I said, and pointed into the ditch.

John's mum put a hand over her mouth. I tried not to look at her as she did that silent crying thing where the shoulders bob up and down. I didn't know what to say.

"Did he look... peaceful?" she said.

"He did," I said, and it was true. Yes, he looked as though something terrible had happened to him, but there was no terror on his face, the only thing that was remarkable about it was the lack of emotion, and I guess that's what peace is all about.

"Why?" she said and buried her face in her hands. "What kind of monster could have done that?"

I hadn't heard him approach, but then Dad was there. He put a hand on my shoulder, and then nodded towards the house, so I slowly walked away. I turned back and Dad was hugging John's mum. I hurried back to the house.

I had an urgent need to beat Super Mario Bros. Luckily Will wasn't already playing. He was sitting on his bed cheating at his Fighting Fantasy book again. So as the Nintendo Entertainment System was free, I could play it all I liked. Will didn't even look up as I ejected Punch Out and put in Mario. He didn't notice me speed through the first few worlds or using the shortcut. He knew all about the first one, where you could skip all of the way from world 1-2 to world 4-1 by running all of the way across the top of the screen to get to the Warp Zone, but he didn't know about skipping from World 4-2 all the way to 8-1. John had showed me this when he came over to play one day when Will was late back because he had a school trip with his class to a museum in Cambridge. To skip from 4-2 to 8-1 you had to find a hidden beanstalk which carried you back up to the top of the screen where you can run to another Warp Zone. World 8-1 is tough because there are so many bad guys and really tough jumps. For the first time ever, I did it without losing a life. I lost a life on world 8-2, due to that stupid cloud that throws out the red spiky things. I hate them! I'm sure I heard Will snort when he heard Mario's death tune, but when I looked round his nose was still buried in the book, with his fingers saving at least two other pages. Even though one of the red things got me I was lucky not to get taken out by the big bullets that get fired across the screen. They normally had me beat and I'd only ever finished the level once before.

When I did get to world 8-3 before it was the Hammer Bros that got me, but this time I ran right under them. That was one of John's tips, telling me that I didn't have to beat every bad guy, just get to the end of each level. There were loads of hammer guys on the level though, some you couldn't run under unless you timed the jumps right, but I did that and was soon through them and onto the last level. Right from the start I mis-pressed the D-pad and fell in the first pool of lava. I was down to my last life and never thought I'd do it. Somehow the flying fish kept launching directly underneath me and dying as they hit my feet, when normally they'd fly at my head and kill me. Even the jellyfish seemed to be swimming away from me instead of towards me.

Then there was Bowser. He was throwing out so many hammers I didn't think it was possible. And when he jumped in the air, there surely wasn't time to run underneath him. The music changed, warning me I was running out of time, so I went for it. As he came forward there was a gap in the hammer stream and I closed my eyes, pushed forward and jumped. I don't know how he missed me. I was expecting to hear the death noise, but instead it was the sound of the bridge falling away. Even as Mario went into the next room, I kept expecting a little mushroom guy to tell me that my princess was in another castle, but she wasn't, she was right there in front of me. THANK YOU, MARIO! YOUR QUEST IS OVER. It said. I'd done it. I turned to get Will's attention, but he was watching anyway.

"Well done, bro," he said.

Will put the football on a little later, but neither of us were watching. It was Cameroon versus Colombia. When the score flashed on the screen at the thirty-minute mark I realised I'd not taken a single bit of it in.

"Remember when John got us all to play as Cameroon?" Will said.

I did. It was on the first Monday we were at school after the World Cup started, the day before he went missing. It was the last normal day we'd had. "He'd be cheering on Cameroon now, wouldn't he?"

We started cheering on Cameroon. A goal soon came in extra time. Me and Will high-fived when Roger Milla put Cameroon in front. Then the funniest thing happened. The Colombian goalkeeper made a massive mistake. He was playing the sweeper-keeper and hanging around half-way between the goal and the halfway line. When a player passed it back to him, he mis-controlled it and Roger Milla took the ball off him. As he was all the way out of goal Milla could just dribble up to the

18-yard line then score from there with no one in the way to stop him.

John would have loved that. A tear trickled down my cheek as they showed another replay.

Even though Colombia scored a goal to make it 2-1, Cameroon held on till the end to make it through to the quarterfinals. Will got up and put their name on his wall chart.

"If England beat Belgium on Tuesday," Will said, "they'll have to play Cameroon."

NOW

"Hullo!" comes a shout from the shed as Charlie and I walk towards the back door of my old house. I turned to see a portly man dressed in the kind of clothes that my dad used to wear, the kind of clothes that you seemingly don't see outside of Fenland farms or Sunday evening dramas on ITV. A checked shirt is tucked into shapeless beige trousers that are held up with suspenders. As he approaches, he rubs his hands on his thighs, adding another layer of grime to them. A grin spreads across his familiar face, and his cheeks begin to redden. Following behind him is a young boy, dressed in near-identical clothes.

"Liam!" I shout, "where's Dad?"

"Where he's been the last month. In bed."

"Are you sure?"

"Of course, Tom."

"Have the police been here?"

"No. You're here now. You can relax. What's got you so wound up?"

I tell him about the police car and the missing girl, and the boy beside him looks up at us.

"That's Jessica Matthews," says the boy.

"Who's this?" I say, smiling at the child.

"This is my boy, Billy," says Liam. He ruffles Billy's hair.

"I didn't know you had a son."

"Yeah, was married for a bit, but that didn't work out. Now Billy comes to stay with me every other weekend, ain't that right, boy?" he strokes Billy's hair.

"What were you saying about the girl, Billy?" I ask.

Billy pulls a phone out of his pocket. It's significantly newer and more expensive than mine. "Saw something on Facebook. Her mum was asking if anyone had seen her."

"No need to worry yourself about that son," says Liam.

"That's the kind of thing they said to us, remember?"

Liam looks at me, puzzled.

"When John was missing, that's what our parents said, 'there's nothing to worry about', only there was, wasn't there?"

Liam pulled Billy close to him. "You'll scare him," he says.

"Maybe he should be scared."

"Billy," says Liam, bending down to talk to the boy, "why don't you take..." he turns to look at my son, "Charlie, isn't it?" Charlie nods and Liam continues, "Why don't you talk Charlie to see the tractor we've been working on?"

Billy practically jumps with excitement and grabs a less-enthusiastic Charlie by the hand. "If our Dads are cousins," says Billy, "does that make us cousins too?"

Once they're out of earshot I lean in close to Liam. "Can't you see? It's happening again, and we're making the same mistakes that they did!"

Liam shakes his head. He takes a handkerchief from his pocket and mops some of the sweat from his brow.

"What are you talking about?"

"Our parents used to send us away when they wanted to talk. Don't you remember all of the whispering? Drove us near crazy?"

"We got caught up in the excitement of it all, that's all. That's what kids are supposed to do."

"You can't keep lying to them."

"What would you do then, Tom, warn them of every possible danger out there, have them worried stiff all the bloody time?"

"Yes. It's what I do. Charlie knows the risks, and he knows the probabilities of them happening too."

"Some childhood that is."

"At least he'll have one," I say.

Liam shakes his head. "How come you never took any of my calls?" he asks.

"I'm sorry," I say. "I couldn't deal with anything that was going on here."

"We could have got your Dad's conviction squashed if you'd have come forward."

Somehow, I resist the urge to correct him. Nothing I could have said would have made my Dad look better, not after what I saw.

Sunday 24ᵗʰ June 1990

After breakfast, Will was dragged out with dad to help stacking the hay bales. While I was relieved that I'd gotten out of it, I also had this horrible feeling because I'd not been asked to help, and it was like I was not good enough.

"Your dad and me think it'll be best if you rest today, and get ready to go back to school tomorrow," Mum had said, and she'd then urged me to go back to my room.

I took advantage of the time and picked up *The Secret of the Scythe* for another play through. With reasonable dice rolls I felt confident that I'd be able to make my way through the game a little better than before. I avoided the witches house, tackled all of the monsters on the way to the Underworld, and then found myself in front of a grotesque living tree. I had to roll a die to test my luck, and unfortunately, I was not lucky, which meant that the tree had tied my legs together with its roots. This meant that I was taking double damage every time it attacked me. I was strong enough to get through it though. I rolled the dice for a strong attack, but one of them hit the corner of the book and bounced off awkwardly under the end of the bed.

As I was crouching down to recover it there was a knock on the door. I thought Mum was in the utility room, because she'd had a basket full of washing with her earlier, but I couldn't hear her go to answer the door, so after a second impatient knock on the door, I went downstairs.

On the stairs, I could hear the washing machine rumbling, and Mum whistling happily to herself. She was deaf to all else outside of that room when the washing machine was clanking away.

I started to think about who could be at the door, and I hoped it was Granddad, but when I opened it, I was disappointed to find this really cheesy looking man standing there with his hair all swooshed over to one side. He had a camera in his hands, and he was holding a little tape recorded.

"Are you Thomas Tilbrook?" he said.

"Who are you?"

"I'm looking for Thomas Tilbrook. It really is rather important that I talk to him."

"What about?"

"Are you Thomas Tilbrook?"

"Might be." There was something about the way he asked questions that made me not want to answer him.

"Listen, if you are Thomas Tilbrook, would you mind answering some questions for me?"

"Who are you?"

"My name is Joseph Price."

"And what do you want?"

"I need to speak to Thomas Tilbrook, who I'm assuming is you. Am I right?"

"What do you want?"

"I'm a journalist. I work for the Daily Report. Have you heard of us?"

I'd seen the paper in the post office but had never read it. Most of the headlines on the front page were stupid, and they normally had a woman in a bra and knickers on the front too. Liam liked to point and laugh at it when we went in for penny sweets. "Yeah."

"Can I come in?"

"No."

"Will you answer a few questions for me about John Glover?"

"No."

"I can pay you."

"No."

"Surely a young man like yourself could think of something to do with one-hundred pounds."

I was tempted, I'd be able to buy enough stickers to complete the World Cup album and a new game too. Maybe enough left over for the next Fighting Fantasy book, but I didn't want to talk about it.

"Go away," I said and tried to push the door closed, but he'd put his foot in the way.

"Mum," I called out, but I could hear the washing machine clunking away, and thought she hadn't heard me.

"Who's this?" I looked up and Dad was standing behind the reporter.

"He won't go away," I said.

"We'll see about that." Dad put his hand around the back of his neck. Dad had huge hands. I could see his sausage fingers clearly on either side of Joseph's neck.

"I wanted to speak to your son about what happened here, Mr Tilbrook."

Dad spun him around with his hand then let him go, only to grab him again by the neck from the front.

"There could be a significant sum of money in it for you, Sir."

"If I ever see you around here again, I will throttle you, understand?" Dad lifted him off the ground and threw him back.

He landed on his bum. He sat up and blew some dust off of his camera. "I could sue you for that," he said in a croaky voice. He brought his hand up to his neck and gave it a rub.

"You better get off my land quick sharp or you'll have a bloody lot more to sue me for."

Joseph was slow getting to his feet until Dad jerked his body towards him then he scrambled up and set off into a run.

"What did you let him in for?" Dad said.

"I didn't. He came to the door. I didn't know who he was."

"Where's your mum?"

She must have heard the commotion because, all of a sudden, she was there with an empty wash basket by her side.

"Where were you?" Dad said.

"What's the matter?"

"This daft boy of ours was about to go tell all of our bloody secrets to some soppy reporter. Bloody ghoul."

"No, I wasn't," I said. What did he mean by ghoul? I wanted to ask, but with him it was impossible.

"I saw you standing in the door talking to him."

"I was trying to close the door. He had his foot in it."

"You shouldn't have opened it to him in the first place."

There was no way to win an argument with him. I turned away and headed upstairs.

"Go on, then, run off," I could hear him say, "Go and cry up in your room." And as soon as he said that I couldn't help but do anything else.

Looking out of the window, I saw Dad go trundling off in the tractor, with Will sat beside him. I watched them go along the drove until they were out of site behind the elderberry bushes. As I was about to move away from the window, I spotted something else. Walking along the drove that ran closest to the house, near to the place where I'd found John there was a man. I leaned in closer to the window. It was Shaky Jake, and he seemed to be peering into the ditches, looking for something right next to the police tape.

I ran downstairs and grabbed Chappie's lead. Reluctantly the dog clambered out of his basket. "I'm taking Chappie for a walk," I yelled, but I don't know if Mum was close enough to hear us.

I moved as quickly as Chappie would allow. We followed the path from the farm onto the drove – the same way that Dad had just taken the tractor, but when we hit the drove, we went the other way, towards the spot where I'd found John.

Shaky Jake was still there. He was wearing some horrible faded green trousers, and he kept rubbing his hands on the side of them, as if they were covered in some disgusting sticky substance that he couldn't get off. Even though it was hot he had a blue jumper on. When he turned to look at me, I realised that he was wearing nothing under the jumper, as a load of curly black hairs sprouted out of the gap in the v-shaped neck.

"'ello," he said, wiping his hands again on his trouser leg.

"What are you doing here?" I asked.

He shrugged his shoulders. "I'm just going for a walk. I like going for walks around here."

"What are you looking for?" I said. I let a little of Chappie's lead out, intending for the dog to take a step closer to Shaky Jake to scare him, but Chappie remained still.

"I heard about that poor boy," said Jake. His head kept bobbing forward as he said it. It was like he was trying to swallow a boiled sweet hole.

I shook Chappie's lead, trying to urge some action from him. He rolled onto his side and exhaled loudly.

"I wis jus' lookin' for clues," said Shaky. "I wanted to help out."

"Do it somewhere else," I said. "Before people start thinking you had something to do with it."

He shook his head wildly, and then almost jumped up and formed a new pose. His feet shoulder-width apart, his body leant forward and crouched down. One hand moved towards his face and the forefinger straightened, vertical, in front of his perfectly circular lips. "Shush," he said in an overly dramatic manner before putting his hands on his hips. "There ain't be no need to go tellin' tales," he said, and then thrust a hand into his pocket with such force I thought his hand was going to burst through it.

From the pocket he pulled a small white packet. "Wanna sweet?" he asked.

Fisherman's Friend. No way. "Get out of here," I said – with Chappie offering none of the required aggression whatsoever.

First, he took a step towards me, and then turned back the other way. He turned again as if he was going to walk past me before finally deciding to stride off in the other direction.

I watched him all of the way to the end of the drove, where it met the bypass, and watched him ponder over which way to go before he finally decided to clamber up the bank and walk along the new bypass.

He was definitely going to need to be watched more closely.

In the evening there was finally a welcome visitor. Granddad looked much older when he came to the door, and actually seemed to need his stick when he walked, rather than carrying it around as a prop.

Mum made everyone a cup of tea, even though it was boiling hot and no one could possibly have wanted a hot drink, but they all sat round the table drinking it anyway.

"It were awful sad to hear that you found your friend," Granddad said, putting his hand on top of mine as I reached for my squash (there was no way I was drinking tea).

All I could do was nod.

"I thought he'd be okay," he said, and took a gulp of his drink.

I looked Granddad in the eye and could tell he felt bad about it.

"Don't get the boy all worked up," Dad said. "He'll be crying his eyes out again if you keep that up."

Crap. I was going to cry.

"Well maybe he should cry. He found the body of his best friend a few minutes from his house. If that ain't worth crying over I don't know what is." Granddad pulled me to him, burying my face into his shoulder.

I cried, but he was hiding it for me. There was no way Dad was going to see this.

"Well, I'm gonna goo check on them chickens and shut 'em up for the night," Dad said, and when he was gone, Granddad let me go and urged me to sit next to him.

"It's alright to be upset," he said.

By then I'd stopped sobbing, though I could still feel some silent tears creeping slowly down my face. "It's not fair," I said.

"What is?" asked Granddad. "There ain't no such thing as fair; we jus' have to deal with whatever hand it is we've been dealt and hope we come out of it better."

"Dad makes me feel worse though."

"Don't you worry about him. Tell him if he upsets you, he's not too big to have his ears boxed."

I smiled. I could never imagine saying that to Dad, but the thought of Granddad telling him off and clipping his ear amused me. It felt like the right time to dob him in. "Earlier a man from the newspaper came to the door," I said, "and Dad told me off because he said I was going to tell him all of our secrets."

"Well, you've got to be careful around folk like that."

"But I wasn't going to tell him anything. I was trying to get rid of him."

"I see. But your Dad never saw that. Fly off the handle, did he?"

"He threw him out of the door by his neck."

"Did he? Well, I imagine he deserved it. Plus, your Dad's a little bit sensitive when it comes to reporters and the like."

Dad? Sensitive? I couldn't see it.

Granddad could see my doubt. "It goes back to when he were young. Your Uncle Rodney he... he did something amazing. But there was this one reporter wanted to twist it into something it wasn't. I reckon the experience of going through that stuck with your dad."

I nodded, but I struggled to picture Dad as a child. "Have you got any old pictures of Dad?" I asked. "From when he was around my age?"

"Reckon I probably do. Swing by after school one day and I'll see what I can dig out."

A few seconds later Dad came back in. He had about six eggs in one hand. "They're some good layers Rodney found for us," Dad said.

And I took that as my cue to disappear to my room for the night.

Monday 25th June 1990

"**Y**ou don't have to go to school today," Mum said. "Not if you don't feel like it." The smell of lard frying was making me feel sick and the sizzling frying pan seemed to be too loud and the sound buzzed around inside my head like an angry wasp. I couldn't think of anything worse than sitting around at home all day.

"I want to go," I said.

"Well, you've got to get a good breakfast inside you," Mum said. Luckily Dad was already out so I didn't have him hassling me as well.

"Can't I just have some toast?"

"Nonsense," Mum said, "I'm doing eggs and bacon, beans and fried bread. That'll set you up for the day."

Because stuffing myself with food was going to get the picture of John's face out of my mind. I hadn't been able to remember it on Sunday for some weird reason, but it was all that was in my head this morning. The purple blotches on his neck had spread so they were like fingers spreading up onto his cheeks and he had dark black circles around his eyes which I didn't remember seeing so I didn't know if I was just making it worse in my memory or if it was really like that. In one of my dreams he was sitting up by the tree and branches had bent down and twigs had grown and stretched out around his neck and got tighter and tighter until his eyes popped out, but I know that didn't really happen because I wouldn't be uncertain about anything if his eyes had exploded out of his face like in my dream.

Will was rubbing him tummy at the breakfast table and already had hold of his knife and fork, ready to tuck in. As soon as his plate hit the table, he started shovelling it into his mouth. I cut a tiny bit of egg white and put it in my mouth. When I tried to swallow, I imagined purple fingers around my neck and coughed it back up onto the plate.

Will looked at me and grinned.

I took a couple of sips of orange juice and after that I was able to eat a few forkfuls of beans and a bit of bacon. I cut the corner off a bit of fried bread, but when fat oozed out of its centre, I put it back down again.

"Thanks for breakfast," I said and took my plate over to the sink, "but we've got to get going."

"You've got plenty of time. Your Aunt Anne's picking you up, so you can finish your breakfast."

I took the plate back to the table and spent a few minutes pushing food around. I managed a bit more of the egg (half white, half yolk forkfuls) and most of the bacon. I wondered if I would be better staying at home, but I could hear Mum singing to herself really quietly as she was wiping down the already clean sink and I wanted to be at school where everything might be normal.

In the car, Liam was quiet. He kept leaning forward, looking at me, opening his mouth and then sitting back again.

Andy had a lot of questions though. "What did he look like?" "Did he smell bad?" "Was his face all gooey?"

But every time he got one of these questions out Aunt Anne shushed him and we went back to having to think about it himself. I tried to ignore the sounds inside the car as I looked across the fields and at the houses, we passed on the way to school. It all seemed much smaller - probably because we passed it so quickly in the car compared to when we walk by. There were a lot of cars on the roads, parents dropping off their children, and also so many more mums walking kids to school.

Aunt Anne leant round from the driver's seat and took hold of my hand after she pulled up outside the car park. She let Will, Andy and Liam get out and then said, "If anyone says anything that upsets you and you want to go home then go to the office and get them to call me."

Liam was waiting outside the car for me. "Sorry about the other day."

I'd forgotten all about how badly he'd taken it when his alien transition idea fell to pieces, and how he'd elbowed me in the stomach.

When we went into the school Mrs Palmer was standing at the entrance. She was sending everyone straight to the hall for an assembly. We never had assemblies on a Monday, but I knew what this one would be about.

The headmaster was at the front of the hall and kept urging everyone to remain silent as we sat down on the floor in our class rows. When we were all sitting down, he noisily cleared his throat. "Many of you will have heard about the disappearance of John Glover, a pupil in Mrs Palmer's class. It is with deep sorrow that I have to tell you that John is dead."

There were gasps in the room and teachers peered down their class rows to quieten their pupils.

"John's body was discovered on Friday, and police investigations are continuing. If anyone has any information that they need to share, please come to my office, or if you just feel that you need someone to talk to about it." I swear the headmaster was staring directly at me when he said this.

"We will be planning a memorial service for John, and I encourage you to share any ideas you may have with your teacher. Now if you could all put your hands together and join me as we say the Lord's Prayer."

I'd never paid attention to the words of the Lord's prayer before, (apart from the end bit being about power and glory, which sounded cool); it was like a chant we did without paying any attention, but this time the line 'Deliver us from evil', stood out at me. Surely John hadn't been delivered from evil? Whatever had killed him must have been evil? Or was the fact that his body came back his being delivered from evil?

Mrs Palmer tapped me on the shoulder. Everyone had already got up and was in a line to go back to class. I stood up quickly and joined the line, looking only at the floor. I went to class, but I don't remember what we did up until break - it was all a bit of a blur. I kept staring at John's drawer and thinking that he'd never be back to clear it out. His pencil case would never be opened again. His books wouldn't be written in ever again. When it came to break time, people headed out onto the pitch as if everything was exactly the same as it always was, as if he'd left school and we were all supposed to get on as if everything was normal.

As soon as we got onto the playing field Liam asked me if I was okay. "So, what's next?" he said.

"Next?"

"What are we going to do about it?"

I hadn't thought about next. In the last week I'd always thought that we'd find John, or if we didn't then he'd just be back at school all of a sudden and everything would be okay. Finding him like he was that seemed like the end of it, I didn't get the concept of a next.

"Don't we have to find out what happened to him?" Liam said.

At least we'd be doing something. "Yeah," I said, "We should do that." I remember Shaky Jake snooping around the drove.

"We need to check the cards again to see what other possibilities there are."

I nodded but got distracted by Will coming towards me. He was with Chris, from his class and he kept trying to stop him walking towards us. When they were really close, I heard Will say, "Chris, leave it." But Chris shrugged him off and came over to me.

"You saw his body," said Chris.

I nodded.

"What did it look like?"

"Like John."

"No, but like was there blood or anything?"

"I don't want to talk about it."

"Were there worms crawling around his face?"

"Chris, he said he doesn't want to talk about it," Will said, coming between Chris and me.

"How come he was found on your land?" said Chris, going up on tiptoes to get over Will. "Maybe your dad ran him over on his tractor."

Chris kept on talking and I put my hands over my ears and then Will swung back his arm thumped him right in the face. Chris was his friend, maybe even his best friend, but he wasn't going to let him upset me like that. I think Will would have punched him again, but Mr Inglehart callout out and Chris ran away.

"Violence will not be tolerated in this school," Mr Inglehart said when he got closer, and told Will to go with him to his office. Liam followed, shouting about what Chris had said, but the headmaster pretended that Liam wasn't there.

Laura came skipping over, with Becky trotting behind her. "Did your brother just punch Chris in the face?"

"Yes," he did. I felt proud of the way he'd stuck up for me like that.

"Why?"

"He was asking horrible questions about John."

"That's mean. He deserved it then. I heard that you found John?"

I really didn't want to talk about it with Laura. I didn't want to cry in front of her.

"That's so terrible. Do you feel okay?"

I managed a nod, and, fortunately, the bell rang to summon us back into school before it went too far.

After break Mrs Palmer had us all doing work in our literacy exercise books. She came over to me and said, "So have you had any thoughts about John's memorial?"

I shrugged my shoulders, "I don't know."

"We were thinking of planting a tree and putting up a plaque by it. How would you feel about that?"

John wasn't really into trees other than climbing them, especially if he'd got a football stuck in one. He did that quite a lot. Then I had an idea. "You know they have that trophy they give out at the end of the year to the person who does best at sports day?" I said, "Could you name that after John?"

Mrs Palmer nodded. "I think that's a lovely idea. I'll tell Mr Inglehart. Now, how are you coping?"

I shrugged again.

"It can't have been very nice to have been the one to find him."

"So, what's... next?" I said.

"Well after lunch we're going to do some painting, but if you don't feel up to it you can sit and read on your own if you like?"

"Sorry, Miss, I meant what's next, with John?"

"In what way?"

"What happens to his body?"

"There will be a funeral, and I don't know if John's parents have decided if they will bury or cremate him..."

"But before that, won't they need to look at the body to work out what happened."

"I imagine so."

"Will they have to cut him open?"

"I don't know, Tom, why?"

"I don't like the idea of him being cut open. He's been through enough."

"I agree."

"Who did it to him?"

"That's for the police to investigate," said Mrs Palmer. She got a tissue from her sleeve and handed it to me. I didn't even realise I'd been crying.

At home the kitchen was shining. The tiles on the floor and the kitchen worktops were bright and the whole place smelt too clean.

"How was your day, boys?" Mum said after Aunt Anne dropped us off.

"Good," we both said, then Will took the letter out of his bag and slid it across the table where Mum was arranging some flowers.

"What's this?" she said.

"Letter."

"Haven't you got one, Tom?"

She looked at the letter than at Will. "Fighting? Whatever is your dad going to say when he sees this?"

"Chris deserved it." I said.

"But I thought Chris was your friend," Mum said, bending down to look Will in the eye.

"He was upsetting Tom."

"He was asking all of these questions about John," I said, and then went to the sink to pour myself a glass of water.

"I see," Mum said. "But still, we didn't bring you up to go around thumping boys on the playground."

"He said Dad ran John over on his tractor," Will said.

"That's ridiculous! Why would he say something like that? What a horrible child. I've got a good mind to have words with his mother."

"He was just being stupid, Mum. Don't worry about it."

"It's not right, people making up stories like that. He'll get someone into trouble."

"Where's Dad?"

"Outside, with the police."

"Can we go see what they're doing?"

"I suppose so, but don't interfere."

I didn't want to go out there, but Will practically dragged me. "Don't you want to find out what happened?" I wasn't sure if I did. I wasn't sure if what had actually happened even mattered anymore. It was only fun trying to solve a mystery when there was going to be something good to come from it, like John coming back. There wasn't going to be anything good from finding out what had happened.

There were loads of them out there. Dad was with a group at the point where the drove led to the field entrance. We walked close enough to see they had tape measures and stuff. At the top of the bypass there were more policemen, and some were climbing up the bank and pacing out how far it was to the markers they'd put in place where the body was.

"They must be working on how the body got into the ditch."

"It looked like he's been running away. There was blood near the tree."

"Maybe he ran away from someone."

"What about the tree? Do you think that had anything to do with it?"

"Don't be silly, that can't do anything."

"It stole Granddad's eye. And don't you remember the wasps?"

It was a few years ago, and we must have felt really brave that day. We'd been out there in the morning helping Dad as he was tinkering with a tractor that had come to a stop on the land, when we heard the tree make a groaning sound. Normally that would have scared us to death, but Will had just got into reading the Hardy Boys books which they had in the school library and he wanted to investigate everything like it was a mystery. So, after lunch, when Dad had finished with the tractor and was busy in another field, we went back. The closer we got to tree the louder the rumble got. There was a deep crack in the tree that got wider at the top. Will had shined his torch in at the bottom of the crack, but it was too narrow to see anything. He'd asked for a boost up, and using my fingers as a step, he was able to shine the light in higher up. With his other hand he poked away with the pen knife, and then he jumped off my hand and told me to run. His voice was quivery, and I knew it was serious. I looked up and there were wasps pouring out of the top of the tree trunk. We both sprinted straight for the bank opposite. We jumped over the ditch and clambered up it and didn't turn around until we were on drove, which Granddad later told us was called Black Fen Drove and would become the bypass. Luckily the wasps hadn't followed us, but it only made me more suspicious of that tree.

Will shook his head, "We've got to think about real possibilities, not trees and monster and all that bullshit." He walked towards the group of policemen standing in the drove, and I walked back to the house.

NOW

It smells exactly the same: an equal mix of ancient engine oil and wasted grain. Billy is pointing at the tractor's engine, and Charlie is nodding, feigning keenness.

"Thought you would have wanted to go straight up to see your Dad," says Liam as we approach our sons.

No. Not yet. Being this close is hard enough. I'm not sure I can bring myself to look at him. I don't know what I expect to see, a man or a monster.

When I get to the tractor, I make the mistake of asking what they've been up to, and Billy goes into great detail about the work he's been doing. He's clearly a smart young lad, and he must have a good relationship with his Dad, so Liam can't have it too far wrong. But then I think back to how close Dad was with Will, and how that all turned out and the bitterness wells up inside me again at being allowed to live in a fantasy land for so long.

As Charlie is listening intently, I don't want to drag him away too quickly. Maybe it's seeing Liam again. I may have shut him out after that summer, but what we had meant something back then, and Charlie's never been allowed that. Cruel of me, I suppose, but I had my own way of protecting him.

I glance around the shed and see an old metal bin lid which reminds me of Andy's Michelangelo costume. "How's Andy?" I ask.

Liam shakes his head. "Same," he says.

Same as what? I want to ask, but then wonder about how many cans of worms I might be opening.

"What about your Mum and Dad?"

"Well, Dad's all right, but... don't you know?"

"Don't I know what?"

Liam takes out the handkerchief out again and squeezes it in one hand.

"She's dead. Cancer. Three years back."

My mouth falls open and I don't know what to say.

"I thought your mum would have told you," says Liam.

And I stand there, flabbergasted, feeling a loss I should have felt long ago, and feeling it harder for the delay. That's what my stupid rules get me.

I want to run into the house and yell at Mum for keeping all of this from me, but then my own voice plays back in my head, telling her clearly that I didn't want to know about anything that was going on in Little Mosswick.

When you've been in the dark too long, a little light sure can be blinding.

Tuesday 26th June 1990

Word must have spread round school that I was the one to have found John because everyone was staring at me, and at break time I could see people pointing at me. Some of the kids who would never have bothered to speak to me before came up to me and started conversations, "Got any swaps?" "See the football last night?" The answer was "No," in both cases and I'd walk away before they got to ask me about what they really wanted to know. Would I have been the same if I wasn't the one to find it? Would I be chasing someone around asking what a dead body looked like? I can't say it was ever on my list of things to do, but when the opportunity is presented to you, I don't know, maybe I would have been curious.

There was another assembly after lunch. We never had them after lunch. The infants were being really noisy and all of the chatter echoing around the hall made me think that my head was going to explode. Maybe I was going to have a case of spontaneous human combustion again. Mr Inglehart came in and settled them down and I was glad of the quiet until he started speaking.

"We have contacted all of your parents in order to make arrangements for everyone to be collected after school. The police have suggested that a curfew is put in place and stated that no children should be allowed to play out after school, effective immediately, until further notice is given."

The hall gasped and the chatter started again. I suppose it didn't make much difference to us, we'd been under a curfew for the last week anyway, with our parents watching us all of the time and telling us not to go out to play, but I thought they were being over-protective. If it was coming from the police then that meant there was something seriously bad out there, and they were worried about it getting more kids.

At the end of the day Mum had walked down to school to pick us up. There were a few police cars about, and policemen and women were going door-to-door to speak to people. There was a car parked up outside Mrs Johnstone's house which made me think about her TCP and soft biscuits. There weren't any police around the farm though, which made a change.

"Do you boys want to go over to watch the football with Liam and Andy tonight?" asked Mum.

I'd forgotten about the World Cup until that moment, but then I remembered that England were playing Belgium for a place in the quarter finals. When England made the second round, I was sure that it meant that John would be okay, but he wasn't. Was everything going wrong? England were going out, I was sure.

Aunt Anne had made a cake with jam and cream and when we arrived, she cut us all a slice.

"Can we take it up to my room?" Liam said. He had his own room. He didn't have to share like Will and I did. Their house had four bedrooms, even though it was just as old looking as ours. I guess Will and I could have had our own separate rooms, because there were other spare rooms in our house, but they were full of junk.

"No, you can watch the football down here," said Auntie Anne.

"But won't you want to watch your programmes?" Liam said.

"Missing them for one night won't do me any harm."

Andy was holding his plate with one hand and not really looking at it as he tore off little mouthfuls. I could see the cake sliding towards the edge of the plate in slow motion. I wanted to say something, but I froze, and it slid off the plate and plopped onto the kitchen floor.

I thought he was going to get told off. He looked at Aunt Anne and I could see his eyes were going all watery. Andy turned into a bit of a cry baby when he was at home, even though he never cried when we were out, even that time he ran into a barbed wire fence and tore his t-shirt open and had blood running down his arm

"Pick it up, then," said Auntie Anne.

He bent down and put it back on his plate. He reached to break off another bit.

"Put it in the bin. I'll cut you another slice."

Andy looked at Aunt Anne then moved very slowly over to the bin. The second slice of cake he got seemed even bigger than the first.

"Now hold it with both hands."

I followed Andy into the living room. Aunt Anne had really plump cushions on her sofa. They were great for plonking down onto and hearing the air whoosh out of them.

We had a bit of time before the game started so we went up to Liam's room. I took out my notebook to show Liam what I'd been thinking about.

Will refused to talk about it and went back downstairs to watch the build-up to the game with Uncle Alan.

I showed Liam what I'd crossed out, and the possibilities that were left in the book, and then we looked again at the Top Trumps, looking for more clues. I held out the pack and Liam pulled one from the centre. It was the stupid beast card, with the monster (with surprisingly good stats) on the stage. It didn't look like what we were after, so we flicked through looking for proper suspects. There was The Fiend. The picture showed him slicing off a man's head at the neck with its really sharp claws. Maybe that's why John's neck was so bruised, because The Fiend was clawing at it. Or there was Talon, which was like a massive bird and that picture had it biting a man's neck. The Lizard Man was strangling a man, so it could have been him, but the worst was the Venusian Death Cell. This weird creature had a bloody curved knife and on the floor was a chopped off head. There was only one thing for it, we were going to have to take a very close look at all of the cards to see exactly how many of them were possibilities.

"It's starting," shouted Will, and we all went traipsing down the stairs, where we found Will sitting alone.

I could hear Mum talking to Aunt Anne in the kitchen, and the clink of teacups.

"Where'd Uncle Alan go?"

"Went off with Dad," Will said as the referee blew the whistle to start the game.

Every time that Belgium came forward, I was certain that they were going to score, but somehow, they didn't. The commentator said that England's goal must have been 'charmed', and maybe it was under some kind of special protection. There was certainly some kind of magic in that England team, and I could see it every time Paul Gascoigne got the ball. Somehow, he could run, and the ball would never be more than a few centimetres from his foot, and it would move from one side to the other, leaving the defenders looking bedazzled. The only thing the Belgians could do to stop him was to kick him in the shins. They must have really annoyed him, because one time, after they got the ball off him, he tried to get it back by kicking them, but the referee said that was a foul and gave him a yellow card.

Neither team scored, so the game went to extra time. Still the Belgian's kept kicking Gazza, and for once he actually got a free kick. There were only a couple of minutes to go, and it looked like there was going to have to be a penalty shootout. Gazza took the free kick. He floated the ball into the air, and it seemed to hang there for ages, giving David Platt enough time to shoot it into the goal with an awesome volley.

England had won.

We were all jumping around on the sofas when Aunt Anne came in, her eyes wide.

"Whatever are you boys doing?"

Will and I dashed off the sofa and stood with our hands behind our backs. Together we said, "Sorry Aunt Anne," while Andy and Liam laughed.

"No need to apologise, boys; with all the noise I thought one of you had had an accident!"

"England won!" Andy said.

"Fantastic," said Anne. "That sounds like a good excuse for more cake."

After we finished our cake, Dad and Uncle Alan came back in.

Uncle Alan dashed over to Liam and Andy, picked one up in each arm and started jumping up and down. "We won!" he cried.

"Come on boys," Dad said. "Time to go." He had a weird smile on his face, which had gone red.

"You okay to drive, dear?" asked Mum.

"What? Course I bloody am."

As we were putting on our shoes Liam asked both my dad and his, "Did you hear anything about John?"

"No, nothing new," said Alan. "It's nothing for you to worry about. Make sure you come straight home from school, and it'll all be back to normal soon."

How could it ever be back to normal again? John was gone, and he wasn't coming back. Something had taken him and killed him. The police were so worried, they'd put a curfew in place to stop the thing from getting us too. How could we not worry about that?

Wednesday 27th June 1990

Chappie wasn't in his bed when I got up, and his dinner bowl was full.

"Have you seen Chappie?" I said to Mum and Dad, who were eating toast at the kitchen table.

"And good morning to you too," Dad said. "Sometimes I think you care more about that daft dog than you do your mum and me."

It was in that half-teasing, half serious way that I never knew how to react to. Maybe that's because the dog doesn't make me feel like a bag of crap, I thought to myself.

Dad flicked out his hand and caught me on the forearm with the tips of his fingers and smiled at me. "I'm only teasing you. He was asleep by the doorstep."

I waited until I was out there before I gave my arm a rub. It was surprising how much it had felt like a burn.

Chappie was in the shade, sleeping. His legs were moving, and his tongue lolled hung out of his mouth. He looked peaceful, so I left him to it.

Aunt Anne arrived a couple of minutes later. Normally they all waited in the car, as we had to hurry to school, but Andy got out, and Aunt Anne followed him. She opened the boot, and he leant in so far that both of his feet were off the ground.

Andy walked towards me, holding something long and brown in both hands. He also had something tucked awkwardly under his arm. "This is for you," he said, holding out the long brown stick, with some masking tape around the middle. "I made it this morning."

"Thanks," I said, trying to sound grateful, but not fully understanding what I was supposed to do with it.

"You can be Donatello," he said, "I made you his staff, so you can fight off the baddies."

I smiled, then realised what he had under his arm. A piece of cardboard cut into the shape of a sword and covered in tinfoil: Leonardo's katana blade for Will.

"Let me take it in," I said. I couldn't bear for Will to start another argument about whether we were the turtles or the crusaders. If Andy wanted us to be the Turtles, I was happy to be a turtle for him.

There wasn't much talk about the football, because everyone had seen something; that's how it seemed. As soon as Aunt Anne dropped us in front of the school gates, we heard bits of people's conversations, and the line, "You won't believe what I saw last night," came up again and again.

Andy ran off to line up for his class and Will stopped to re-tie his shoelace, but I stopped by Laura Matthews and Becky Reid who were having a similar conversation.

"What did you see?" I said.

Laura looked at me funny, probably because I don't often just go up to girls and start chatting. Also, it was probably obvious we'd all been earwigging into her conversation with her friend. "Nothing," she said.

"But I just heard you. 'You won't believe what I saw', that's what you said."

"Well maybe you should have listened a bit longer instead of interrupting us," said Becky. She tucked her arm around Laura's and pulled her away from me.

"Sorry," I said, after jogging to get back in front of them. "But what did you see?"

"Why should I tell you?"

"Because we're investigating," Liam said.

"Don't tell anyone else, then," said Laura.

"Okay," I said

"Can we write it down? You know, in our evidence book," Liam said.

"Only if you show us it," said Laura.

"We don't have it with us now," I said

"Then how are you going to write it down?" said Becky. Smarty-pants.

"We'll record it when I get home," I said.

"Okay. But don't laugh."

Me and Liam nodded. Laura leant in and the four us made an enclosed circle. "You know, where I live?" I nodded. Of course I knew where Laura lived. She lived on the other corner of Downham close and Main Street. "And you know who lives opposite?" It was Shaky Jake. "Well I swear I heard him howling like a wolf last night."

We all took a step back.

"What?" Liam said.

"I don't know what time it was, but it was dark, and something had woken me. I had the window open because it was so hot, and that's when I heard it."

"How do you know it was him?" I asked.

"I looked out of the window and his front door was open."

"That is weird," Liam said.

"He is weird though," I said, and Laura smiled at me.

At lunch Liam and I went around talking to as many people as we could, and there had been sightings of things everywhere. Brian had seen something running across the field out the back of his house at around ten o'clock. Sarah saw something that must have been a ghost, moving around quickly, like the Tasmanian Devil when she got up to go to the loo. Half a dozen people heard weird noises at different points during the night. We had a map of the village and charted everything on it, but it was all over the place. None of it made any sense. What was out there that could be causing so much weird stuff to go on? Were the dead rising from the graves and attempting to capture the living? Why was John the only one who had been targeted, and why did everyone think we were in so much danger? It all had to come from one place. I drew lines between each even and noticed that the centre was in line with our house, and with the tree too.

Adults didn't help. "I'm sure the police are working their hardest on it." But when did the police ever solve anything like this? This kind of thing normally only happened on TV and was left to the likes of Captain Caveman and Scooby Doo to sort out. The only time the police showed up was at the end once the mystery was solved. If it was a regular crime then it was up to them, but there was no way that had had happened to John was any kind of regular crime.

Mum came to pick us up from school. She had to go to the Post Office though, so we had to walk along with her.

"Have the police been back again today?" asked Will.

"Yes, I think there were a couple of cars today, but they're gone now."

"Did they find anything?"

"Oh, I don't know, Will, they don't come and tell us about every little development. How was school?"

Will muttered something about his teacher, and I wanted to say that school was a mess because no one knows what's going on and we get distracted and can't concentrate on a single thing, but Mum wouldn't have wanted to hear about all of that, so I kept walking behind her. Liam and Andy were with us too. Liam was walking beside me, and I think he could see how wound up I was, but he didn't say anything. Andy had run on a little ahead, but after being warned by Mum not to get out of sight he had stopped and was waiting further up the path for us. We'd reached Downham Close. The Post Office was a couple of houses further along Main Street. Andy was standing on the path pointing across the road. We looked over and there was a police car parked outside Shaky Jake's house.

"Stay here," I said to Liam and then I ran across the road (after checking it was clear).

"Thomas!" shouted Mum, but I blocked her out.

There were no policemen in the car. I tiptoed across his lawn and peered into his front room, but there was no one in there, even though the TV was on. He had a lacy white tablecloth, like an old lady would have, on his coffee table. He'd tidied his magazines away.

"Tom, what are you doing here?"

I turned around and Laura was on the pavement in front of me with her mum and her little brother.

My face felt hot. "Nothing," I said.

"Thomas you get back over here right now," shouted Mum and I wanted to hide away.

"Well, I better go," said Laura, and she crossed Downham Close and went into her house.

I went back across Main Street and Mum cuffed me on top of the head.

"Don't run away like that. That's the kind of behaviour I'd expect from a toddler, Thomas, not you."

Liam jabbed me in the ribs and made a face at me, so I didn't talk to him until we got inside the Post Office.

"Can I have a Calippo, Mum?" Will said. Mum was at the counter talking to Sheila who runs the post office.

She was old. She had white hair and glasses with a blue rim, and her arms really wobbled when she got something down from the top shelf. I know this because John and I once made her get down loads of different sweets from the top shelf so we could see just how much they wobbled. I ate so many Cola Cubes that day that my whole jaw ached.

Will asked Mum for a Calippo, so I said I wanted one too. In the end we all had one. I took mine to the counter where I spotted a box of Fisherman's Friends.

"Excuse me," I said, and looked up at Sheila, "Who buys these?"

"Lots of people."

"Could you give me a list?"

"I'm sorry," Mum said, and pushed me away from the counter, "Ignore him, he's just being a bit daft today."

I leant round the other side of Mum, "No, really, a list of all the people that buy them would be fantastic."

"I couldn't do that anyway, love," said Sheila. "My customers don't want me keeping tabs on them."

"I'll take a pack," Mum said, then she looked down at me, "Your dad likes them. Now stop being so silly."

Embarrassed, I shuffled towards the door where Liam was staring up at the top magazine shelf. He pointed at Fiesta. "Look," he said. "They sell it here."

Mum caught up with us. "Liam Carter, what are you gawping at?"

And Liam went redder than I was.

As we were walking back towards our house, we could see police cars were back outside again.

"How would you boys like to visit your Granddad?" asked Mum and stopped us from heading home.

Andy sprinted off along the path, and Will joined in, calling out, "Race you to the telegraph pole."

Liam and I watched as Will overtook Andy, but then slowed at the last second to let Andy win.

Andy jumped up and down excitedly. "I'm the fastest!"

Liam laughed. "I can't believe you got beat by a year three."

Will smiled, and ruffled Andy's hair.

Andy was so excited when we reached Granddad's cottage that he blurted out about his victory as he pushed the door open.

Granddad peered round the doorway from the kitchen. "Well done, little man," he said before looking up at the rest of us. "I wasn't expecting you lot to call in on me today. Is it my birthday or something?"

"Sorry to turn up unannounced, Norman," Mum said. It sounded weird to hear his name.

"Always a pleasure to see you," Granddad said. "Got... company at yours?"

"It looked busy, yes," Mum said.

"You boys don't want to sit and listen to us blather on," Granddad said. "Why don't you have a look in the garage, see if you can find those old photographs I was talking to Tom about the other day?"

I let Will, Andy and Liam head out the back door first and hung back a little.

"Found out?" I heard Granddad say.

"They might have done, but they've not told us anything. By the looks on their faces they don't seem to be getting anywhere fast." Mum looked up and saw me by the door. She nodded in my direction.

Granddad spun round, quicker than I thought he was able, and tiled his head so that he was looking at me with his good eye (he had the green glass-eye in today, which was one of the least scary ones). "Try looking in the cabinet right in the back corner – the one I keep my tackle box on top of."

I left and caught up with Liam, Andy and Will who were looking in a box in the opposite corner to where Granddad had suggested.

"Found anything?" I asked, knowing they wouldn't have.

"Just a load of rusty nails and screws," Will said. "Oh, your friends are still here." He pointed behind me.

I turned, and I knew what it was from the foul smell. Two of the three pheasants that had been there when we went fishing still hung from hooks through their beaks. They had lost most of their colour and the feathers looked greasy. The necks also seemed longer, as if the weight of the body was stretching them out of shape. I quickly turned away from it and covered my nose with the sleeve of my jumper. "We should look over here," I said, my voice muffled by my clothes. With my other hand I pointed to the cabinet in the corner.

Liam was first over there. He looked inside the tackle box and pulled out the pot Granddad had got from Teddy Barnham. "Hey Andy, wanna play with the maggots?" As he held it in the air, he must have heard something, as he said, "Shush," and then held the tub to his ear. He looked at us, his eyes wide and his mouth open. "It's buzzing!"

"Open it," Will said.

"No, Liam. Don't," Andy said, shaking his head and backing out of the garage.

"Go on!" Will said. "Don't be chicken."

I wanted to see what was inside, but I didn't want to get on Liam's bad side. "You don't have to if you don't want," I said.

"Why, are you scared?" asked Liam, and he placed the tub down on the cabinet, and gripped the lid. He looked up at each of us. Will was smiling, eager to see what was inside. I was apprehensive, fearing the worst, but knowing it couldn't be anything too bad in so small a box, and Andy was practically outside.

When Liam tore the lid off two plump flies buzzed out and flew in opposite directions. One hit the dusty window and crashed to the floor, and the other headed for one of the pheasants and came to rest on its greasy feathers.

"Tom, catch!" shouted Liam, and tossed the pot towards me.

Instead, I moved away and let it hit the floor. It turned on its side, and the crispy carcasses of the remaining maggots fell to the floor.

"Out of the way," I said to Liam, and brushed him aside.

He huffed, and then went to join Andy by the door.

I opened the cabinet, and inside were a couple of battered boxes. As I pulled the first out it tore along an edge, and I could clearly see that there were no photographs in there. I pulled it out anyway, but it was full of boring bits of material. The second box was much heavier. Carefully I placed a hand underneath it to help guide it out as the box felt a little damp in my hands, and I didn't want it to tear. It was full of old photographs, but it was near impossible to see them in the dim light of the garage. Will helped me to shuffle the box out into the daylight. We picked up the first photograph. With his slender figure, huge hands, and wild hair it was clearly a picture of Uncle Rodney. Even though he was just a child in the picture he looked almost the same, only bigger now, with a few wrinkles and redder cheeks.

Andy and Liam dashed over to the box and plucked out the picture underneath. In it, were a young boy and a girl. "Look," Andy said. "It's your dad."

I didn't believe it at first, but the shape of the eyes and the nose gave it away.

"He looks just like Will!" Liam said.

Will glanced at it. "Shut up," he said. "My hair's nothing like that."

But the rest of the face was similar.

"Who's that beside him?" asked Liam.

"Is it my mum?" asked Andy.

The gap-toothed girl with the pudding-bowl haircut was barely recognisable as Aunt Anne, but it had to be.

"Found 'em then," Granddad said, emerging from his cottage.

"You've still got pheasants in there," Will said.

"Oh, I'd darn well near forgot about them. They'll be jus' right for my dinner."

"Can I take them home?" I asked.

"The pheasants?" Granddad said.

"Urgh! No! the pictures."

Mum had also emerged from the house after Granddad. "They look a bit heavy to carry," she said.

"I'll tell you what," Granddad said. "Help me get them onto my kitchen table, and I'll bring them over to you another time. How's that sound?"

I picked the box up, on my own this time, and struggled into the cottage and through into the kitchen. As I popped the box down, I noticed that there was a piece of paper stuck to the bottom of it. I tilted the box forward and picked it off. Half of the page was still stuck to the bottom of the box, but I could see that it was an old newspaper. The headline read 'MISSING BOY FOUND BY LOCAL TEEN', and the picture beside it, though almost faded completely, looked much like the picture of Uncle Rodney that we'd just seen.

I heard people moving back into the house and quickly jammed the paper back into the box to look at once it all arrived back home.

NOW

I walk in through the back door without knocking and am immediately met by a blast of hot air. I breathe it in, but it's utterly devoid of oxygen. I can't breathe. I gasp at the thick air, my lungs working overtime to try to extract something worthwhile from it. Charlie's behind me, and I go into a momentary panic thinking that he won't be able to breathe either. I see myself on a plane, the pressure dropping when oxygen masks fall in front of my face. I desperately want to pull one over Charlie's face to save him, but there are no masks, and I'm struggling to grasp at the air before me.

Charlie tugs at my arm. I look round, expecting to see him suffocating, but, other than the look of concern on his face, he's fine.

Knowing that he's okay allows me to breathe more easily. Yes, it's warm, the aga is still firing away in full, but it's more the shock of being back here that I'm struggling with.

I look down at where we used to keep Chappie's bed and a smile forms on my face, and then I take in the rest of the furniture, which hasn't changed.

The one thing that's new is an armchair in the corner - though the armchair itself looks ancient, and the person sitting in the armchair looks older than time.

He's asleep, so he hasn't seen me come in. Somehow, his white hair is thicker than ever. The skin on his face is so heavily wrinkled that it looks like the earth on the droves after a particularly long dry spell. Somehow, it seems, Granddad Norman is going to outlive all of his children and I'm glad that he's still alive.

Charlie is looking up at his face in fascination.

"That's your great grandfather," I say.

"What's wrong with his eye?" Asks Charlie.

Grandad Norman doesn't have a glass in, leaving a gap where an eye should be, and I realise that I never told Charlie the story.

Our words make him stir in the chair, and his eye ebbs open.

"Will?" he says, his voice rattling through thick phlegm.

I can't help but sigh.

Granddad's eye opens a little further. The colour of the pupil has faded behind thick cataracts, and I wonder if he can see at all.

"Thomas!" he says, his voice raising in pitch a little.

There is a flutter inside. A brief feeling of elation that I chase back down. I'm not here to rebuild the bridges I burned down; I'm here to make sure nothing can possibly rise from the ashes.

Granddad reaches for his cane and grabs it on the second attempt. He leans forward on it, closer to Charlie who is captured in the cyclops glare. "This your boy, then?" he asks.

"I'm Charlie." Charlie holds out a hand which Granddad swallows with his own.

"Well, aren't you a polite young man."

Where is everyone?" I ask.

"Your mum's just taken some food up to your dad. He won't eat it."

"It's happening again," I say, thinking of that photograph of the girl, and picturing the wounds around John's neck around hers.

"What is?"

"A kid's gone missing."

"Won't be the same."

"How do you know?"

"Can't be, can it, Tom?"

I pull a chair from under the table and sink into it. "I don't know," I say rubbing at my temples. "I really don't know."

Thursday 28th June 1990

Chappie hadn't eaten his food again. His bowl was still full, though his water bowl was empty. I filled a glass at the kitchen sink and topped up his bowl. He didn't even notice. He was lying on his side, fast asleep. He was whimpering, and I thought he might be having a nightmare. I stroked him. His fur felt thinner, and his ribs were prominent.

"Don't wake him up, love."

I looked up and Mum was standing over me.

"He's not eaten, Mum."

"He's probably not hungry. It has been hot."

"He's ever so thin."

"I could make an appointment to see the vet, but you know, Thomas, he is getting old..." Mum looked away, and then she made a show of looking at the clock. "Oh, is that the time? You'd better get your shoes on, and I'll walk with you and Will to school. Go make sure he's ready."

As I was one of John's best friends, Mrs Palmer wanted me to dig the hole to put John's memorial tree in. I was taken out of class in the morning by Mr Inglehart and he walked me onto the school field, past the infants' play garden to the spot where the tree was going to be. It was a good spot, in view of the swimming pool and the football pitch, the kind of place that I could imagine me and John sitting under on a hot day.

"We've already dug up the spot," said Mr Inglehart. "So, all that we'll need you to do is to dig the spade in and lift the top layer of turf out of the hole."

"What, just the grass?" I said.

"Yes, take a look and you can see where it needs to come out of."

"But that won't be deep enough for a whole tree."

"No, once you've taken the top layer off Mr Jenkins will remove a little more of the soil."

Mr Jenkins was standing nearby leaning on a shovel. He gave me the slightest nod of his head.

"Would you like to see the tree?" asked Mr Inglehart.

I nodded and the headmaster led me around to the side of the swimming pool where this puny looking thing was leant against the fence. It was shorter than me.

"What do you think?"

He must have seen the disappointment on my face.

"It's a Monkey Puzzle Tree."

I smiled.

"Yes, I thought you'd like that. They have to be planted while still quite young, but they're fast growers.

"John would have liked that." I said.

"That's one of the reasons why we chose it."

"What happened to John?" I said.

The headmaster crouched down, "I understand the police are still investigating."

"But it's been ages. Shouldn't they have found something by now?"

"Thomas, it's best you don't let such things concern you and try to strive on with your life."

"But we're not even allowed out after school. Why not?"

"Until the police have concluded their investigation, they believe that it is in your best interest to be under the constant care of an adult."

"Then how am I supposed to forget about the police and what happened when we can't even do the stuff we used to do?"

"I think it's time you went back to class, Thomas."

"But Sir, it's not fair."

"That's life, I'm afraid. Now you're sure that you will be okay with the ceremony this afternoon?"

John's parents were there. The school had invited them to come along, and they were standing at the back, watching. It was only our class, with us all sitting on the grass and Mrs Palmer out the front with Mr Inglehart. He gave a speech first about how John was a special child. He was my friend and everything and I really liked him, but it felt funny only saying all of this good stuff. It didn't seem true. He didn't find maths easy at school and I always had to help him, and he could be a bit of a show-off, but I guess when someone dies, they only want to talk about all of the good stuff. I suppose if I was gone and people were talking about me, I wouldn't want them bringing up that I was a bit puny, and I couldn't lift a hay bale over my head. But there was great stuff that should have been said about John that wasn't. He had the power to make me laugh when I was feeling down, he was generous and would share anything without being asked, and he made me believe that I could achieve anything that I wanted to.

"Thomas, can you come up here?"

I hadn't been paying attention and didn't realise they were ready for me. I went up to the front and Mr Inglehart handed me the spade. Mr Jenkins came along with a wheelbarrow and plonked it down beside me. John's Mum and Dad were still standing at the back. She looked much smarter than the other day when she'd come to the house. She was wearing this posh black dress, and her lipstick was really red, but her eyes were all black and she kept dabbing at them with a handkerchief. John's Dad was in a suit. I don't think I'd ever seen him before. He probably wore a suit every day for work. John said he had an important job 'in the city' and I don't think he meant Ely, or even Cambridge.

I put the spade into the ground, and then lifted the clump of grass into the wheelbarrow. People started clapping, and then Mrs Palmer pointed back to where I was sitting before, so I sat down again. Mr Jenkins had dug out a bit more mud and as he wheeled the wheelbarrow away Mr Inglehart brought the tree out from round the back. I could tell everyone was looking at it the same way I did: it was a too small and didn't do a good job of representing John at all. I whispered to Daniel, who was sitting next to me, "It's a monkey puzzle tree, spread it." That made people giggle, and I think John would have been happy with that.

After the ceremony we were allowed to stay out on the field to "share memories of John," as Mr Inglehart put it. I was standing on my own when Laura came over to me.

"I'm glad that you're on your own," she said.

"Oh," was all I could mutter.

She must have seen that I was hurt. "No, I don't mean it like that. I'm glad your friends aren't here because they can be a bit... silly."

I figured that she was talking about Liam.

"I wanted to tell you something, something that I've never told anyone."

"Not even Becky?"

"No, not even Becky."

Was she going to declare her love for me? If she did, I would say that I liked her too.

"It's hard to say."

"Go on."

"I... I really liked John."

"Oh."

"I had a huge crush on him, and now he's gone there's nothing I can do about it, so I'm telling you because you were his friend. Is that okay?"

I nodded. John was my best friend, and he was dead, and for a second, I hated him because of what Laura had said, but then I was overcome by guilt and took back all of those terrible thoughts. Of course, Laura fancied John. He was the cool one. No one would ever fancy me. But it also made me realise something else about John. He was the only one that liked me for being me, not because we were related, not because of who my brother was, not because a teacher had made us work together. Now I'd lost him and was left with people in my life who tolerated me because they had to.

Aunt Anne dropped us at the end of the drive, and as Will and I walked towards the house, I could see that it looked different. As we got closer, I knew why. Half of the ivy had been pulled off, and Mum was busy tackling the rest.

"Afternoon, boys," Mum said. She mopped at her forehead with the back of her hand and took a deep breath. "I don't suppose one of you would grab your mum a glass of water?"

With a puzzled expression on his face, Will went into the house.

"What are you doing?" I said.

"Taking down the ivy."

I looked up at the house. The ivy had been there as long as I could remember, and the brickwork appeared strange without it. Where the ivy had grown into the brick, it left a pink trail, like veins spreading across the face of the house.

Mum snipped again with the sheers and then set them down to grab the vines.

"Why?" I asked.

Mum pulled at the ivy and stepped back. As the ivy tore away from the wall, flakes of loose brick drifted towards us. Mum stepped back into a rose bush and grunted in annoyance. She stopped what she was doing and turned to face at me. "It makes it look like we've got something to hide," she said before stepping aside, away from the rose bush.

I noticed that her dress had snagged on the thorns, and, seeing a couple of other small tears, I realised it wasn't the first time she'd stepped into it.

Mum tugged at the vines again, stepping back and yanking at them until they'd either come away from the house or snapped, leaving small worms of vine clinging to the house.

Will returned holding a glass of water. He handed it to Mum. "Do you need some help?" he asked.

"No thanks, love," she said before taking a gulp of the water. "You don't know how long I've wanted to do this." She put the half-empty glass down on the ground, unfazed by the odd angle at which it sat, and picked up the sheers again, pretending we weren't even there.

I went inside, through the scorching kitchen and upstairs to the bedroom. I picked up the Secret of the Scythe. The dice were kind; I went inside, through the scorching kitchen and upstairs to the bedroom. I picked up the Secret of the Scythe. The dice were kind; I had a good chance as long as I made sensible decisions. I ventured into the witch's house to explore, knowing I was strong enough to take on any surprises that the book offered. It was worth going in too. Written on a scrap of paper, hidden behind a broomstick in the witch's kitchen cupboard, I discovered the secret of the path to the Underworld. You had to push on a tiny branch on the trunk of the tree that looked like a disgusting wart near its mouth. I thought of the tree in our field, visible from our window, sure that it had a similar knot. That damn thing was responsible in some way. That damn tree was covered in ivy, just like the house. But if the house could be freed from its dark influence, the tree could be defeated too.

Friday 29ᵗʰ June 1990

They'd taken the name from John's peg, and his P.E. bag was gone. It left a gap between Steven Farley and Brian Harper. For the first time since he'd gone missing Mrs Palmer also completed the register, flowing from Steven to Brian smoothly, not even stumbling at the point where John used to be. They'd had their memorial and they'd moved on. Even his name sticker had been torn from his tray, but not cleanly, so it left jagged white fragments and sticky patches. They were all ready to move on. Was that also the influence of the Underworld? Was the tree sending out some kind of brainwaves to erase John from people's memories?

"We can't let it go," I said after finding Will at break time.

"What else can we do?" he said.

"Keep an eye on the tree. See if anyone else is visiting it. Follow Shaky Jake."

"Shouldn't we let the police get on with it?"

"They've done nothing."

"We're stuck though. We're not allowed out after school, so we can't follow anyone. You can sit around watching a tree if you want, but I've got better things to do with my time."

"He was your friend too," I called out as he started to walk away.

"And I can't bring him back. What do you expect from me?"

To be the hero. That's all.

There was a surprise waiting for us on the playground after school: Uncle Alan.

"Hey boys," he said as Liam and I came out of school. Andy was already with him.

"What are you doing here?" Liam asked.

"Car's had its M.O.T. Got to pick it up from the garage."

Once Will came out (almost last) we made our way to the garage. It was next to the post office, and unfortunately, we were walking not far behind Laura and her family. We were also much quicker than they were as her little brother was on a tricycle, which made him slower than walking pace. I desperately didn't want to have to pass them or talk to Laura at all. I'd done such a good job of avoiding her during the day. Andy went marching in front of them first of all, and then they came to a stop, ready to cross the road. I was going to have to pass them. Laura didn't even look back though. She crossed beside her mum, who was holding her brother's tricycle in one hand, and his hand in the other. If she knew I was there, she didn't care enough to even look at me.

There was a low wall outside the garage which Uncle Alan told us all to sit and wait on while he collected the car. I was still looking over at Laura's house, having watched her and her family go in a minute ago.

"Look who's coming," said Liam.

Shaky Jake was crossing the road almost directly opposite us. Andy leant back, hiding himself behind Will, who was staring up at Jake. Shaky hadn't noticed us until he was halfway across the road, and when he did, he swerved back into the road, turning back on us, only to snake back the other way again, and walk down the middle of the road in the direction of the Post Office.

"Shit, look," said Will.

A car had come around the corner and was heading straight for Jake. It blared its horn and came to an abrupt stop. Jake hurried onto the pavement and shrunk into himself as the driving started shouting abuse out of the window.

"At least we're not the only ones who think he's a freak," I said.

A couple of minutes later Uncle Alan pulled up in his car, which shone in the sun having been washed and polished. "Hop in," he called.

We all got in the car and buckled our seatbelts. As he was about to pull off the man with the Fu-Manchu moustache came running out of the garage.

"Mr Carter," he cried. "Don't forget your receipt."

As Uncle Alan was thanking him, I saw Shaky Jake walk by, having left the Post Office. Under his arm was a copy of Fiesta. It had to have been him that was spying on kids outside the school.

When we got home, Will was in no mood to talk, so I picked up my notebook and took it downstairs. I was sitting at the kitchen table drawing a map of the farm, marking out the drove and the tree and the bypass and the spot where I found John's body and there was a knock at the door.

Mum was peeling potatoes at the sink. I don't think she'd noticed me come down and sit at the table, but she rested her hand on my shoulder as she went by to get the door. I looked around. It was John's mum. I closed the book.

"Hello Mrs Tilbrook," she said, "I just wanted to pop around to let you know that John's funeral will be on Monday."

"Thank you for letting us know."

John's mum leant around my mum a little to look at me.

"Thanks for what you did at the school, Tom," she said.

I didn't know what to say, so I smiled, and she looked back at my mum.

"If Tom wants to come along to the service that's quite alright. I know they did their own thing at the school, but he was John's best friend."

"We'll see," Mum said, then John's mum backed away from the door.

"Okay, goodbye. Bye Tom," she said, but before I could say goodbye Mum pushed the door closed.

"Can I, Mum?"

"Can I what?" she said as she headed back towards the sink.

"Go to the funeral?"

"I don't know, Tom. Funerals are really quite difficult things, and you've already had the memorial service at the school, as Mrs Glover was saying."

"But she also said that I was his best friend."

"Let me speak to your dad about it," she said.

"I know it's a sad thing, but I want to be there."

"See what Dad thinks," she said, and she started on the spuds again.

Saturday 30th June 1990

ad had said I could go, but that meant I needed a suit. The most smartly I'd ever dressed before was for school, and that wasn't even a proper uniform. For this I was going to need a proper shirt and tie.

Dad knew a tailor who had a shop in Ely. It was a man he'd gone to school with, though you wouldn't have thought that from looking at him. He was half the size of Dad, and the only hair he had on top of his head was a thin comb-over from the side. He had round little glasses which were slid all the way down to the point of his particularly long nose, a tape measure hanging around his neck, and a pencil tucked behind his ear.

"Do my eyes deceive me or is that Trevor Tilbrook?" said the tailor as he came over to Dad and shook his hand.

"Alright Fred, how's business?"

"We have thin days and fat ones. I prefer the fat ones; they use more material."

He was odd.

"Still at Little Mosswick?" he said, and he rubbed his hands together.

"Yep, we don't go far."

"I drove through a week or two back – I won't be doing that much longer, what with the bypass and all that."

Dad cleared his throat.

"So, what can I do for you today? New suit?"

"It's for my son."

"Ah, is this one your eldest? Will, is it?"

I shook my head.

"No, this is my young 'un. Thomas."

"And what's the occasion?"

"It's for my friend's..." I muttered, but Dad cut in.

"Funeral."

"Ah," said Fred. "Not that young lad that was killed in your village?"

"Yep, that's the one," Dad said with a sigh.

"Terrible business that. Has anyone been arrested?"

"Not as far as I know. Police are struggling to come up with anything. They keep combing over my land, looking for clues, but they ain't getting nowhere."

"Of course, it was on your farm that the body was found. Terrible."

"It was Tom here that found it."

I looked up at Fred and he stared down at me. I was worried his glasses were going to fall off and hit me in the face.

"And he was a friend of yours?"

"Yes, Sir."

He sighed, shook his head, and then took the tape measure from round his neck. "Let me measure you up and we'll see what we can do for you."

He took his tape measure from around his neck and measured up my leg. He scrawled something on a pad of paper with a little pencil he took from behind his ear. Then he asked me to hold out my arms. He demonstrated; "Like this," he said, and put his arms out in an airplane pose. When he did so his shirt rode up his arms on both sides and I was amazed by how hairy the tops of his arms were. It was like he had a full-on hairy sweater underneath his shirt. I glanced at his hands as he held the tape around me. No wonder he didn't wear a watch, it would forever be getting caught up in his arm hair.

He breathed out heavily onto my face, probably accidentally, but that didn't stop it smelling like the tubs of maggots in Granddad's garage. It made me think of The Maggot from the Top Trumps cards, but other than the smell Fred was nothing like him. He didn't look like any of the cards I could think of, but those arms put the werewolf into my head. The Top Trump werewolf was even wearing a fancy blue suit. I made a mental note to check if it was a full moon when John went missing.

Fred looked at the numbers he'd written down.

"Yes, we should have something in black in your size, young man. You're lucky; we only have a limited stock of junior-sized suits."

He went into the back room and came out a minute later with a black jacket and trousers in one hand, and a white shirt in the other. He handed them both to me. "Would you like to try them on?"

I had to hold them up high to stop them trailing all over the carpet. I went into the changing room and stripped off. I could hear Dad talking to Fred.

"It must have been hard on the young man, finding the body of his friend like that."

"He could do with some toughening up."

I started to hum to myself to drown out the rest of the conversation. I didn't want to hear what else Dad had to say about me, but it was no good. I heard every word.

"Yes, but I wouldn't wish a sight like that on anyone, especially one so young."

I got the shirt buttons in a muddle first time and had it lop-sided. When I undid them all and put it on again it was much better.

"Was the young boy interfered with in any way?" said Fred.

"Police aren't saying, but there's some weird fuckers about."

I pulled on the trousers.

"A beastly business," said Fred. "There's some real monsters out there."

I heard a rustle from behind me and stepped out of the changing room, straight through the curtain without lifting it. The trousers were long, and I was stepping on the backs of them when I came out.

"Ah," said Fred, "Yes they'll need turning up a touch, come here."

He had me lift my arms up again and he looked at the shirt. He put a finger between the collar and my neck which caused me to bend my neck over to that side, so he had to struggle to get his finger out.

"Jacket and shirt fit fine," he said.

Then he put his finger into the front of my trousers.

"Not too tight?" he said and took his finger out again. I could feel his wiry hand hair scratching at my skin.

"No, they're okay, just a bit long," I said.

"Are you happy with that, Trevor?"

"Looks fine to me."

"When is the funeral?"

"It's on Monday."

"Ah," said Fred. "Well I have to make the alterations. How long are you going to be in town for?"

"Wasn't planning on stopping."

"Could you pick it up on Monday, first thing?"

Dad sighed. "I should think so. We'll come back then."

"Okay, thank you Trevor. Good to see you again. Send my regards to the missus."

We left and Dad shook his head. "Monday? All that time to turn up a pair of trousers. Probably charge the earth for it too."

"So, did you know him then, Dad?" I said, trying to change the subject.

"We went to secondary school together. He was a twat then and he hasn't changed."

"Oh." I said.

"Come on, boy, let's get home."

But before we got to the car park, he stopped walking. He put out his hand and stopped me too.

"Wait here a minute," he said, then he turned around and he was gone.

He'd left me outside the haberdashery. Mum sometimes went in there to get a bit of material. It always took ages because she'd get speaking to the woman behind the counter and they'd go on and on and on for ages. I think they knew each other from school too. I guess no one moves far from Little Mosswick.

It seemed like ages before Dad finally came back. He was carrying a bag from the tailor shop. When he caught up to me, he pushed it into my chest, and I had to quickly reach out and grab it before it fell to the ground. It was my suit. Dad's face was red. He put two fingers into his collar, and you could almost see the steam bursting out.

"I thought it wouldn't be ready until Monday." I said.

"I had another word with him to see if he could speed it along."

On the way back to Little Mosswick, Dad had me get a sweet out of his glove box for him. They were those horrible Fisherman's Friends.

"You can have one if you like," he said as I fished into the packet and took one out.

"They're yucky," I said.

"Suit yourself. You won't get nothing else."

They reminded me of the time we found the empty packet of them and that magazine. I peered into Dad's glove box as I put the sweets away. If that's where he'd shoved the magazine it was gone now. I poked about among the oily rags in the foot-well with my feet. It wasn't down there either.

As we got close to Little Mosswick we had to go around the new roundabout. Soon, you'd be able to go straight over and drive all the way around the village without going in. At the moment there were some cones blocking people from driving down that way, but that was all that was there. It would be easy enough to move them out of the way and get down there. Most of the work was finished. The road was complete. There was a police car just the other side of the cones, and further down the road I could just about see two policemen walking down the road, but then we were around the roundabout and heading into Little Mosswick I couldn't see them anymore.

Instead of turning down our drive, Dad kept going. I daren't ask where. We left the village, and a minute or so later, he turned off the road, and I knew where we were going: Greater Mosswick; I had no idea why we'd want to go there though. Dad took the turning that led to the river, and pulled over by the pub, The Merry Maidens.

"Wait here," he said, and left me in the car.

Two minutes later he was back.

"Thought Rodney might be here," he said. "I needed to have a word with him."

"The man in the suit shop said there are real monsters out there," I said to Will who was busy filling out his Italia 90 World Cup wall chart. We didn't buy the TV times, probably because Mum and Dad always used to watch the same programmes anyway, so there was no point, but Will had seen that this one had the chart in it and had asked Mum to get it for him. He had to forfeit his ice-cream that day, but he said it was worth it.

He'd not kept up with it since early in the tournament, but he'd put all of the results in, and was writing in the teams for the quarter finals.

"You've made me smudge it now," Will said.

He was right at the bottom of the quarter final teams. It was 'ENGLAND' that he'd smudged.

"If they don't win now," he said, "it's all your fault."

"Real monsters, Will. That's what he said."

"He can't have meant real monsters though, can he? That's all made up stuff to scare kids."

"Or is it?"

"Why don't you go ask Mum what she thinks."

As I was heading for the door Will said, "And pass the Tip-Ex."

Mum was sitting outside on one of the patio chairs. We didn't have a patio, just patio furniture on the lawn. She was looking out across the fields. I thought she was staring at the tree.

"Mum," I said.

She kept staring dead ahead. It was like it was hypnotising her or something.

"Mum," I said again.

She turned her head and looked at me.

"Are you okay?"

"Do you think the bypass will ruin the view?"

I looked out, past the tree. I could see two policemen out there, probably the same two I'd seen at the top end of the bypass.

"Listen to how quiet it is."

I listened. I could make out a lorry rumbling down Main Street.

"It'll never be this quiet again once that road opens."

It had been noisy for months though, when they'd been working on the road, and I figured it would be the same traffic as goes down Main Street, only now it would be going around the village instead. But all of that was distracting me from the reason I'd come down to talk to Mum in the first place.

"Mum, do you believe in monsters?"

"No, don't be daft."

"It's just, Dad was talking to the man in the suit shop, Fred, and he was said there were some real monster out there."

Mum stared at me. "Did he say that to you?"

"No. I was getting changed. I overheard him say it to Dad when they were talking about John."

"What he meant, honey, was that some people could be monsters."

"So, there aren't real monsters, but people can be monsters? That doesn't make sense."

"Don't worry about that. How's your suit? Can I see it on?"

"Okay," I said and ran back upstairs to put it on. When I came back down Mum wasn't sitting outside anymore.

I wandered into the yard to see if she was out there anywhere, maybe talking to Dad. He was out there, she wasn't.

"What the fuck are you doing out here in that?"

I looked down at my suit.

He was marching towards me. "You've not had it five minutes. Do you want to get it covered in dust and dirt? Do you want to get grease and oil slarred all over it?"

He grabbed me by the head. His hands were that big that he could do that. They felt like they could wrap around my entire skull and crush it in an instant if he wanted to. He turned me around and guided me back into the house. "Now what in God's name are you playing at?"

"Mum wanted to see."

"And what made you think she'd be standing in the middle of the yard?"

"She was outside before."

"Before what."

"Before I got changed."

"Get out of that suit before it gets wrecked. I don't want to see you in it again till the funeral."

As I slinked back through the kitchen towards the stairs mum popped her head out of the utility room door. "That looks nice, dear."

I remained upstairs for the rest of the afternoon. I didn't want to look at either my mum or my dad. I picked up *The Secret of the Scythe,* and remembered where I'd left it previously, having discovered the secret way to enter the Underworld. I read on and was making good progress through the book until a series of poor dice rolls left me very weak after a battle with a creature called a 'dead-eyed wanderer'. It was all getting a bit intense, and when I put the book down Will was fiddling with the TV. I looked at my watch. It was time for the first of the quarter matches. It was another excuse not to leave the room. Argentina versus Yugoslavia wasn't a brilliant match, there were no goals at all in normal time or extra time, but something weird and wrong happened during penalties. Maradona, one of the best players in the world, one of the footballing magicians, one of the superstars of the game, the man who claimed to have God on his side, missed. His penalty didn't go in. I looked at Will and he looked as puzzled as me. It was more proof, if more proof was needed, that there was something wrong with the balance of the world, and it was quite possibly because of the evil emerging from the tree I could see out of my bedroom window.

Sunday 1ˢᵗ July 1990

The more I read of *The Secret of the Scythe,* the more convinced I became that the old oak tree was also a link to the Underworld. The description seemed to be almost identical, though I was going from memory, as it had been a while since I'd studied the tree closely.

"Will," I called. He was still under the covers, though I knew he was awake.

"What?" he groaned.

"Wanna come for a walk with me?"

"No."

"Why not?"

"We won't be allowed to go anywhere."

I could barely hear him as his mouth was muffled by his blankets. I got off my bed and moved over towards his. "I only want to go out to the field. I need to look at the tree."

"Why?"

"I need to check something."

Will pushed the covers away from his mouth. "What do you need me for?"

"This is going to sound stupid…"

"What else is new?"

"Listen, Will. Something's wrong with the tree. I think it might be a pathway to the Underworld."

"You're right, it does sound stupid."

"It's all linked: Granddad's eye, the wasps, John, the thing that chased me the other day."

"If I go along with this, what's in it for me?"

"Don't you want to be the hero? Don't you want to solve the mystery?"

"No, I want gold and riches." Will jumped out of bed.

"I don't have any of those."

"Okay, but if I come with you will you stop all of this fantasy crap?"

"If you see what I think you'll see, will you start to believe me?"

"Tom, I..." Will rubbed his forehead. "I don't think this is going to turn out as some great fantasy."

"What do you think then?"

"Someone kidnapped John. They kidnapped him and tortured him. Somehow, he got away, and he ran, but he couldn't make it. Some evil bastard as good as killed him. That's what I think, Tom."

"What just a man?"

"Just a man."

"A madman?"

"Maybe."

"Like Shaky Jake...?"

"Maybe."

"So maybe it was just a man, but maybe he's involved in the Underworld..."

Will sighed. He looked at the clothes strewn around his half of the room, then selected an appropriate pair of shorts and a t-shirt.

I found the page in my book with the description of the demon tree and slid a bookmark in place. If this was the same tree, what would we do? And who would believe us?

"Take Chappie," Mum said, when we told her where we were going. "And don't go any further than that field, you hear me?"

Chappie barely raised his head when I picked up his lead. He used to go crazy the second he heard the metal hoops clicking together, but if anything, he buried his head further into his basket to try to avoid coming with us. He did perk up when Will started to stroke him, and he arched his neck to try to lick Will's wrist, and when the lead was around his neck he did hop out of his basket quite enthusiastically, but by the time we got to the door we were practically dragging him.

The fresh air seemed to do him good, and he took advantage of the opportunity to pee on a few weeds, but when we got close to that awful tree he stopped. He didn't want to go near it any more than I did.

"So, what did you need to show me?" asked Will.

I fumbled with the book, eventually opening it on the right page, but I daren't look down at the page in case the tree did something while my guard was down. I held the book out for Will to have a look.

Will looked at the passage.

"Read it out," I said.

Will held the book in both hands. "After emerging from the thick brambles, you see a tree in front of you, and a feeling of intense dread surges through your body. Its thick trunk is scarred by a great scorch mark which runs from one side to the other and looks like a cruel mouth. Above it, two sunken knotholes which appear to have no end make eyes, and on one side, between the eyes and mouth is a tiny broken branch that looks like a wart.

Do you:

Wait in the bushes to see what happens 359

Put your finger in an eye hole 24

Stick you knife in the mouth 234

Twist the wart 112."

"It's the same," I said.

Will looked from the book to the tree. A wrinkle formed on his brow. "I just don't see it."

"What do you mean you don't see it? It's exactly the same!"

"If you squint, maybe."

"It's close enough though, right?"

"Close enough for what?"

"In the book, the tree is a gateway to the underworld."

"So?"

"Maybe that's why it's all going wrong. We have to find a way to block it."

"That's ridiculous."

"No, it isn't. Don't you see, with everything that we've found out, that it all makes sense."

"Why can't you see this for what it is? Someone killed John because they're crazy."

"What's inside the tree made them crazy. Ever since it first tasted blood, maybe when it took Granddad's eye, its power has been building. We have to stop it."

"You have to stop it, Tom."

"I can't do it by myself."

"No Tom, you don't have to stop the tree, you have to stop talking like that. It's time you grew up and stopped making up silly stories."

"That's not you talking. That's Dad. That's what he'd say."

"Well maybe Dad's right. I'm going back."

I didn't turn to watch him go. I stood looking at the tree. The upper branches shook, though there was no wind. I stared into the eyes, long and hard, even while Chappie started whining and pulling away until it stopped shaking. There was a single tear running down my cheek. Fucking cry baby. That's what Dad would say.

I turned to walk back to the house, Chappie glad to be hurrying away from the tree. I could see a figure on the drove, walking slowly and turning his head from side to side. Shaky Jake. I wanted to go over to confront him, to stop him from getting near the tree to get more orders from the underworld, but then he'd see my face and know I'd been crying. He'd know I was weak, and he'd use it against me. I couldn't have that.

Instead, when I got in, I watched him from the bedroom window. There was a moment where I swear he looked up to me and I'm sure he was laughing.

I'd managed to avoid Will for the rest of the morning and afternoon by reading *The Secret of the Scythe*. It took a couple of play-throughs, but I got all of the way to the end. There were monsters in the Underworld worse than in any of the other books I had played through. I solved the mystery of the dead-eyes wanderers, who were said to slip through from the Underworld and possess the bodies of the living, their purpose being to bring fresh souls to the Underworld for the demons to feast upon. The book also featured the cruellest trick in the series. Often you would meet a fellow traveller who would help you overcome some obstacles, such as Sym in *The Crypt of the Sorcerer*, but Kyle, the traveller that you meet in *The Secret of the Scythe,* turns out to be possessed by the dead-eyed wanderers, and if you trust him, then, when you are confronted by another dead-eyed wanderer, he stabs you in the back. Literally. There are no friends to be found in the Underworld, and no one you can trust.

Eventually I made it through to the end, and gambled for the life of my master, but the game doesn't end there. The Grim Reaper honours the deal but sets the rest of his demons on you. You are first of all forced to fight the chief demon, who is one of the strongest enemies in the series, and the only one I've ever found with the ability to heal himself by sapping your stamina. After beating him his skin peels off and he turns into a fire demon, an even stronger enemy, and I used all of my provisions to get my health up enough to be able to beat him. After that you have to flee the underworld, testing your luck to avoid being consumed by a fast-spreading fire, which the fire demon spreads with the last of his strength. But I was lucky, and I escaped. The fire chased me all of the way back through the entrance to the Underworld and then, just after I burst through, the tree is engulfed in flame, and burns down to nothing, closing the door to the Underworld forever.

I didn't want to go down and watch the football with the rest of them, but Dad made me. "Waste of bloody electricity," he said. "You watching it up here, all on your own, like some kind of demented hermit, when we've got it on downstairs."

I was tempted to say that I didn't want to watch it, but I did, and if I said that there would be no way that Dad would let me watch it.

I came downstairs as one of the reporters was talking to a man standing outside a mud hut. He was wearing a grass skirt and had a big mask over his face.

"That's a witch doctor from Cameroon," Will said.

I stared at the TV just as he said, "Cameroon will win, 2-1."

"Bloody mumbo jumbo," Dad said.

Part of me wanted the witch doctor to be right, just so I could rub it in Dad's face (in my head), but only for a second. I needed England to win the game. They had Gazza, and his magic was surely more powerful.

When the game started, we were all silent. England had a lot of the ball but didn't make many chances. Cameroon had the first good chance, when Omam was one-on-one with Peter Shilton, but Peter Shilton was a giant and Omam must have been terrified to be confronted with such might. He tried to shoot around Shilton, but it was impossible, and he saved the shot. Cameroon had a couple more good chances, but Shilton was massive and there was no way round him.

After about 25 minutes England finally had a run with the ball. It got crossed into the box and David Platt was there again. It was like he'd magically teleported into the box to arrive just in time to head the ball into the goal, and England were winning. Even Dad gave a little cheer. It was all going to be okay.

In the second half, Cameroon brought on Roger Milla, and I was worried. I looked at Will, and he was worried too. Milla had been amazing in the tournament so far, and there was every chance it was about to get tough. It was Milla who won the penalty. Gazza, of all people, brought him down in the box. I know he was only trying to get the ball back, but Dad doesn't understand football, and he said, "Daft prick."

I clenched my fists together tightly and hoped Cameroon would miss. At least Milla wasn't taking it. I thought that maybe they were giving England a chance, but they weren't. Shilton dived the wrong way and all of a sudden it was 1-1.

Everyone in the crowd was cheering on Cameroon, and England seemed to be weighed down by all of the cheering for their opponents. Roger Milla was practically dancing around the England players. It was like his feet had been enchanted, and I thought of the witch doctor and the spell he said he was putting on the team, and I could see it was true. Milla beat Gazza, he beat Wright, and he beat Platt to be through on goal. There was no way he could get it round Shilton though, and he knew that. Instead he passed the ball across the goal to another one of Cameroon's substitutes who kicked the ball into the net, with Shilton nowhere near it. 2-1. The witch doctor knew.

When Cameroon had another chance, I knew they wouldn't score from it. Milla was still magic, and he played Omam through on goal. Shilton might have put him off, but for me that meant nothing. The witch doctor had called 2-1 and it was going to end 2-1. Omam's shot missed the goal entirely.

And when England got the ball up the other end and Wright slotted a perfect ball through to Lineker I knew he wouldn't score. He didn't even have the chance to, because one of Cameroon's defenders slid in and took his legs away. The referee pointed to the spot, but it didn't matter. England weren't going to score. Lineker took the penalty himself. He was good, but he was going to miss this one. He ran up to the ball, and he kicked it high, and I knew it was going to go over the bar and sail off into orbit, but then the net bulged, and I didn't understand what had happened. It was 2-2. "The witch doctor was wrong!" I cried out as I stood up.

Dad turned his head to look at me and frowned.

I sat back on the sofa, with my heart pounding. What did this mean? Was it more proof that magic wasn't working? Or was there a stronger force working for England? I didn't know what to think anymore, and suddenly the football became interesting again. It was no longer a foregone conclusion.

Cameroon had a couple of good chances, but Shilton wouldn't let them by. Eventually England started to pass the ball better, and Gazza looked like magic again. He slid a perfect ball in to Lineker, but he never got to it because two of Cameroon's players squished him like a piece of meat in a sandwich. Another penalty. Lineker must have been scared of missing this one, because instead of kicking it high up where the goalkeeper couldn't reach it, he hit it hard right down the middle. The keeper dived to the side where he's shot last time, and England were back in front. The Cameroon players looked exhausted. It was like the spell had worn off them, and they couldn't get the ball back. England had won. We were in the semi-final of the world cup.

"You boys had better get to bed," Dad said before they'd even cut away from the pitch and gone back to the studio. He stared directly at me. "You've got a big day tomorrow."

Of course. John's funeral. How had I forgotten about that?

NOW

When Mum comes down the stairs, I'm drinking tea with Granddad having a very safe conversation about how I've been over the last few years. I came in defenceless, but managed to put the barrier up in time to not let the sadness that hangs on his face get to me, though he did manage to recount my Dad's steps in the years since I last saw him, so I know when he got out of prison, and the terrible condition that his lungs were in at the time. What he doesn't tell me, is what caused it.

Charlie runs at Mum and hugs her around the midriff, and she nearly drops the tray of untouched food that she's carrying. However hard I tried to keep them apart, there seemed to be a special bond between them. I get up and take the tray from her, allowing her to put her arms around Charlie and give him a proper hug. She looks older too. She's aged significantly in the months since I saw her last. The skin is loose around her face, and her hair is thin and lacking colour.

"Let me make you a tea," I say.

At first, she refuses and insists upon doing it herself, and I realise that, in this house, I never once made her a cup of tea.

Charlie manages to convince her by saying, "Dad makes nice tea," and she sits with Charlie pulling his own chair close to hers.

"There's cake in the pantry too if you want some."

I head in there, unsurprised to find the layout as it ever was, and grab the half-eaten Victoria sponge cake from the shelf and take it back into the kitchen. The knives are still in the same place. Yesterday, had you asked me to draw this kitchen I doubt I would have been able to do so with any accuracy. Now, I could tell you the home of every utensil.

"I saw Liam outside," I say.

"He's done a great job keeping this place ticking over."

"How's Andy?"

"He's not so good."

"I figured. Liam just said he was the same."

"He didn't take his mum's death too well."

"Why didn't you tell me about that?" I ask, and a pang of guilt hits me hard when I see Mum's face strain to breaking point. "Sorry," I say, hoping I've caught it before it's too late. "That's my fault. They were my stupid rules."

"That boy can't see sense no more," says Granddad. "He's thrown away the sense he had. Poor bugger."

"Drugs," says Mum.

It wouldn't just have been his Mum's death that damaged him. What I put him through would have hurt him too, and him being that little bit younger it must have left him badly scarred.

"Alan does his best," says Mum.

Charlie finishes his cake and starts fishing around inside his mouth.

"Charlie," I say, and give him the look.

"What you got going on in there?" Asks Granddad.

"Wobbly tooth."

"Come here, and I'll give it a yank."

Charlie shakes his head, and Granddad laughs.

"If you don't let it come out naturally, the tooth fairy won't come," says Mum.

"I don't believe in the tooth fairy," says Charlie.

"Then what happens to your teeth when they fall out?" asks Granddad.

"Dad throws them in the bin and gives me a pound."

"Oh."

Mum gives me a look, but I don't feel guilty. Leading Charlie to believe in the tooth fairy would only lead to him finding out I was lying to him later on. What good could it possibly do?

Monday 2nd July 1990

T he last time that I had a day off school and Will didn't he had a bit of a tantrum and insisted that it wasn't fair. Not this time. He was in his school uniform, which I suppose is quite smart, but he looked a bit of a scruff compared to me in my suit. He didn't say anything, just put a hand on my shoulder before he left the house.

Mum was already in her dress, but Dad was nowhere to be seen.

"Where's Dad?" I asked.

"He's out tinkering with something. He'll have work to do when he gets back."

"But haven't we got to get going?"

"We've got hours yet, love."

"But we've got to get all of the way to Cambridge."

John was being cremated. They were going to burn his body. I didn't understand why.

"Your dad knows what he's doing."

"Why isn't he being buried?"

"Well..." Mum came over and sat at the table beside me. "Some people prefer it that way. They don't like the idea of burying the people they love in the ground. I imagine they want to spread his ashes somewhere special."

"His what?"

"Ashes."

"Where do they come from?"

"Oh, dear, I don't want you to worry about this too much. After the body is burned, they collect the ashes and put them in an urn."

"Why isn't he being buried in a graveyard?"

"I don't know, son. Maybe his mum and dad aren't very religious? They might want to do it in their own way. Why don't you sit and watch some telly until it's time to go, hey?"

Dad didn't come in for ages, and when he did, he was at the sink scrubbing away at his hands for so long. I was standing in the kitchen looking at my watch, but I daren't say anything. When he stepped away from the sink, I could see that his hands still had dark smears on them in the creases. "Don't worry, boy," he said. "We've got plenty of time." And he went up the stairs.

When he came down, he was in his smart suit. His hands were pink, with only slight spider-webs of grease still on them. His face was red, and though he hadn't shaved for a number of days, he looked like he was supposed to have a beard, rather than just looking a mess. His suit was the same colour as mine. It was the smartest I'd ever seen him, apart from the picture of him and Mum on their wedding day. "Ready, boy?" he asked, and then he came over and adjusted my lapels. "Very smart," he said.

I was waiting for the 'but', or for some kind of criticism, but it never came. Mum came down the stairs a second later. She glanced nervously at the clock, but neither of us said anything about how late we were running.

He drove like a loony. He was overtaking cars on the approach to bends, but he was lucky because nothing was coming the other way, apart from one time when the car flashed its lights at us and had to swerve into a layby. Mum was holding on to the door handle, and I could see beads of sweat on Dad's forehead.

I kept looking at my watch. Dad must have seen me in the rear-view mirror.

"Take that bloody thing off," he said, and turned around to glare at me.

Look at the road, I kept thinking, but he wouldn't turn back. I pulled the watch off quickly, tearing the strap in the process. Once it was off, he turned back to the road, and then yanked at the steering wheel to pull us back into the right lane. The horn of the car we'd almost hit, without any of use even having seen it, blared.

"Spend a bloody fortune on a nice suit, and he's wearing a cheap plastic watch."

It wasn't a cheap plastic watch. It was a Casio calculator watch. It was a birthday present from Mum and Dad. I doubt Dad had much to do with it. I'd torn the strap between two of the holes. I could probably still wear it, but it would either be too loose and fall off, or too tight and uncomfortable.

Where Dad had been sweating his hair at the front had darkened, and it was scruffy where he'd mopped at his brow. He started digging his fingers into his collar and breathing heavily.

As we pulled in the car park Mum turned to look at him. "Let me just sort you out," she said, and reached towards him with her hankie.

Dad batted her hand away. "Leave it."

When we got out of the car a group of people came towards us. Some were holding cameras. Among them was the man who had come to my door before, Joseph Price. "Thomas!" he said. "Have you got anything to say?"

Dad glared at him, and he stopped.

We went into the chapel. Soft music was playing, music that John wouldn't have liked at all. We must have been quite late because most of the pews were already filled up and we had to sit near the back. There were a few people from the village I recognised, but most I didn't who must have been John's family. The dark wood of the pews and the old brick made the place look gloomy. At the front was a podium, which looked wonky because the wood on one side was bowed. There were small round stained-glass windows on either side, but they were just split into blocks of colour, red and yellow on one side, green and blue on the other. It wasn't like the stained glass at church. There was no Jesus with his disciples or carrying his cross. There was no Jesus in the chapel at all. You could take a church being dark and dingy, because it was a church and it was hundreds of years old, but the newest and brightest thing in the chapel was the red curtain at the front, just behind the coffin.

I'd not really thought about the coffin. John was in there. My friend, John, who let me borrow his imported Gameboy before anyone else; who knew all of the words to John Barnes rap from 'World in Motion', and could sing it perfectly; who'd picked me first in the football on days when I was feeling down, even though I was crap, was inside that wooden box with that horrible red mark around his neck, with the hole in his head which got bigger, darker, and angrier every time I pictured it, and with his body twisted at that awkward angle. John was inside that coffin because something had killed him, and I hadn't even gotten around to finding out what or why. Thinking about John, in that tiny box, I felt the roof of the chapel drop. The walls started to close in. I couldn't breathe. I wanted to get up and run, and Dad must have felt me fidgeting because he put a heavy hand on my leg and stared at me.

The sun must have come out from behind the clouds, because, as Dad was staring at me, his face went red. I looked up at the beam of light that seemed to be shining on only him through the red stained-glass panel. When I looked closer, I could see a slight yellow hint on the wall behind him, but it was nowhere near as prominent as the red on his face. It was getting hot in there, and my suit felt too tight and Dad's hand felt like a claw digging into my leg.

My eyes darted around the room looking for an escape route. A man emerged from behind a pillar, perhaps having come from a back room, and took his place on the podium. He cleared his voice and all of a sudden all of the attention was on him. His words didn't sink in, but I started to calm down. I watched John's parents. His dad's arm was around his mum, who dabbed at her eyes with a handkerchief. Occasionally I looked up at Dad, whose face was still illuminated in red light, giving him the look of a demon, and I had to look away.

When the man at the front stepped down, I realised I'd missed his whole speech. John wouldn't have been able to sit through it either. Then he must have pushed a button or something, because the curtain opened, and two men helped guide the coffin through the hatch behind the curtain. I could imagine it opening up into a giant furnace which would swallow up the coffin whole and spit out the ashes. For some reason, when the coffin had gone through and the curtains closed the Mario death tune played in my head. But John can't play on; he doesn't have another life.

As soon as we got outside Joseph Price came up to us. "How do you feel, Tom, that whoever did this to your friend is still out there?"

I've never seen Dad move so fast. He had the front of Joseph's shirt balled up in his fist, and he used it to pick him up off the ground. "I told you to leave my boy alone," he said, and he threw Joseph to the ground. Dad then loosened his tie open, opened the top button of his shirt, and stomped off towards the car.

Dad diverted on the route home to stop by Uncle Rodney's house in Greater Mosswick. He knocked on the door, and then a few seconds later he peered through the pane of glass beside the door. After that he went to the next window along (I think it was the living room; it had been a long time since we'd been over to Uncle Rodney's house) and peered in through there.

"Not home," he said as he got back into the car. He drove off, and again stopped by the Merry Maidens.

While he went inside, I started at the pub's sign. I'd never noticed that the three women dancing on the sign (presumably maidens) had their boobies out. I felt uncomfortable and looked away, so that when Dad opened the door, it made me jump.

"Well I don't know where he is," he said shaking his head. "It's like he's disappeared off the face of the Earth."

Had the Underworld taken him too? He was an adult. He was tall, and strong. If it had grown powerful enough to take him, then it wouldn't be long before it was too powerful to be stopped.

We were back in Little Mosswick before the end of the school day. Dad dropped me and Mum off outside the post office, and we were going to walk down to the school, then walk home with Will. We left the post office (armed with a Sherbet DibDab for me, and a Sherbet Fountain for Will) and started to walk towards the school. As we passed Downham Close spotted a couple of police cars outside Shaky Jake's house. He had to be involved in what happened to John.

"My shoelace is untied," I said to Mum, and crouched down, staring across the road the whole time. Had they discovered that he was possessed by a dead-eyed wanderer? Had they made connections with the Underworld? The front door opened, and two police officers came out. Shaky was standing at the door, looking shakier than ever.

"Come on," Mum said, "Will'll be out in a minute."

"The other one needs re-tying too," I said and watched the police get into their cars, leaving Jake at his door. He closed it quickly, and before the police had even started their engines, I could see his living room curtains twitch.

"Why didn't the police arrest him?" I said as we started walking again.

"How do you even know he did anything wrong? The police have questioned a lot of people."

"But Mum, he's a weirdo!"

Mum stopped walking and put her hands on my shoulders. "Thomas Tilbrook, you do not speak about people in such a way. Jacob Radford may have his problems, but you can't go around accusing him of being a child murderer without any kind of evidence."

"But Mum...!" I didn't have an argument, but I knew there was something wrong with him. He was an agent of evil, and all I needed was proof.

Aunt Anne was already waiting on the playground for Liam and Andy. I moved over to the door to Andy's classroom in order to catch him first. When he came out, I said to him, "Don't you think it would be a good idea to go see Granddad today?"

"Brilliant!" he said. "Let's go."

"You have to ask your mum. She'll definitely say yes."

So, Andy dashed over to Aunt Anne while I strolled back with an innocent look on my face.

"Andy wants to go over to see Granddad, is that okay with you?" Mum said.

Perfect. We could talk through some of our ideas with him, and he could help us come up with a plan to get rid of the portal to the Underworld and bring Shaky Jake to justice.

Granddad was in his garden with trowel in hand.

"Hi Dad," said Aunt Anne. "The boys wanted to come over and say hello."

"Hello boys, you can go now," Granddad said.

"No!" cried Andy, and Granddad laughed and opened his arms for Andy to run into.

"You can leave us here, if you like. Granddad will walk us home later," Liam said.

"Oh, will I?" Granddad said.

"If that's okay, I mean," Liam said.

"Of course that's okay."

"Well if you're dropping them back, why not come in for dinner?" asked Mum.

"That's an offer I can refuse," Granddad said, and then he got up and went to talk to Mum and Aunt Anne quietly.

Will started prodding around in the ground with the trowel Granddad had left on the ground, and Liam and Andy were peering into the holes he made, looking for worms.

"Now," Granddad said, looking directly at me as I bent over the border, "that's not your school uniform. You better step away from the dirt or your mum will have me hung, drawn and quartered."

I stepped back, just as Andy spotted a fat worm and plunged his fingers into the black mud to grab it. "It was John's funeral today."

"I see. Well, you scrub up pretty well."

I moved closer to Granddad. "Why do some people get cremated?"

"Some folk prefer it that way."

"It seems wrong to burn the body."

"No, there's nothing wrong with that. He's at peace now, and they can scatter his ashes someplace nice."

"Will you be cremated when you die?"

"When I die? What makes you think I'm going to die?"

"You're not... but."

"I've already got a spot in the graveyard. Next to your nan. Couldn't leave her by herself."

"I saw the police today. Outside Jake's place. How come they didn't arrest him?"

"Why should they?"

I sighed. I was going to have to explain the whole thing. "You know that tree that took your eye?"

"Of course I know it. Damned thing."

"It's a portal to the Underworld. Maybe when it took your eye it got this thirst for blood, or it might have been before. Do you know about anything else that happened with the tree before that?"

"Well this is a tall tale," Granddad said. He straightened his back and then bent down to my height again. "Nothing before that I know of, but it was a fair old tree then, and I don't know its entire history. Tell us the rest of this tale."

"It's not a tale, Granddad, It's true."

"That may be so but let me hear it."

I told him about the dead-eyes wanderers, and how they possess regular people and force them to bring healthy souls into the Underworld for the demons to feed on. Will, Liam and

Andy had stopped playing with worms and were listening in to my story.

"And that's why that poor boy's body was found not far from the tree?"

"Exactly." I said. "He escaped and was coming to me for help. So how do we stop it."

"You've got a good imagination, and that's normally a healthy thing, but you're getting yourself all tied up in knots. There's nothing so complicated going on here. There's no Underworld. Someone killed that boy, that's right, and we might never know why. It was a nasty, evil thing that was done, and we've all got to live with that."

"But the evil's got to come from somewhere, right? People don't just murder people for no reason?"

Granddad couldn't answer. "Let's rewind a bit. You said something about old Jakey, what's he got to do with this?"

"I think it was him that took John."

"Oh, you can't go around accusing people of things like that. That's up to the police to do."

"The police were at his today."

"That don't mean a great deal. They've been down to speak to Teddy a couple of times lately too. They've been back here more than once. Jake's got enough to worry about without you spreading rumours."

"So, what can we do?"

"You don't need to do nothing. Soon enough the police will work it out, and things will go back to the way they were."

"But the tree, there's something wrong there."

"You've got some imagination; I'll give you that."

"There's more. I think it's taken Rodney."

"Rodney? What's he got to do with this?" Granddad appeared to be shaking.

"Dad was looking for him and couldn't find him anywhere. Said he might have disappeared off the face of the Earth."

"I think it's time I walked you boys home." He looked round at Andy. "Go wash your hands under the tap before you go, or your mum will have me strung up."

Granddad walked beside his pushbike, the box of photographs I'd found the other day in the basket at the front. "You have a look through these," he'd said as he picked them up. "That'll take your mind off the underworld and murderous trees."

The road was strangely quiet as Granddad first dropped off Liam and Andy, and then walked up to ours. When our house was in view, we realised why.

"Bypass is open then," Granddad said, as we looked at the stream of traffic on the new road. It was far enough away to not be able to hear it well, unless you really concentrated on it.

Mum and Dad were sitting outside on a couple of kitchen chairs when we arrived home, looking out at the bypass.

"Bloody glad I stood my ground about my land," Dad said when he saw Granddad. "Any bleeding closer and we'd be choking on the fumes."

I couldn't even see any exhaust smoke from the cars, they were that far away. They never sat out here anyway and were only doing it to have something to complain about. I wished it was closer. I wish Dad had sold the land to the developers. They would have flattened the tree and closed the portal. John would still be alive. Or when they tore it open the creatures inside might have flown out and consumed us all.

Granddad stopped outside with Mum and Dad, the three of them looking out at the road, and Will urged me to follow him up to our bedroom.

"Look, Tom," he said. "You have to stop all of this talk about the Underworld. People are going to start thinking you're weird."

"Will, I don't care if you don't believe me. There are two ways you can look at this. Either someone killed John, because that's what people do; they go around killing each other when they feel like it. Or people do bad things because some kind of evil being overtakes them, but it's something you can stop. I know what I'd rather believe."

"But we're not going to bring John back."

"Don't you think I know that? I saw his coffin go through the curtain. His body was in there, and it was going to be burned into ashes. I know more than anyone that he's not coming back, but shouldn't we be doing all we can to make sure the person who did this to him gets caught?"

"What can we do though?"

"Nobody is going to suspect that we're investigating this. I've seen Shaky Jake come backwards and forwards to the tree. We might be able to see something that no one else has seen yet."

"Okay," Will said. "We'll do something, but please, just give it a rest for tonight. You're driving me crazy. Go have a look at those photographs or something. Take your mind off it."

Will had agreed to help. That's all I needed. Maybe the distraction would be good for me. I went back to the box, and the newspaper article I'd glanced at the other day was still tucked down the side, where I'd left it. I looked again at the headline, 'MISSING BOY FOUND BY LOCAL TEEN', and stared at the picture. It was definitely Uncle Rodney.

It was hard to make out all of the words on the paper as it was so badly faded, but it turned out that the boy had been missing for a couple of weeks. I moved it closer to my face as I tried to make out the name. There was a rot hole right in the middle of it, but it left 'Jac   ord'. The boy was found close to death, with heavy bruises on his neck. Further in the article his forename was repeated. Jacob. Could it have been Jacob Radford? Shaky Jake? Skimming through the rest of the article as best I could I saw words like 'deeply traumatised', and 'hasn't spoken since the incident'. The article finished with the phrase, 'police are still investigating.' Was this the moment that Shaky Jake was enlisted by the Underworld? He had to be stopped.

Tuesday 3rd July 1990

We had a plan. We'd need Liam and Andy to help out, and we wouldn't have long to pull it off, but it was a chance to start checking things out. Before school I had another look through my investigation notes. So many ideas had been crossed through. All of the possibilities where John was still alive had been crossed out. Anything that involved his body being destroyed (such as spontaneous human combustion) was gone. We'd put the idea about alien transition to bed. There were a couple of persons of interest listed, but most of those were based on the fact that they looked like Top Trumps. The only idea that added up was the one about the Underworld, and the only person who we had serious suspicions about was Shaky Jake. I stuffed it into my bag and set off for school.

The plan was simple. Me, Liam and Will had to sneak out of school after lunch and go snoop around Shaky Jake's until we found evidence that he was some kind of psycho-killer. We'd be back in school before the end of the day, or close enough for Andy to be able to blag us enough extra minutes. It was a perfectly constructed plan.

After lunch, just after Mrs Palmer had got us started on some maths problems Liam grunted.

"What is it Liam?" said Mrs Palmer, clearly annoyed to be distracted from working with the kids on the blue table.

"It's my stomach Miss," Liam said. He scrunched up his face in feigned agony.

"Well I suppose you'd best go to the office to see Miss Harding," she said. Miss Harding was secretary, school nurse, and occasional dinner-lady all rolled into one.

"I feel so dizzy," Liam said. "I'm not sure I can stand."

"Oh Liam, that doesn't sound good," Mrs Palmer said, and dashed over to him. She put a hand on his forehead. "Oh, you do feel hot."

Liam groaned.

He was over-doing it, I though. She wouldn't trust me with him if she thought he was seriously ill. "Do you want me to take him to Mrs Harding?" I blurted out.

"No, I think it's best if he gets some air." She moved over to the window and pushed it open. "Come sit here, Liam."

"I think I'm going to be sick," Liam said, clutching his stomach.

"I've seen him like this before, Miss." I said. "He'll projectile vomit."

"Well you better go then," she said and ushered him towards the door. "Are you sure that you'll be okay with him, Thomas?"

"Oh, I'm used to it Miss. I've been on holiday with him when he's eaten too many donuts." This wasn't a lie. It was gross.

"Okay, but you hurry back to class once he's at medical, okay Thomas?"

Once we were outside the door and a little way down the corridor Liam straightened up. He pulled the prepared note out of his pocket, then knocked on Will's classroom door. He sheepishly put his head in, and then looked at the note. "Sorry, Miss, but could Mr Inglehart see Will Tilbrook in his office please."

A few seconds later the three of us were in the corridor together, where we saw Mr Jenkins. He wasn't part of the plan.

"What are you boys doing out of class?"

"We were sent to find you, Mr Jenkins," Will said.

"Whatever for?"

"There was a small boy stuck in the toilets by Mrs Harding's office."

Mr Jenkins shook his head and went marching off, leaving the path to Andy's class clear. There was an exit down to the field and swimming pool beside it. Carefully I pushed open the door, and Liam did the secret knock, quietly on the window. This was Andy's cue to put his hand up and ask for help. His teacher, Miss Norris, bustled her way over to him, and while she was bending over his work, we ducked down past the classroom window and hurried along, as best we could, to the fence that surrounded the swimming pool. We took a moment to catch our breath, knowing that we were out of sight, and then continued along the edge of the field. If we were caught, we were going to be in huge trouble. They'd phone home, for sure, and that would be worse than any punishment the school could come up with. I looked back over my shoulder at the monkey puzzle tree that we'd planted for John. That was why we were doing this. The risk had to be taken.

At the bottom of the field we scrambled into the ditch between the two elderberry bushes and jumped across the trickle of water at the bottom of the ditch. We were then on the drove, not far from where we'd found the sweet wrapper and the magazine. If we followed that around, we'd come out not far from Downham Close, and Shaky Jake's house.

The road was clear. That was the advantage of the bypass - we wouldn't have to stand for long at the side of the road. Of course, the only people driving through the village were likely to be villagers, people we knew, and more importantly, people that knew our parents. There wasn't a single car to be seen on our way to Jake's house. First of all, we followed his fence around to the back. It was five-feet tall all around the back of his property, but there were a few knotholes in the wood. Peering through, I saw that his garden was surprisingly tidy. There was a slab path in the middle of it, and either side grass which had been recently cut. In the corner, was a shed. Jake was in there.

"Maybe that's where he's hiding something," Liam said.

"The police might not have looked there," I said.

"Liam, go knock on his door. When he goes to answer it, I'll jump over the fence and have a look what's inside," Will said.

We heard the doorbell from where we were. Shaky Jake started muttering to himself, and then closed the shed door. As soon as he was through the back door, I gave Will a boost up and he was over the fence. He dashed over to the shed and peered inside.

"How's he doing?" I looked round, and Liam was beside me.

"Aren't you delaying Jake?"

"I did a knock door bunk. I didn't want him to see me."

"Will, hide." I called out in a loud whisper.

He emerged from the shed and then slipped behind it.

"Go back and knock again. Give Will time to get out of there."

Liam went back round to the front of the house and rang the doorbell again.

Shaky Jake had just stepped onto his back garden again. "Rotters!" he cried when he heard the bell, but instead of going straight back out there he went to his grass pile and picked up a pair of shears from the top of it. "Bloody rotters," he said and went back into the house.

"Will, quick!" I said.

Will popped his head into the shed again, and then pulled out a thick blue rope, and a dusty white t-shirt.

"I've got to warn Liam," I said, "Can you get back over okay?"

Will nodded. He dropped the rope on the floor, but stuffed the t-shirt half in his pocket, and started running towards the fence.

I ran myself around the side of the house towards the front, and almost ran into Liam.

"Thank God," I said, "I didn't want you there when he opened the door."

"I saw him through the front panel. He was holding some kind of knife, so I scarpered."

"Bloody rotters. I'll have you. One day I'll have you!" we could hear him shouting at the front of the house. We made our way round to the back where Will was dusting some of the grass from his school uniform.

"What is it?" I said.

Will took the t-shirt and held it out. We could all see the Little Mosswick Primary School logo on it and recognised it immediately as a P.E. top.

"We better get back," I said.

"No," Will said. "Let's see what he does."

We were all peering through the knot holes when he returned to his back garden. He saw the rope on the floor and dashed over to it then fell to his knees. He picked it up and cradled it in his arms for a minute. He then got up and went to the shed. He threw the rope inside then looked from side to side, He checked behind the shed, and then looked over his shoulder again. When he was sure there was no one there he went over to the grass pile. He grabbed his rake and pulled the whole pile to one side and dusted away some of the mud. He lifted the slab it had been hiding and pulled out a pair of gloves. Mopping the sweat from his forehead with the back of his hand he called out again, "Rotters. I didn't do nothing. Why do you punish me?" He buried the gloves again, pushed the grass-pile back into place, and sat rocking on the ground.

On the way back to the school, Will pulled out the P.E. top.

"We've got to phone the police," Liam said.

"We can't," I said.

"Why not?" asked Will.

"They'll know we bunked school, and broke into his shed," I said.

"We can call anonymously," Will said. "We'll leave a note in a box, telling them what we saw, and where."

"We can draw them a map," Liam said.

"Good idea," Will said.

"We'll leave it all somewhere they can find it, and then call them from a phone box," I said.

It was really dodgy that Jake had that school uniform, but what proof was there that it was even John's? "Name tag!" I blurted out, and Liam and Will looked at me. "All of John's clothes had name tags in. Check the t-shirt."

Will pulled the t-shirt back out of his pocket again and peered into the neck hole. "Torn out," he said and looked at me blankly.

I snatched it from him and looked myself. There was a small tear in the back of the neck where the little white label used to be.

When we were nearly back at the school, it started to rain, and not gently. The sky opened up and we had to hug the edge of the drove to get some kind of cover from the wild trees and bushes. It has been so dry, that most of the droves had turned dusty, but now that was like a thick paste that was sticking to our trousers.

We got back into the school without being spotted, but we were leaving filthy wet mud-prints behind us. Jenkins would be furious.

I popped my head inside my classroom door. "Liam's still in the toilet, Miss," I said.

"Do you need some help?"

"It's okay, I've been to the office. Mrs Harding has called him Mum, and she's coming to get him."

"Well, if he's waiting for Mum, you'd better come back to us now."

"I can't."

"Why not?"

"He sicked on my leg. It smells. I better not come in."

Mrs Palmer sighed. "Don't bring it in here. Can you borrow anything from the lost property?"

"I rinsed most of it off... but it's all wet. I don't think I can sit down."

"I suppose the best thing for you to do is to wait with Liam then. You will have to catch up on these maths problems tomorrow though."

"No problem. Thanks Mrs Palmer."

Aunt Anne was waiting for us on the playground under a huge umbrella. All of the parents had umbrellas open which made a huge covered canopy. She looked down at us when we got to her. "How'd you three get so wet?" she said, looking at Liam, Will and me, and then at Andy, who was bone dry.

"Dodgy tap in the toilets," Will said.

"And trust you three to be there when it went wrong. I don't know. Anyway, Tom, Will, a bit of bad news, you'll have to come home with me."

I was pleased. This would give us the opportunity to put together our evidence box.

"Why, what's up?" Will said.

"The police are back at your house again. Your mum phoned and asked if I could feed you some tea. Come on, let's get you out of the rain."

Back at Aunt Anne's, after she pulled out some of Liam's clothes for Will and me to wear, Liam found a suitable shoe box, and we started to put our note together. We were honest, in as far as we said that we climbed into his garden, then we listed what we'd found. The t-shirt we put in the box, along with the map that Liam put together, indicating the spot where the gloves were hidden.

"Should we sign it?" Andy said.

"We can't," Will said. "It's anonymous."

"But we could sign it as the Turtles?"

"We're not the Turtles."

"The Crusaders then?"

"All of that stuff was a game, Andy. This isn't a game. We can't put our names to it."

So, it was done. Just the facts. What we'd seen, and none of the speculation that had no doubt been running through our heads. Was the rope tied around John's neck? Was he wearing the gloves when he tried to strangle John? Why did he keep the t-shirt in his shed, and what other souvenirs were hiding in there?

Once complete, we had to convince Aunt Anne to let us out. There was a phone box outside the house next door, so we didn't need long, and Liam had us all kitted out in raincoats and old trousers so the rain wouldn't be an excuse.

"Can we watch the rain run off Mr Wilson's shed?" Liam asked. There was a gap in his guttering, and it would cascade down the side like a waterfall, and it would have been tainted green from all of the moss and sludge on the top of his shed.

"You'll get soaked," said Aunt Anne.

"We've got our raincoats on, and it looks so cool!" said Andy.

"Okay, but only five minutes."

Liam had had to convince Andy to give up the only ten pence piece in his moneybox, and he held it out proudly as we walked for the telephone box.

"Where should we leave our evidence?" Liam asked.

"Here," Will said.

"In the phone box?"

It'll stay dry and be easy to find."

"What if someone else takes it?"

"They won't. The police will be here within minutes to pick it up."

"Who's going to make the call?"

"I will," I said. I felt it was my duty.

I picked up the handset, put the money in, and dialled 999.

The operator on the other end asked what my emergency was, and I asked for the police. Within seconds I was put through and asked for my name.

"I can't tell you my name, but we have evidence for the murder of John Glover in Little Mosswick." They tried to cut in, but I kept talking. "I am leaving it in a shoe box in this telephone box on Main Street, around about number twenty-six. It is evidence that shows that Jake, who lives at the corner of Downham Lane and Main Street is hiding something. Please check it out as soon as possible." I clicked the phone back into place, and there was a tinkle as the ten pence piece came back out again.

"Hey, I got my money back," Andy said.

We were back in place, watching Mr Wilson's shed by the time Aunt Anne called us in, and though my legs were soaked, they were soaking so much, I couldn't feel a thing.

"What were they doing?" I asked Mum when we got home.

"They were searching the whole field."

"I'll tell you what they were doing," Dad said. "They were cutting up the land, fucking up the potato crop, and finding the sum total of bugger all new. Waste of bloody time."

"What are they looking for?"

"A clue, because they haven't got one."

There was no way I was going to get any sense out of Dad. He looked wound up. His hair was sticking up in crazy tufts, almost as if he'd grabbed handfuls of it, and his beard was bushy and wild. I couldn't look at him, so I gazed into the corner. Chappie's basket caught my eye. It was empty. His food bowl was still full, and I'd put that food in there in the morning before I left for school.

"Where's Chappie?"

"How the fuck should I know? Police have probably taken him in for questioning. They need to eliminate him from their enquiries. Maybe they've promoted him to lead detective, because the current lot are bloody clueless."

"Mum have you seen him?"

"Sorry?" she'd tuned us out. Maybe that was the best way to cope with Dad.

"Have you seen Chappie?"

"Not since I let him out this morning. He's probably shielding away from the rain somewhere."

I put my coat back on. "I'm going to look for him."

"Stay in sight," Mum yelled, panic in her voice as she followed me out the door and repeated the instruction that I had no intention of obeying.

I kept looking over at the tree. Chappie wouldn't have gone there, I was sure. Not after the way he froze in fear when close to it before. He knew better than that. He also knew the location of all of our hideouts. I went to them one-by-one to see if he'd gone there. Narnia was flooded, which reminded me why we'd abandoned it in the first place. Moon Base One was deserted. We'd not been there for days because of the curfew. I walked around the edge of the field, peering into the overgrown ditches as I went. There were a couple of runs where animals had gone in and out, and I tried calling Chappie, but there was no reply. I walked past the place where I'd been chased a few weeks ago and kept my eyes on the spot, but there was no movement. I walked around the top of the field, with the bypass only metres away, at the top of the bank. I could see where the police had been. They'd staked off a larger area of the field with police tape, and they'd turned the ground over, leaving dark ridges and darker troughs over half of the field. Any sign of the potato plants on that part of the field was gone. I looked across to the house, and my eyes fell upon the tree first, and then on Chappie.

I could only make out the white tops of his ears first of all, as his coat was both camouflaged by, and covered in, mud. I scrambled down into the field from the drove and struggled through the mangled earth over to Chappie. "Hey Chappie," I said, but there was no movement. The ground around him was soft and I could feel my feet sinking into the mud. "Chappie," I called again, and reached out to stroke him. He was still. "Chappie?" I touched his head and it flopped over, lifeless. "No, Chappie!" I said. "You can't be dead. Not here." I put my arms around him and tried to lift him up, but the mud was sucking him back in. I could hear laughing. I looked up and the tree was shaking its branches over me. The rainwater had weighed the branches down and they seemed to be lurking over me, occasionally cascading their collected water down on to me. I hugged Chappie again and tried to pull him to me. I slid my arms down, so my face was on his cold, wet, body and pulled at him from lower down and he started to lift out of the mud. I fell back as his body came free and he fell on top of me. I lifted him gently off to the side, away from the tree, where the ground looked firmer. I shuffled back and could feel my shoe held by the ground. It was trying to pull me in. Thankfully I was around the back of the tree. Surely it couldn't pull me into its mouth from there? I imagined it spinning round to face me, the mouth coming open, and the branches dropping behind me and pushing me towards the entrance. I could sense the dead-eyed wanderers inside, ready to pull me in, and despite being soaked through, I could feel my temperature rising due to the presence of the fire demon inside. I shook my head and banished the vision. I couldn't let them inside my brain. It was the back of the tree that was in front of me; surely that was its weakest point. I yanked my foot back, and out it came, without the shoe. I reached forward and grabbed my shoes by the laces and gave then a good yank. They were going to snap, surely. Somehow though, it held. I put it back on my foot and felt the mud inside squelch into all of the gaps. I picked up Chappie and took the safest path back to the house.

"They got him," I said when I bundled inside.

"Who?" Mum said, before she turned to look at me.

I must have looked some sight, soaked through and covered in mud, with Chappie in my arms.

"Don't bring him in here all covered in muck," Dad said, getting up from his chair and putting the paper down on the table. Normally they were so careful to hide the news from me. On the front cover was a picture of John, and beside it a picture of the crematorium, with the headline, 'REST IN PEACE'. Under that, a related story. 'New lead in Mosswick Murder Case?'

"He's dead, Dad," I said, and put Chappie on the table.

I didn't see his hand coming. A sideways swipe caught me on the side of the head and sent me flying to the floor. Then he must have realised what I'd said, and he looked at the dog.

Mum stepped away from the cooker and looked at the table.

Will must have heard the commotion because I heard his feet on the stairs next, and a few seconds later he was peering at us too. I was on the floor, covered in mud, my face burning;

Dad was standing in the middle of the kitchen, his chest heaving as he breathed heavily; and on the table, the mud and water on him soaking into the table cloth and turning it from white into a murky grey, was my pet, my friend, my dog, Chappie.

Mum was first to move, and it was over to me.

"Come on, let's get you out of those filthy clothes. Will," she looked up at him, "Start a bath running for your brother."

Will turned and went up the stairs, and Mum helped me up.

"Trevor, go take Chappie out to the barn. We can sort out cleaning him up and burying him later."

I let Mum help me up. It was the first time I'd heard her call Dad by his name. In front of us they always used 'Mum' and 'Dad'. I was so confused, that I was utterly under her spell. I let her lead me into the utility room and whip off my clothes. She picked the barely used picnic blanket (I say barely used, it had been used to make bases a few times inside the house) and wrapped me in it to keep me warm. She rubbed my arms to get warmth back into them, "You poor thing," she said. "Finding your dog like that." And she stayed with me, saying sympathetic words until Will shouted out that the bath was ready. She led me upstairs then left me alone to wash.

As I sat soaking in the tub, I played it all through in my head. We'd gotten close to catching out Shaky Jake, and the Underworld had responded by taking Chappie. Getting Jake arrested would not be the end of it. There would be repercussions. It was possible that the armies of the undead were gathering for an assault, or they could send more dead-eyes wanderers through. Leaving Chappie on their doorstep was supposed to be a warning. It was the Underworld showing me that they could get me here, and that I had to leave them alone. There was no way I was going to let them get away with it.

"Will," I said, wrapped in a towel and dripping onto our bedroom floor.

He looked up from the Nintendo.

"I know you don't believe me about the Underworld, but I want you to help me."

We spent the rest of the evening formulating our plan.

NOW

"**D**o you want to go up and see your Dad then?" Asks Mum, the tea drank, the cake eaten, and the conversation long since ceased.

I want to say "No". There's a certain level of comfort sitting here but seeing Dad will spoil all of that.

"Come on," she says, and I'm obliged to do as she says.

Like when I was a child, she's decided that she's going with me. She opens the door and I peer up the stairs. They stretch out, endlessly. She glides up them, and, tentatively, I climb onto the bottom step. As soon as I touch it, I shrink, making the next step almost insurmountable. I use the handrail to pull myself up and stretch my leg up as far as possible to reach the next step. This one feels like it's made of marshmallow, and I'm sinking into it. Under the heat of the stairs, it's melting. I grab onto the next step but part of it comes away in my hand.

"Close the door," calls Mum from the top.

I turn, reach out for the handle, and pull the enormous door towards me. It slams just like the door of the aga.

I clamber the rest of the way up the steps under her watchful eye.

"Sit down," she says.

I sit on the top step, and she sits down next to me. "I suppose there's no Father Christmas in your house either?"

If I was at home, I would have told her that it was none of her business. I would have threatened to stop her from seeing Charlie. But in my old home, I was just as powerless as I was when I was ten. I manage a nod.

"Don't you feel that Charlie is missing out?"

I shrug. I want to tell her that he's not missing out. I want to tell her that he's experiencing these things on a much higher level than other children, but I can't think how to get the words out.

"Look in here," Mum says. She pushes herself up from the step, finding it much more difficult than I thought she would. She opens the door to my old bedroom, the room I shared with Will.

"See that poster on the wall?"

It has Bowser on it. I remember Will tearing it out of a magazine that John gave us when he had finished with it.

"Does Charlie have any posters on his wall?"

"Yes," I say. He has a poster of the periodic table.

"Any kids' posters?" says Mum, seeing right through me.

I shake my head.

Mum goes into Will's cupboard and takes out a box while I wait at the door, afraid to cross the threshold.

"I kept all of these," she says as she struggles across the room with the box. She places it at my feet and pulls it open. The sun emerges from behind a cloud to shine through the window and illuminate the row of green spines. "I know that you wanted to throw them all out, but I couldn't let you."

I look at some of the titles, *The Caverns of the Snow Witch, Appointment with F.E.A.R* and of course, *Secrets of the Scythe.*

"Does Charlie have any books?"

"Of course he does!" I picture his bookshelf, the rows of encyclopaedias, *Horrible Histories,* and the collection of magazines about rocks.

"Does he have any stories, Thomas, real stories?"

"No, Mum!" I say, raising my voice at her for the first time in my life.

"You can't blame stories for what happened."

No. I blame myself. But before I can tell her that a booming voice comes from the room down the hall, a voice I've not heard for a very long time, and a voice that scares me as much as it always has. "Stay out of Will's room."

I run.

Wednesday 4th July 1990

At school, all anyone could talk about was the World Cup semi-final. England were playing West Germany for the right to play Argentina in the final, who had knocked out Italy the night before. The West German team lacked magic. They played without any kind of flair. Their approach seemed to be to bore the opposition to sleep by passing the ball from side-to-side, and then kick the ball into the net. England, on the other hand, had Gazza. He was a proper player. Then there were Waddle and Beardsley, and David Platt had turned up out of nowhere and become some kind of goal-scoring wonder. All of those players had the ability to get the ball to Lineker, and he was the best striker in the world, so he wouldn't miss. All of the skill was with England. Even if the German's did manage to lull England to sleep, they'd have to get past Shilton the giant.

The only person who didn't want to talk football was Liam. "Do you think they got our message?" he said as soon as he saw us on the playground.

"They must have done. They couldn't have ignored the call," Will said.

We'd talked last night about involving Liam and Andy in our plan but had decided that they were best left out of it. Liam had never fully been behind the Underworld idea, being more convinced that aliens had invaded the school, and now his thoughts were pinned entirely on Shaky Jake.

"After school," Liam said, "we should find an excuse to walk down to the Post Office to see if there's anything going on at his house. They might be digging up his whole garden." Liam must have noticed that I wasn't very enthusiastic about his plan. "What's wrong with him?" he said to Will.

"Chappie died."

"Damn. Sorry about that."

Liam had been with us on some of the best times we'd had with Chappie, just walking through the droves, making our own bow and arrows, and building bases. Chappie was always up for a game of fetch too. He was one of the gang. I felt myself welling up again and had to run off to the toilet.

Tears clouded my eyes. I headed towards the toilets to wipe my face. Laura stood by the entrance. The closer I got to her, the more she smiled. I wasn't even embarrassed by the tears in my eyes. I could tell her about Chappie. She'd understand; she'd make me feel better.

But as I got closer, I realised that she wasn't making eye-contact with me; she was looking over my shoulder. She was looking at someone else. Once inside I turned and looked back through the window. She hugged Chris Jackson, and they walked off holding hands. I lost sight of them as my eyes clouded with tears.

"We've had a thought," Mum said when she came to pick us up at the end of the day. "Wouldn't it be fun for Liam and Andy to stay over tonight so we could all watch the football together?"

Andy practically jumped for joy, and Liam gave him a high-five. I looked at Will and he kind of shrugged. "Yeah, that would be cool."

"Ace," I said, with a new version of the plan already working itself out inside my head.

"We've got a bit of business to deal with first though," Mum said, "but if you come over for around six?"

That bit of business was putting Chappie to rest. Thankfully it had stopped raining by the time we got home, but the sky was still dark, and the clouds still looked heavy.

Chappie was clean again, and he had a red handkerchief tied around his neck. He used to like to wear that when he was younger, but in the last few years it had seemed to irritate him. Dad had dug a hole in our garden under one of the bushes where he often liked to lie. It was the right place to put him.

"Am I okay to put him in?" asked Dad. He was looking at Mum.

I nodded, and Mum nodded at Dad, and he carefully moved Chappie from the blanket and into the hole.

"Well?" he said, and my first thought was that I'd done something wrong. "Have you got any last words for him?"

"Bye Chappie." I said. "You were a good friend."

A raindrop fell on my face.

"Will?"

"We had fun together," Will said.

Dad held the shovel out for Will to take. He took a little of the dirt from the top of the pile of tipped it on top of Chappie.

Will then passed the shovel to me. The rain had started to fall a little harder now. One drip landed in the gap between by hair and my collar on the back of my neck and followed the path of my spine all the way down my back. I looked down at Chappie for the last time as I tipped a little of the dirt onto his head.

"Leave it to me now boys. Get inside before you get too wet."

And as we were leaving, I heard Dad say, "You were a good dog."

We didn't mention the plan to Liam and Andy. We figured that we could fill them in after the game. The start was so hectic, that I almost forgot about the plan altogether, with England winning three corners, and coming close to scoring each time. Gazza was playing well too, with the ball held magically to his boot, and he forced the German keeper into a couple of good saves.

England were definitely the better team, but there were no goals in the first half. Somehow Chris Waddle hit the bar from almost halfway, but there were no goals. England were playing better than they had done in the whole tournament. There was still some good in the world, it was obvious. West Germany had a few chances at the end of the half, but nothing to trouble super Shilton.

West Germany took the lead, and in the only way possible, with a deflection. They had a free kick, which was taken short to Brehme. Paul Parker tried to block his shot, which Shilton was already diving to save, but the ball hit Parker and looped up in the air. Shilton was already in mid-air, going the wrong way. There was no way back, and the ball fell into the net. It wasn't over though. I believed in England, and they didn't let me down. They made chance after chance, but it looked like they weren't going to score. I didn't give up on them. When Waddle was brought down in the box, and the referee waved play on I still had a feeling that we were going to be okay. Paul Parker, no doubt trying to make up for the ball going off him for the German goal ran up the field and smashed in a cross towards Lineker. It bounced off a German player's leg, then Lineker controlled it with his knee, and knocked it into the only bit of space in the penalty box which was swarming with West German defenders, then he kicked it hard into the opposite corner of the goal, giving their keeper no chance. John Motson, who was commentating for the BBC described him as an 'Ace marksman', and he was. We had ten minutes to win it, and then we had some more important business to deal with.

No goal came in the last ten minutes, so it meant extra time, and a much later night than planned. It was extra time for the third England match in a row. They'd scored in extra time in the last two games, so why should this be any different? When Klinsmann jumped to meet a cross and headed the ball towards the bottom corner of the goal, I didn't doubt that Shilton would be able to save it, and when the ball dropped to the same player in the box I knew that he was going to miss. But then Gazza went sliding into a tackle and it felt as though something had gone very badly wrong with the word. It seemed to take an age for the referee to pull out the yellow card, but Gazza knew it was coming. You could see it on his face; he was going to miss the World Cup Final.

Until that moment I was so sure that England would do it, but that card caused the doubt to flood over me. I could see the tree out there and knew that it would be laughing at us in here. Its powers were strong if it could influence events in Italy. I wanted the game to be over so that I could go out there and put that damned tree to rest forever. Instead, I had to sit and watch the inevitable.

Waddle hit the post. The ball seemed to swerve off target. There was no way it was going into the net again tonight; I was sure of it. So, when the ball did go into the West German net, I had a sick feeling in my stomach. Maybe there was enough good in the world? David Platt again! But I hadn't heard the whistle or spotted the referee with his hand up. Offside. Goal disallowed. That wasn't the end of the action; Shilton made a superb save and Germany hit the post, but there were no more goals. That meant there was going to be a penalty shootout.

The first six penalties were all scored before Stuart Pearce stepped up. I hadn't been able to watch any of England's other penalties, and this one was no different. I closed my eyes and put my hand in front of them too for double cover. The blackness in front of me formed into an image of shaking branches and a cruel mouth. Before Dad even cried out, "You bugger," I knew he'd missed. The Germans scored the next one. They had to miss one, or it was over. I made myself watch Waddle's penalty, afraid to close my eyes again, and I watched him kick the ball over the bar and into the crowd. England were out, and it was my fault for playing with forces I didn't understand.

I went straight up the stairs to prepare for the assault. The first part of that plan meant cleaning my teeth and putting on my pyjamas. Will wasn't far behind, and Liam and Andy were hurried upstairs by Mum minutes later. We had to go to bed, or at least pretend to. Everything had to seem normal until after Mum and Dad had gone to bed.

We filled Liam and Andy in on the plan. Earlier in the day Will had gone out to the barn and moved a can of petrol to near the back door. I'd taken a box of matches from the kitchen cupboard. All we had to do was go down to the tree, cover it in petrol, and set it alight, closing the door to the Underworld and trapping the evil beings inside

"Will, I was speaking to you the other day about this," Liam said, awkwardly nodding his head towards me.

"We're doing this. I don't believe the Underworld theory, I don't believe in aliens, but I do believe that when that tree is gone, all of this will settle down."

"But why?"

Will pulled Liam to him and whispered something in his ear, and then, for the benefit of all of us, "I just want to get my life back. In three weeks' time, it's the summer holidays, my last summer holidays before secondary school. We have to end this before then, or how can we possibly enjoy it?"

We waited until we could hear Dad snoring. It didn't take long on those nights where he'd had a can or two of beer, and he'd certainly had a few while the football was on. Will went first and expertly took the stairs, missing the creakers. I waited in the corridor while Liam and Andy crept down. They weren't so familiar with the floorboards in the house though, and a creak made the whole house gasp.

"That you, Thomas?" It was Mum's voice.

"Just getting a drink."

"Okay, love. Night."

"Night Mum," I said, and we all continued on our way.

It had continued to rain while the football was on, and while it had stopped, thick purplish clouds still hung in the sky. It was around eleven o'clock, and I felt as though it should have been darker. I guess it was unusual for us to be up so late. We traipsed around the edge of the field, with the ground very soft under our feet. A couple of times Andy lost his balance. He was much shorter than us, and had trouble picking his feet up high enough to stop them getting stuck.

We stopped in front of the tree. The light of the moon had crept between the clouds and now shone on his twisted face.

"So, it has come to this," I heard the tree say in my head.

There was a rumble.

"He's hungry," Andy said and took a couple of steps back, but then the sky was lit up with a flash of sheet lightning, and he froze.

I realised that he'd brought his nun-chucks with him. He was too young for all of this.

"You don't have what it takes to stop me," I heard the tree say.

"Splash it on, Will," I said.

He moved forward and unscrewed the petrol canister. He moved his nose to the spout and sniffed, and immediately reeled back.

"Death juice!" Liam said, and raised a stick, which I'd not seen him pick up, in the air. I wondered what he intended to do with it.

Will swung the can so a load of petrol gushed out the end and splashed around the base of the tree.

The first spots of rain had started to fall, and another rumble made us jump back.

"You don't know what you're doing," said the tree.

With the flash of lightning, which was no more than two seconds later, the rain gushed down. With the moon lost behind the clouds, darkness had descended upon us.

"Is it done?" I said to Will.

"We're empty."

I pulled the matches from my pocket and lit the first one. It fizzled out as soon as it sparked up. I tried another and the same thing happened.

"You are doomed to failure, boy," said the tree.

"Liam, Andy, Will, come here."

They stumbled over to me. By the time the next flash of lightning came we were gathered together.

"Shield me from the rain," I said.

Huddled together, we were able to get a match lit. I threw it towards the tree, but a gust of wind blew it back at us, dead.

The tree laughed.

"We'll have to get closer." I had to almost shout, as the wind was now howling.

We moved together, but I felt our group get smaller.

"Who's not with us?" I said.

"It's Andy," Liam said.

"Andy, come on!" cried Will. "Join us!"

"No. It'll get me."

A flash of lightning illuminated Andy's terrified face.

"You stay there, then Andy. We'll be back with you in a second," I said.

We started to edge towards the tree.

"Come on... come closer."

Liam suddenly fell away from us.

"Liam!" I called.

"I tripped," he said. "I'm going back to Andy, he's too scared."

He was scared. We all were. I don't blame him for giving up on us.

We were close to the tree now. Almost within arms' reach.

"Okay, do it," Will said.

On the third attempt I got a match lit, and I tossed it at the tree. It fizzed for a second, and then went out.

"It's too wet," Will said. "It's not going to work."

He stepped back, and as he pulled my hand, I fell.

"I will consume you!" cried the tree.

Lightning flashed and I saw that its mouth was starting to open. Inside I could see a glimpse of the Underworld. A tree-lined pathway. Chasms of fire. Creatures shuffling towards me.

I tried to move, but my foot was stuck. It wasn't like when my shoe was stuck in the mud, this was a different kind of grip, more powerful. I tried to yank my foot away but felt something pulling the other way, grazing against my ankle. A root was wrapped around my leg. It was pulling me in. The hordes of evil creatures were waiting to feast on my soul.

I opened the soggy matchbox and pulled out a match. It didn't feel solid enough to light a match with, but when I brushed it against the side it sparked up. I put the match inside the box with the others, causing them all to light at once and tossed the box onto the base of the tree. A wall of fire flared up briefly, its heat washing over my body.

I wasn't sure if it was the fire roaring or the tree, crying out in pain. Will had hold of one arm, and Liam grabbed another. Together they pulled. Something was sticking into the side of my foot and I felt it tear at the flesh as they tugged me free.

"Run," shouted Liam, and he took off for the bank behind the tree. Andy quickly followed, and Will helped me along. It took me back to the time Will and I had fled from the wasps that lived inside the tree and we'd got up onto the drove and fell flat on our backs. That was before they started the construction work. There was no drove now; the bypass had taken its place. I hobbled up the side of the bank and Will laid me down about halfway up, a couple of metres from the road.

"Get off the road!" I heard Will shout. I looked round to see the lights. Will moved quickly, and all I heard was a screech, a thud, and a scream.

"What are you doing out here on the road?" the driver said. He was an oldish man, older than Dad, but not nearly as old as Granddad. He'd gotten out of his car and he was staring at Liam who nearby, for the first time in his life, looking completely white. "What did I hit? Oh God, what did I hit?"

Andy was lying in the road. Liam dashed over to him, and I managed to get to my feet. Liam knelt by Andy.

"Is he okay?" said the man, he started towards Andy then stopped when he saw headlights coming the other way, and something else in the road.

Andy sat up. "Will pushed me," he said. He rubbed his head. "Why'd he do that?"

The man was walking down the road. "Oh God," I could hear him mutter again and again. There was another flash of lightning and on the object in the road I could just make out the colour of Will's red pyjamas.

"No!" I said and started to follow the man. Every time I put my foot down pain shot through my body.

"What were you doing in the road!" cried the man. I waited for an answer from Will, for some kind of noise, but there was nothing to be heard over the lashing rain and the approaching car, which stopped just short of Will's body, where the man was standing, waving his arms.

"Go get help," said the man. "For God's sake, there's a boy on the road. I hit him."

The car sped off, and as it approached me, I could see a trainer a few feet from me. I hobbled over and picked it up. It was warm and wet, sticky with blood and mud, and it reeked of petrol.

I turned and looked down towards the farmhouse, and between me and home, the tree. The fire had put itself out, and I swear to God that evil bastard tree laughed.

PART THREE

Thursday 5th July 1990

So many questions. 'How' and 'why' over and again. I couldn't answer them. It all seemed too stupid. I'd played the whole thing over in my head on the way to the hospital. People were dashing around, and at first, they seemed to ignore me. A nurse eventually led me into a room, where my foot was cleaned up and stitches were put in it. I didn't know where the rest of my family were until Uncle Alan popped his head around the curtain, where I was waiting with a nurse.

"Are you this boy's father?" she asked.

"His Uncle."

"Okay. He's free to go. Standard pain medication will be okay. Keep the wound clean."

Alan helped me off the bed, and then sat with me in the waiting area. "Liam said it was all your idea. What were you thinking?"

"Is Andy okay?"

"He's has a bump on the head, but he'll be fine."

There was no point in asking about Will. We all knew he was dead long before the ambulance arrived.

"How's the foot?" said Uncle Alan.

I looked down at the four stitches. "It itches."

"I just don't understand what you were doing out on the road at almost midnight?"

I couldn't explain it. Maybe Will had been right all along, and bad stuff just happens. In the back of my mind was this idea that Will had only been killed because of the powers of the Underworld. That they'd made the car appear there, and that they planned to take Andy. Will saw it just in time and pushed him out of the way, but as a result was hit by the car himself. Will would have said that that was ridiculous. If I'd have listened to him, and stopped going on about The Underworld, we never would have gone out there, and he'd still be alive. It was my fault.

Uncle Alan passed me a tissue.

"It was my fault," I said. "I had this stupid idea, and now Will's dead."

"No, no," said Alan. "It was an accident, that's all. You didn't make that car hit him. Whatever you did do, you can't blame yourself."

"Where's Mum?"

"They're with the police. You're going to come home with me once they give Andy the all clear."

Liam wasn't speaking to me. He didn't make a big show of it or anything, but he didn't let himself get drawn into conversation. Andy was better. He made me feel the bump on his head, and he said he couldn't really remember anything that had happened the previous night. I sat around feeling lousy and thinking of Will.

Aunt Anne came in. She'd been nice to me. She gave me a hug when she saw me and pulled me to her and gave me a kiss on the forehead. She offered to cook me anything I wanted, but I wasn't hungry, and made do with a bit of toast. "The police are here to speak to you," she said, and sat down.

P.C. Wade followed her into the room. He didn't have that normal chirpy grin on his face from the road safety awareness days. "How are you feeling, Thomas?" he said.

I shrugged. "Horrible."

"I need to ask you a few questions to get to the bottom of this."

I nodded. "It's my fault," I said. "It was my idea to go out there."

"Why were you out on the bypass?"

"We weren't meant to be. It was the tree in the field."

"What about it?"

"We were going to destroy it."

P.C. Wade held his pen close to his pad but wrote nothing. "Why did you want to destroy the tree?"

"I had this idea," I said, but I wasn't sure how to explain it to an adult. "The tree is evil."

"Go on."

"Chappie died there. It's near where I found John.

It took Granddad's eye, and we'd seen Shaky Jake hanging around, looking at it..."

"And you thought all of these things were related."

"Yes," I said. I didn't want to talk about the portal.

"When you say Shaky Jake, you mean Jacob Radford?"

"Yes."

"And how is he involved in this? Been telling you boys stories?"

"He's the murderer."

"What proof do you have of that?"

"We sent you a box! It had John's P.E. kit in, and a map..."

"Ah, so that was you."

"It was. Did you arrest him?"

"I shouldn't be telling you this. We checked with Mrs Glover. John's P.E. kit was at home."

"So, it wasn't John's?"

"No. But let's get back to the events of last night. You arranged for your cousins to sleep over, so you could sneak out and attack the tree?"

"It was only supposed to be Will and me," I said. "But when Liam and Andy were stopping over to watch the football, we changed our plans."

"Why last night?"

"It was stupid. I was certain that if we didn't get rid of it, something else bad would happen."

"Something bad did happen. Why didn't you tell anyone about this?"

"I tried! People said I was being silly."

From the hall the phone rang. Aunt Anne started to get up but heard Uncle Alan answer.

"So you didn't listen to them?" said PC Wade.

"They wouldn't tell me what was going on with John. They kept on saying that sometimes bad things happen. I was looking for the reason why."

"I see," said Wade. "It's a terrible tragedy, and we've had too many in the village." He stood up and as he got to the door, he turned back to look at me. "I'm sorry for your loss."

After seeing Wade out, Uncle Alan beckoned Aunt Anne out of the room. More whispered secrets.

Aunt Anne came back in and took my hand. "That was your Mum on the phone. She thinks it would probably be best if you stayed here tonight. Is that okay?"

NOW

I practically run into Liam in the doorway. I push past him and suck in the clean air.

"Hey Tom," he says, oblivious to the state I'm in. Some things, some people, never change. "Some parents are searching the area, looking for Jessica."

What's the point? She's probably already dead.

"I figure, who knows these old droves better than you and me?"

Even his grin is exactly the same as it was when he was ten.

"It'll be like old times," he says.

Like those old times we actually thought that we could make a difference? That we searched the droves like a bunch of idiots, led by some bullshit cards thinking we'd be heroes? Those old times where my stupid plan killed my brother?

I glance over at the ditch I found John's body in. I look over to where we found Chappie's body, but that field is now covered by solar panels. I wonder if the tree stump is beneath them. I look over to the bypass, now a constant stream of traffic and see Will's trainer, the pool of blood, and his lifeless body. Then I think about what's beyond that if you follow the droves for long enough.

"Come on," I say to Liam. "I know where she'll be."

I start down the drove, with Liam following behind me. I glance into the drove and see discoloured crisp packets, crushed cans of beer, and sweet wrappers. I don't remember all of the litter being there in my childhood.

We keep going until we pass the bridge. I gaze into the water, and what used to be a constant stream is a dirty trickle. I look further down to where the ditches used to drain into the river and see a couple of old tyres. I look over the other side to see a stagnant pool, trapped by a wall of sludge. The bridge creaks beneath my feet. I kick at the posts at the edge of the bridge, and rotten wood flakes off and sinks into the dirty water below. It's all tainted, and rotten. I know I won't find any good here.

Friday 6th July 1990

Aunt Anne ran me home in the middle of the morning. She was quiet in the car, and I had nothing to say either.

Mum was waiting for me in the kitchen. "Hi, love," she said. "How are you feeling?" Her voice sounded forced and she looked really grey and had big bags under her eyes. Her hair was all over the place.

I shrugged. I could feel the tears coming again, and I tried to fight then back as I ran to meet her.

She pulled her to me, and I could tell that she was crying too by the jerky breaths that she took. She let go of me, then bent down to my level. "We've had to... make some changes."

"What?"

"Your dad wanted to keep Will's bedroom the way it was."

"What do you mean?"

"We've made a bed up for you in the spare room. Your new room."

I went upstairs. The door was closed to my bedroom, my old bedroom that I'd shared with Will, but the spare room, my new bedroom, was open. All of the boxes had been stacked up on one side, uncovering the bed that had been in there, unoccupied, for years. Clean bedding had been put on it. As I went in, I sneezed. Dust hung in the room from where so many boxes had been for so long. This was junk that Granddad had put there when he lived in the house. There was room for nothing else other than the bed and the boxes. On the bed was the box that I'd recovered from Granddad's house that contained all of the photographs, and on top of that someone had placed a book from my bedroom, the only one of my possessions that had been recovered. It was *The Secret of the Scythe*.

I wanted to go and look at some of Will's things. I left my room and approached my old door. Inside I could hear sobbing.

I pushed the door open a crack, and could see Dad in there, sitting on the floor.

"Dad," I said.

"Keep out!" he cried.

I pulled the door closed, but not before I heard him mutter, "Why did it have to be you Will? Why you?"

I wished it was me too. I couldn't take that horrible feeling anymore, knowing that I was responsible for Will's death. Dad knew it too, and he was practically wishing me dead instead. Even the way that Mum had held me suggested that she didn't love me as much anymore.

I went back into my new bedroom and picked up *The Secret of the Scythe*. I was going to tear it to pieces. It was that book that had given me the idea about the Underworld. Without that book, and its stupid tree I would never have come up with such a ridiculous story. I grabbed the book and tossed it onto the bed, where it struck the box of photographs. I gave it a shove, hoping to push it to the end of the bed, out of the way, but I failed at that too, and the box tipped over.

Pictures of Dad, Aunt Anne and Uncle Rodney spread over the bed. In some of them I could clearly make out Granddad Norman, and I vaguely recognised Nanna Betty. Among the photographs were various news clippings. A single column story headlined 'Hero teen runs away from home' told the story of Uncle Rodney leaving Little Mosswick to join a travelling theatre company, just as Granddad had told. Another story told of the ongoing suffering of 'kidnapping victim, Jacob Radford', and I started to sympathise with him. Maybe what he'd been through as a youngster had made him the way he was.

Then I found a large A3 sheet of paper, folder in two. It was yellow with age, and I feared it would tear as I unfolded it. There was an image of a tree on it with partially faded ink on the branches revealing plenty of names on it I knew. At the top it said, 'Tilbrook Family Tree'. Norman Tilbrook was written roughly in the middle, and his children beneath that. My name and Will's were on the bottom row. Enid Tilbrook was on there too, on the same level as Granddad's. So, she must have been his cousin, but there was another name beneath hers that I recognised too, Jacob Radford. I was related to Shaky Jake? I remembered all of the things that I'd written about him in my book of investigation, and I remembered that my book was still in my old bedroom, right beside where Dad was weeping. I had to get it back, but I'd have to wait for the right time.

I delved deeper into the box. It was full of decades old paperwork and letters. Enid Tilbrook, it seemed, had had a relationship with a young man from Little Mosswick, who had later been called up to fight in the Korean War. There was a child, and Enid died giving birth to him. This child, born outside of marriage was taken into care, and given up for adoption. His adoptive parents gave him a new surname, and he became Jacob Radford.

Looking at the picture of the family tree again it struck me as odd how much death there was in it. Many of the branches had died, and not many men with the Tilbrook name still lived. There was Uncle Rodney, but he didn't have children, Granddad, Dad and me. I was the only one of my generation. How weird was that?

"Thomas," there was a shout from downstairs. It was Mum, her voice cold and lifeless.

I trudged down the stairs, unsure whether I could bear her judgemental eyes on me again, but when I opened the door there was a kind voice.

"How's Tom?" Granddad said. While he looked upset, he still had some of his old colour. He sat down and rested with one arm on his walking stick. His other arm was open and welcoming me in.

I shuffled over to him, and he wrapped his big arm around me. As he hugged, he exhaled loudly, and sounded in pain. I leant back and could see him grimacing.

"You okay, Granddad?"

"Finally got around to finishing off those pheasants. I think it was past best. How are you doing, anyway? Tough day?" he said. He was always the master of the understatement, when he wanted to be. He knew when to play up a story, and when to play it down.

"I'll make some tea," Mum said, still struggling to hide how hard it was to stop her voice from breaking.

"Listen Tom," Granddad said, quiet enough so that Mum wouldn't hear. "You mustn't blame yourself for this."

I tried to squirm away. I didn't want to hear it.

"You're a good lad."

I wriggled, and tried to shrink into myself, cover my ears with my shoulders.

"But you're like me, Thomas, that's the problem."

I stopped struggling. I was ready to listen.

"You love a good story, and you want others to share in it. You know how I lost my eye?"

"The tree. The tree tried to take it."

"Farming accident. That's all. An unfortunate incident."

I nodded.

"But what kind of a story is that? No kind; that's what. You get caught up in stories because it's in your blood. If that's anyone's fault, it's mine."

"No, Granddad, you weren't there."

"But I've been planting seeds in your head all your life. No wonder you got caught up in your own fantasy."

"I'm sorry."

"Never be sorry for that, Thomas. Your Dad don't understand you. He was never one for stories and don't understand how they work. But I understand, and I say don't ever change. Okay?"

He let me go, and a little bit of the shell around me broke.

"I think your Dad needs me. I understand he's been in Will's room all night." He pushed himself up using his stick, and then made his way up the stairs, grunting all of the way.

Later, Granddad managed to talk Dad downstairs. He convinced him that he needed some fresh air. It was my chance to get back into my old room and destroy my book. This story had gone on far enough.

"Thomas," Mum said, as I was about to go up the stairs. "We do love you, you know." She opened her arms.

We cried. We spoke, though I doubt either of us could remember what about, and eventually the book went out of my mind, and a tremendous tiredness spread through my body.

"I need a nap, Mum," I said, and we parted. When I got to the top of the stairs, I saw my old bedroom door open, and I remembered what I had to do. I went inside, picked the book off the bedside table, and started to flick through it. It was a story. Fiction. Full of ideas that we'd come up with together. Crazy theories. As I was going to take it to my new room a shadow fell in front of me. Dad was blocking out the light from the hall.

"Stay out of Will's room," Dad said. He grabbed the book out of my hand. "What's this?"

"It's nothing."

"Where did it come from?"

"It was on my table..."

"In Will's room?"

"It was mine."

"It stays in his room." He started to flick through the pages. "John's killer? What's this?"

"Don't look at it, Dad."

"I asked you a question. What is this?"

"We had ideas about who killed John, and how his body ended up where it did..."

Dad continued to flick through the book. "You blamed a tree? That's what you were doing out there?"

"It's stupid. It was an idea we had."

"What this tells me, is that if you weren't fooling around, Will would never have died."

"I'm sorry. It wasn't supposed to happen."

He turned back another page. "What's this about Shaky Jake?"

"If it really was him, the police would have arrested him."

Dad froze. He was staring over my shoulder. "The bastard. Returning to the scene of the crime. I'll show him." He darted down the stairs.

I turned around and looked out the window. Walking along the drove, peering into the ditches was Shaky Jake.

"Thomas?" called Mum, and I followed quickly down the stairs. "Where's your Dad going?"

"Call the police," I said. "Quick."

Dad had Jake by his hair. He was dragging him across the field. Over his shoulder he had a coil of rope, and in his other hand the red petrol canister.

Granddad Norman started out across the field after him, with Mum behind him, and me following. I was immediately hit by the heat of the day. After the rain of the last few days the sun was back with a vengeance.

"Trevor," Granddad said. "Come back in the house."

Dad didn't even turn around. He kept pulling Jake across the field, dragging him over divots to keep him stumbling along.

The whole time Jake was making this low-pitched whining sound, like something inhuman. With his hands, he was gripping on to Dad's hand; whether he was trying to free his hair from Dad's grasp or simply trying to stop his scalp from being torn off, I don't know.

Granddad Norman stopped moving and leant on his stick, gasping for breath. Mum reached him and placed a hand on his back to support him. He let the stick go and put both hands to his stomach, before collapsing onto his knees.

I kept moving beyond them as Dad hurled Jake towards the tree. All of the air rushed from his body and he turned around. "No," he said. "I never... I never..." but he couldn't get the words out. Even from a distance I could see that he was shaking worse than ever.

Dad wrapped the rope around him and the tree.

"Dad, don't!" I said as I continued across the field.

"This is what you wanted, boy," Dad said.

"It's not," I said, as Jake kept muttering incoherently.

"It ends here."

"We were only messing around!" I said. "Let the police decide."

"It's too late for that, boy." Dad's eyes were glassy, and the brown iris had become so dark it was almost black. He twisted the cap off the petrol canister and tossed it to the ground and started to splash petrol onto Jake.

I could hear the police sirens in the distance. "The police are coming. They'll know what to do."

"If they knew they would have done it already. Then you and Will would never have got so crazy about all this."

I looked round for help. Granddad was now lying on his side with Mum over him. "Something's wrong with Granddad," I said. "Look."

Dad looked over at him. For a second the true colour returned to his eyes. The petrol canister dropped from his hands.

"I... never..." muttered Jake, his chin wet and shiny with drool.

The dead-eyed look returned to Dad's face. He put both hands to his head and scrunched his hair, leaving it sticking up in wild tufts when he removed his hands. His face was beaded with sweat, and his beard glistened with it. He reached into the deep pocket of his overalls and pulled out a box of matches.

"But he's family," I said. I ran towards him, thinking that I could knock the match box from his hand before he had the chance to do anything with it. I reached out, got my fingers into the matchbox and got hold of a few matches. Pathetic.

With the hand that was holding the match he struck out at me, the back of his hand catching me across the bridge of the nose which knocked me to the ground. He stared at me, his eyes scanning from my feet, to my head, with a look of absolute disgust on his face. "Families make mistakes," he said. He struck the match and tossed it at Jake's feet.

Flames immediately engulfed his shoes, and were licking at his trousers, climbing up his legs. He was still protesting, "I never. I never."

But I couldn't take my eyes off Dad. He was focused only on the flames, almost hypnotised by the way they danced. I could see the fire reflecting in his eyes. It was like he'd been possessed. He couldn't take his eyes from the fire, and I couldn't take my eyes off of him.

Jake's protests turned to screams.

I turned to look at him, and the flames had covered him completely. The rope must have burned through because Jake fell forward. He rolled over in the mud until the fire was out, and then lay there twitching, smouldering.

The tree was fully aflame now. It had spread to some of the higher branches and was dropping flaming debris.

Dad still stared at the tree. The fire was so bright that his face was glowing orange. His eyes were almost entirely flame. His face was entirely without emotion. His dry, cracked lips parted as he seemed to inhale the smoke. His hair, where he had earlier pulled at it, had formed into horns.

I felt into my back pocket. Liam's Top Trumps were there. On top was the picture of the Fire Demon. I looked from the card to Dad. He looked more than human, as if he had the strength of a demon. I looked at the card again and the vision became clearer. It wasn't the flame that was making him appear orange, it was his skin. He was orange. Those were horns on his head, not tufts of hair. My father was a fire demon.

I ran. Not up the bank and onto the bypass. I'd never do that ever again. I headed across one field and into another. I ran through the oilseed rape, no longer a bright yellow, having dropped its flowers, but green, tall and thick. I pushed through until I hit Catchwater Drove and I followed it up along the river. I could feel heat on my back, chasing me, closing in on me. I daren't turn around. When I reached the bridge, I turned to the left and followed the path of the river, all of the way past where it went under the new bypass. The old pumping station came into sight. I cast a glance behind me, fearing that it would be my last and the demon would be upon me, but he was not in sight. I daren't slow down though, not until I was in the shade of the crumbly old brick building.

Around the side was a door, which was slightly ajar. I pushed it open further and edged in, only to be met by an almighty stench. There were steps that led down a little way, and then there was a little more space, before it dropped down into a massive hole, which had a low metal frame all around it as an ineffective barrier. Whatever machinery used to be in there had been recovered, and it looked like the inside of an empty shell. Part of me wanted to shout to see if there was an echo, but I didn't want anyone to hear me. I took the steps, slowly and carefully, with one hand over my nose. The steps were slimy, and slippery, and I had to hold on carefully to avoid falling. At the bottom, as I stepped on something, I heard a rustle. Looking down I saw some familiar sweet wrappers: Bamse mums and Stratos bars. Not the typical sweets that you could buy at Little Mosswick Post Office.

I crept towards the pit and looked down, not knowing what to expect. It was too dark to make much out. I couldn't see the bottom. I felt around on the ground and found a stone. I dropped it in, and a couple of second later heard a plop. There was water, but it wasn't deep. My eyes started to adjust to the lack of light, and I thought I could make out chains hanging down the opposite side.

Light flowed into the chamber, and I looked to the door to see a tall silhouette with enormous hands and wild hair.

"Uncle Rodney!" I cried.

"Shush, Thomas, dear boy," he said. "Your father will hear you. He's gone crazy." He came down the steps towards me.

"How did you know where to find me?"

"I saw the fire across the fields from where I was having a quick drink, and saw you running off. I ran as fast as I could and thought I might find you somewhere near here."

"Is dad out there?"

"Keep your voice down. He looks wild." Uncle Rodney's eyes grew large as he reached the end of the sentence, and he continued to walk towards me. "Stay here with your Uncle Rodney." He said in a comforting whisper, "I'll look after you."

Rodney wrapped his arms around me. He was breathing heavily, and it stunk of alcohol. "There's a place in here you can hide. No one will know you're here." He led me around the pit where it was almost completely dark. He grabbed something, which sounded like a piece of thick board, and dragged it aside.

"Through there," he said, and guided me into a gap. I felt myself passing under an old sack, and then I found my way to the end. There were cushions to sit on, but little else.

"Wait there," said Uncle Rodney. "I'm going to check to see if your father is still on the rampage."

I heard the board slide back across the entrance to the hole, and then something else being placed in front of it.

I tried to open my eyes wider to see anything, but it was pitch black. I touched the walls. I could make out some kind of scratches in the wall, but nothing else. I leaned forward and pushed at the board in front of the entrance, but it wasn't moving. Dad would never find me in here. I sat back on the cushions and tried to make myself comfortable. I was sitting on something which was an awkward shape. I reached into my pocket and pulled out Liam's Top Trumps and tossed them in front of me. There was something else in my pockets too. Some of the matches I'd grabbed from Dad. If I could light one, I thought, I would be able to have a better look at my surroundings.

The first one I struck against the wall snapped in half. That was no good. I tried again with a second, and with a satisfying fizz it erupted into life. On either side were old fashioned slightly pink bricks, thick with years of grime and in from of me the piece of board. On the floor the Top trumps were scattered. The Beast, the creature with a horror rating of 98, the creature pictured on stage, was on top of the pile. I turned to look closer at the bricks. Something had been carved into them. Lyrics. Lyrics about holding and giving and doing it at the right time. It was John Barnes' rap from New Order's England World Cup anthem, 'World in Motion'. There was only one person I knew who knew and loved that song so well that he'd turn to it in his darkest hour. John. He'd been trapped here, and now I was stuck in the very same place.

The match fizzled out on my fingers and I yelped.

"Quiet," cried Uncle Rodney from the other side. "He'll hear you."

I lay on my back and kicked at the board. It barely moved.

"Stop it," said Uncle Rodney, "Or I'll have to silence you."

"It was you!" I shouted. "You killed John."

"No one can prove that, dear boy."

I kicked at the board again and again. Pain arched down my leg, and I could feel bleeding from where my stiches must have split open.

"It's no good. You don't have the strength, my boy."

I was sick of being told I was too weak. I held nothing back and gave one more almighty kick. I felt it move further. I squirmed around so that I was facing forward, and I was able to push my arm out of the gap. I pushed forward, edging the board, and whatever was holding it in place, forward, millimetre by millimetre until I could get my head out. I wriggled forward, trying to force my body through.

"I told you it's no good," said Rodney, and I saw him move towards me. He put a piece of cloth over my mouth and a sickly-sweet smell hit me like a Bullet Bill. I tried to hold my breath, but then a slither of light appeared over by the door and I gasped.

"Rodney!" called a gruff voice.

He dropped the rag from my face and stood up.

I felt dizzy and was struggling to keep my eyes open. The figure at the door was surrounded by a fiery glow.

"Turn around, Trevor. The boy wants to be here with me."

"It was you, wasn't it?"

"I don't have the faintest idea what you're talking about."

"It's always been you." Dad moved quickly down the steps, and I could feel a wave a heat wash over me. "You never rescued Jacob Radford. You'd kidnapped him."

"Why don't you ask him, see what he says? Oh, that's right; you toasted him like a marshmallow."

"That boy, John. That was you too." Dad was beside Rodney now. The Beast versus Fire Demon. Every statistic was in The Beast's favour.

"Dad," I managed to murmur.

He looked down at me, and as he did so he seemed to weaken. Rodney was taller and he was bending Dad's hands back. Of course, he was. The Beast had 87 physical strength, and the Fire Demon only had 71. They came together in a flurry of blows, and I could no longer see my father and my uncle, but the two monsters. They locked their massive hands together, grappling, trying to overpower one another. The Beast loomed over The Fire Demon, and pushed down hard, forcing it onto one knee. He was losing. He looked weaker. I was going to be left to be consumed by The Beast. He seemed to be shrinking into himself, and all of a sudden, he was my dad again. He roared, "I've lost one of my boys. I won't let you take the other." He let go of The Beast's hands and threw his body forward, his shoulder crashing into its stomach, orange sparks flying from his body.

The Beast came forward again and kicked Dad, who was still on the floor having thrown himself forward, in the ribs. The Beast took a step back and joined his hands into a mighty club. He ran towards Dad again, but Dad moved too quickly. He arched forward, under The Beast's blow, and stood up, lifting it over his shoulders and letting it crash against the metal barrier with a sickening crunch.

"You okay, boy?" called Dad.

I managed a feeble, "Yes."

The Beast had gotten back onto his knees, but it wasn't The Beast anymore. He was Rodney again, with his ridiculous clown hair. His back was twisted, and he couldn't straighten his body. Dad kicked out, planting his foot right on Uncle Rodney's chest. He tumbled back, over the low metal barrier and fell into the pit below, screaming weakly until he hit the water with a splash.

Dad hurled the board away, and started to come towards me, flames flickering in his eyes. He placed his hands on me, and the last thing I remember is an intense heat washing over me.

NOW

We keep moving along Catchwater Drove, and I begin to look around frantically.

"It's gone," says Liam.

I break into a run and stop where it should be. A brink scar remains, running up from the river. You can see the outline of where the pumping station used to be, and the huge pits have been filled with the bricks that once made up the station.

"They tore it down not long after what happened there."

There is a low fence around it, with barbed wire at the top, and a sign that warns of danger.

"What did happen there?" I say.

"You were there, Tom; you should know."

I stare at the place that Uncle Rodney had held me and think back to what Dad did. I can't shake the vision of the two monsters going at it, but then I remember that I'd been drugged. The whole reason that Liam and are out here is because we're looking for a missing child. What would I do if Charlie was in danger? Would it give me super-human strength? Would it allow me to kill? I hope it would.

"But I don't know," I said. "My Dad turned into a monster. He burned Jake to death, and then killed Rodney."

"He did it for you, Tom."

I see those burning eyes coming towards me again.

"Do you remember what happened when you left the pumping station?"

I remembered waking in my bed. Everything was hazy. I had a feeling as if I'd been plucked from a nightmare by a guardian angel. Then the sun had shone through a window, I thought I was burning, and I started screaming. After that was the hospital.

"Your Dad carried you all the way home. Three police officers tried to take you from him, but he refused to let you go until you were safe."

I was shivering as we stood on the drove, the cool breeze blowing from the river on to us. "Then what happened?"

"They took your Dad away."

"And I told everyone that he was a monster."

Liam put an arm on my shoulder.

"What did they tell you about me?"

"They said you'd be okay. They told me not to worry."

"More lies."

"I don't know. I look at you now, and you're not doing so bad."

When I first saw Liam again, I couldn't see a change. He'd seemed like a giant version of himself, with a little Liam clone behind him, but maybe there was more to him than that. "What would you know?" I said, brushing Liam's arm off.

Liam moved round to look me in the eye. "You and Charlie are all your Mum ever talks about – once she's stopped bossing me around with what to do on the farm."

"Really?"

"Yeah. The solar farm was all her idea. That really got us out of a hole."

Same old Liam, getting the wrong end of the stick. "No, I meant, does she really talk about us?"

"All of the time. So does your dad."

Now I knew he was lying. I started to walk back towards the house.

"He does. He says that he always knew you were the smart one."

I move faster.

With the extra weight he's carrying, he can't keep up. "He says he's proud of you."

I leave Liam behind.

When I get back to the farmhouse, I'll grab Charlie, and go. I can't take all of these lies. I won't even have to go back into the house, I realise, as Charlie is sitting on the patio outside, drinking juice with Billy.

"Where's Dad?" asks Billy.

"He's coming," I say, and suspect it's true.

"They found Jessica," he says.

I see the photograph the police officer had flashed in front of me, now stained with blood.

"Her Dad had taken her."

"She's okay?"

"See, Dad," says Charlie. "There wasn't anything to worry about."

Mum comes out of the house. She ruffles the hair of both boys, and then places her hand on my wrist. "We thought you'd gone again."

"I'm going," I say.

"Your Dad was so upset when you ran off like that."

"Why was he shouting?"

"Shouting? He can barely whisper, Tom."

Mum was still sticking up for him. Or maybe it was another echo from the past.

"He won't want me to tell you this, but he wept when you went back down them stairs. All he wants is to see you again."

"No, Mum."

"He talks about that day all of the time."

I see his mud-smeared face, wild beard and fiery eyes, and can hear him boasting about killing two men.

"He blames himself. Says part of him always suspected Rodney, but he didn't want to believe it. Then, when he saw the fear on your face, he knew that he had to save you."

I try to pull myself away from her, but her grip on my arm is strong.

"I saw you two coming down the drove. He was batting them police officers away like flies. 'Leave my boy alone' he was saying. 'You can take me when I know he's safe.' When he placed you in my arms what I saw on his face was pure relief."

I imagine Jessica's mum is feeling the same kind of relief, knowing that her child is safe. So, I guess there really was nothing to worry about. Almost every day there's nothing to worry about. There are monsters out there, but they're not on every street corner. They're not hiding behind every twitching curtain. They're not upstairs, in a bedroom of your childhood home, waiting for you to come home so that they can finally devour you.

I look up at the house, and into his bedroom window. It's time.

I climb the stairs alone. I don't need my Mum to hold my hand. I push open the door, and I'm unsurprised to be hit by a blast of heat. I look at the bed. He doesn't take up as much space as I thought he would. It's as if he's shrunk, though of course, I realise, I've grown significantly since I last saw him. And the last time I saw him, he'd become a monster in order to save me.

His eyes open. I should say something. How about I'm sorry that I haven't spoken to you in twenty-five years. How about I'm sorry that you spent years in prison, partially because I refused to tell my side of the story.

How about I'm sorry that I thought you were a monster.

"Hey, Thomas, my boy." His voice is still loud, but it has a quiver of weakness.

That's what he used to call me, 'my boy'.

We chat about everything. We chat about nothing. At some point he says, "I hear you've got a boy of your own now."

"Do you want to meet him?" I ask.

He smiles, and I remember that he used to do it all of the time, before that summer when he was so worried about trying to protect Will and me.

"Charlie," I call, and he comes flying up the steps.

"This is your Granddad," I say.

Charlie reaches out a hand and takes my father's. "Pleased to meet you," he says. He takes a second to assess my dad, and then reaches across to hug him.

Moments later Mum comes in. She had to check that we were all okay, like she always has. "Made you a tea," she says, and rests a hand on my shoulder. I've missed that.

"We'll be back," I say to Dad.

When he tries to reply, a cough catches in his throat, and I don't know how many opportunities I'll have to make it right with him.

I take Charlie by the hand and lead him down the stairs. I may not be able to make it right with Dad, but I can with Charlie. As we re-enter the kitchen, Granddad stirs in his chair.

"Granddad," I say, "why don't you tell Charlie how you lost your eye?"

"Farming accident," he says with a frown.

"No Granddad," I say, giving him a very obvious wink, "tell him the real story."

ABOUT THE AUTHOR

Benjamin Langley has been writing since he could hold a pen and has always been drawn to dark tales. He has had short stories published in over a dozen publications including *Crescendo of Darkness*, *Deadman's Tome*, and *The Manchester Review*. He has also written Sherlock Holmes adventures that have featured in Adventures in the Realm of H.G. Wells, Adventures Beyond the Canon, and Adventures in the Realm of Steampunk. Benjamin has also written comedy sketches that have been performed on stage, radio and television.

He lives, writes, and teaches in Cambridgeshire, UK, where he also studied at Anglia Ruskin University. He was awarded the prize for best Major Writing Project while studying for his BA in Writing and English. He completed his MA in Creative Writing in 2015. An earlier version of *Dead Branches* was part of Benjamin's final project. He has recently finished work on a second novel, a supernatural horror titled *Is She Dead in Your Dreams?* and is now working on a third called *Normal*.

WELCOME TO THE BLACK
MOUNTAIN CAMP FOR BOYS!

Summer,1989. It is a time for splashing in the lake and exploring the wilderness, for nine teenagers to bond together and create friendships that could last the rest of their lives.

But among this group there is a young man with a secret-a secret that, in this time and place, is unthinkable to his peers.

When the others discover the truth, it will change each of them forever. They will all have blood on their hands.

ODD MAN OUT is a heart-wrenching tale of bullies and bigotry, a story that explores what happens when good people don't stand up for what's right. It is a tale of how far we have come . . . and how far we still have left to go.

Available in paperback or Kindle on Amazon.com

http://bit.ly/OddManKindle

I KNOW WHAT YOU HAVE HEARD ABOUT ME

You say that I am a madman. You say that I am dangerous. You say that I am the one who has been abducting women, slaughtering them, and burying their corpses all around this city for years. You are wrong, because only part of that statement is true...

I AM NOT A KILLER

I know that you probably won't believe me. Not now. Not after all that has happened, but I need to tell my side of the story. You need to know how this all began. You need to hear about the birds, but most of all, you need to understand...

I AM NOT THE BOULEVARD MONSTER

Available in paperback or Kindle on Amazon.com

http://bit.ly/B0ulevard

A TERRIFYING HAUNTING

This is the place where the harrowed ghosts of a dozen generations whisper in the shadows of their ancestral home, where one family's dreams of a new beginning turned into a nightmare that ended in tragedy.

A CURSED BLOODLINE

This is the place where a line of witches bound themselves—in blood—to a primeval entity. Here, nightmare and reality meet beneath frozen skies, and even time and space fall under the power of the demonic being that rules this remote northern wood.

A CHANCE ENCOUNTER

This is the place where the path of a tormented survivor meets that of an unknowing innocent. Past and present collide, and secrets long buried crawl back into the pallid light of day as the shadow of the Beast falls over them both. But even the bloodiest dreams of that demonic being may pale in comparison to what lies buried within the human heart.

This is the place where evil dwells... **ABODE**

Available in paperback or Kindle on Amazon.com

http://bit.ly/Ab0de

ON THE HORIZON FROM
BLOODSHOT BOOKS
2019-20*

Jimmy the Freak – Mark Steensland & Charles Colyott

The October Boys – Adam Millard

Dead Sea Chronicles – Tim Curran

The Hag Witch of Tripp Creek – Somer Canon

Behemoth – H.P. Newquist

Dead in the U.S.A. – David Price

Blood Mother: A Novel of Terror – Pete Kahle

Not Your Average Monster – World Tour

The Abomination (The Riders Saga #2) – Pete Kahle

The Horsemen (The Riders Saga #3) – Pete Kahle

*other titles to be added when confirmed

BLOODSHOT BOOKS

READ UNTIL YOU BLEED